"I don't want to hurt you the way my father hurt my mother. I don't want to be like the other men that hurt my mother." His voice was as raw as his emotions.

"You won't hurt me, Garret."

"How can you say that after everything you've been through? How do you know I won't do what Henry did to you?"

"I believe in you."

Garret grabbed her and crushed his lips on hers. This was a different kiss from the other ones they'd shared. There was a desperation in this kiss; he hungrily sucked at her tongue—his mouth bruising hers. Dragging his lips away from hers, he pulled away and said, "I need you, Callie."

Callie nodded her head.

"But I can't promise you anything. I know that my parents loved each other at one time, but that love turned into something bad. My father's blood runs through my veins. I can't tell you that I won't turn out to be like him."

BOOK YOUR PLACE ON OUR WEBSITE AND MAKE THE READING CONNECTION!

We've created a customized website just for our very special readers, where you can get the inside scoop on everything that's going on with Zebra, Pinnacle and Kensington books.

When you come online, you'll have the exciting opportunity to:

- View covers of upcoming books
- Read sample chapters
- Learn about our future publishing schedule (listed by publication month *and author*)
- Find out when your favorite authors will be visiting a city near you
- Search for and order backlist books from our online catalog
- Check out author bios and background information
- Send e-mail to your favorite authors
- Meet the Kensington staff online
- Join us in weekly chats with authors, readers and other guests
- Get writing guidelines
- AND MUCH MORE!

Visit our website at
http://www.kensingtonbooks.com

SMOOTH OPERATOR

Janette McCarthy Louard

KENSINGTON PUBLISHING CORP.
http://www.kensingtonbooks.com

DAFINA BOOKS are published by

Kensington Publishing Corp.
850 Third Avenue
New York, NY 10022

Copyright © 2005 by Janette McCarthy Louard

All rights reserved. No part of this book may be reproduced in any form or by any means without the prior written consent of the Publisher, excepting brief quotes used in reviews.

All Kensington titles, imprints and distributed lines are available at special quantity discounts for bulk purchases for sales promotion, premiums, fund-raising, educational or institutional use.

Special book excerpts or customized printings can also be created to fit specific needs. For details, write or phone the office of the Kensington Special Sales Manager: Kensington Publishing Corp., 850 Third Avenue, New York, NY 10022. Attn. Special Sales Department. Phone: 1-800-221-2647.

If you purchased this book without a cover, you should be aware that this book is stolen property. It was reported as "unsold and destroyed" to the Publisher and neither the Author nor the Publisher has received any payment for this "stripped book."

Dafina Books and the Dafina logo Reg. U.S. Pat. & TM Off.

First Printing: August 2005
10 9 8 7 6 5 4 3 2 1

Printed in the United States of America

*This novel is dedicated
to my beloved son
Jamaal.*

Mommy loves you!

ACKNOWLEDGMENTS

Giving glory to God for His many blessings. I would like to thank my husband Ken for his love and support throughout the years, and my darling son, Jamaal who is my inspiration. As always, I thank little Michael for being a writing companion for me. My love and thanks go to the extraordinary McCarthy family, Mummy, Paul, Mark—my "peeps"—who, no matter what, always have my back! Big ups go to my girlfriends, Kathi, Lessie, Robyn, Stephanie, Vonda, Charmaine, Guilene, Diane, Joyce and Angie, whose gentle encouragement and wise words always follow me wherever I go. Thanks, Ladies! Many, many thanks to Leah Williams who encouraged me to write a steamier romance and was a wonderful editor! Thanks to Karen Thomas for her guidance and her patience. Thanks to the readers of my novels. I am humbled and grateful that you took the time to hang with me. Finally, I want to thank my father. Daddy, you're my shining star—now and forever! Amen.

Chapter 1

Callie Hopewell was predictable, reliable and filled with common sense. As a child, Callie was the one who could always be depended on to make sure her four wild sisters did their homework, brushed their teeth, and said their nightly prayers. She kept the house clean and her sisters fed and out of trouble while her mother worked the late shift at the hospital. She was the daughter who brought home straight A's, sang alto in the church choir, and went to two Ivy League schools on full scholarships. She had a good job and a decent bank account. Her mother would tell anyone who cared to listen that from the day Callie was born, she never gave her any trouble. Callie always did the right thing—the appropriate thing. So, on that gray February morning, four days before Valentine's Day, as Callie sat in the first-class cabin on Caribbean Air Flight 057 bound for the island of St. Christopher, on her way to see a man who didn't know that she was coming, she was more than just a little nervous.

She stared out the window of the airplane at the outline of the tall buildings of Manhattan in the distance. She worked in one of those tall buildings. She'd worked in her office on Park Avenue for seven years now—toiling diligently as an associate in her law firm hoping to make partner one day. For a moment she thought about all the work she was leaving behind. Even though she'd spent the entire weekend getting all of her cases in order, she knew there was still more work to do. There was always more work to do. She'd finally decided to get off the work treadmill—even if it was only for a week. She was going to take a vacation in a place she'd never been. She was going to spend some quality time with the man of her dreams. To be honest, Henry Kincaid wasn't exactly the man of her dreams, but he possessed all the attributes that she was looking for in a man—handsome, smart, dependable. She'd waited a long time to find someone like Henry, and although the all-consuming passion that she'd dreamt about wasn't there, she'd made up her mind that she wasn't going to walk away from another relationship. This vacation to see Henry was long overdue. She hadn't taken a real vacation in over two years. Long weekends and business trips to foreign places did not count.

The partners at her law firm viewed vacations as an explicit admission that the lawyer in question did not belong in the legal profession. For many, it was a matter of personal pride that they had steadily clawed their way up the partnership ladder, neglecting family along the way. Divorces, nervous breakdowns, heart attacks, juvenile delinquent children notwithstanding, the lawyers at Buford, James & Osborne prided themselves on their dedication—their single-minded focus on work. When Callie told Blair Osborne, the partner with whom she was currently working on yet another trial involving two companies at war, that she was taking a vacation, he had stared at her dumbfounded. He had been silent for about a full minute before barking, "A vacation! We're going to trial in six weeks!" Callie had explained that everything that needed to be done at this point was done and she'd secured the services of two other associates who were thoroughly familiar with the case to help out in the unlikely event of an emergency. Besides, she'd gently reminded Blair, the remaining time after her trip to St. Christopher would give them more than enough time to prepare for trial. Blair had not look convinced. In fact, Blair had looked downright unhappy. When she finally escaped his office, she'd left him muttering dire comments about associates who shirked their responsibility and their short-lived careers at the firm.

Callie didn't care. Blair Osborne was on his third wife and wife number three didn't look any happier than wife number one or two. Callie had lived the first thirty-four years of her life afraid of people like Blair—people whose goodwill, or lack thereof, impacted her paycheck. It was time to get off that train. It wasn't that she had any desire to be unemployed, but lately when she found herself sitting at her desk late at night, eating yet another sandwich for dinner, and examining legal documents clearly designed to piss off lawyers on the other side of the case, she wondered if there wasn't more to life than this. Her sisters and even her mother had worried about Callie's single-minded focus on her work. They'd worried that she'd grow old alone in her Harlem apartment, ending up with innumerable cats for company. Even though Callie thought they were all being a little dramatic—they did have a point. It was time for a change. She didn't intend to live another thirty-four years of her life with nothing but her job and her accomplishments at work to keep her company. She was going to have what other people took for granted: A life. A husband. A child. Maybe a dog thrown in. She was going to be more than a "damn good attorney."

Six months ago this would have seemed impossible. Six months ago, her job and her crazy family consumed her life to a degree that her therapist had long ago declared to be "unnatural." Between putting out fires at work, listening to her mother complain about her sisters and her sisters complain about her mother, their men, their jobs, their lives, their latest haircut, there hadn't been much room for fun or excitement. Her love life wasn't dead, but it was definitely on life support. The few relationships she'd had were with men who all had one thing in common—an aversion to commitment. When Callie met Henry Kincaid, she'd been dating (the polite word for it) Augustus Williams, a self-involved investment banker who struggled mightily between love of his huge salary and TriBeCa loft and his desire to go to Central America to help the underprivileged grow coffee beans and "throw off the mighty chains of their oppressors" (his words). Callie's relationship with Augustus was based on mutual convenience. Both were workaholics, and weeks would go by with only perfunctory telephone calls and occasional, scheduled, quick (very quick) sex.

Henry Kincaid was different. From their initial meeting at a party her sister had dragged her to, kicking and screaming, Henry had consumed every free moment she had. Although his family's textile company kept him busy with their New York operations, they still managed to spend a lot of time together. When Callie was not working at the firm, she was with Henry. For the first time she was with a man who made spending time with her a top priority. Tall, slender, with skin the color of coffee and cream, Henry was undeniably handsome. His chiseled looks, brilliant mind, warm smile and baritone West Indian accent sealed the deal.

Her mother and her sisters were suspicious. Why hadn't someone snatched up a man as good-looking and, judging from his free spending ways, wealthy as Henry? Something about Henry put her sisters' collective teeth on edge. Even her sister, Phoebe, who never had anything bad to say about anyone—even when they deserved it—had said "something's not right, Callie. His aura is not good—not good at all." Her friends were worried about the suddenness and the intensity of Callie's focus on Henry. Her therapist advised caution. But Callie didn't care.

Henry was easily the most fascinating man she'd ever met. He'd lived all over the world, having recently come to New York from Geneva, where his family also had some business concerns. He spoke five different languages fluently: English, French, German, Spanish, and Patois, sent her French poetry and fresh white roses regularly, and the passion he brought to her life had been like a long, tall glass of water after a drought. When he proposed three months after their meeting she'd said yes immediately, but the practical side of her asked him to wait a year before their marriage. She wanted to get used to the idea of marriage and ultimately moving to another country. Agreeing to marry a man three months after she met him didn't say much for Callie's well-known quality of being sensible. It was too soon, her family said, and there was a part of her—the sensible part—that agreed. But sensible Callie had been single for a long time. Sensible Callie had been in too many ugly bridesmaid dresses. Sensible Callie had given up any hope that she would meet a man who would look beyond her sensible shoes, sensible suits, and sensible life to see that there was an interesting, funny woman hiding behind all that sensibleness.

She said "yes" to a future as Mrs. Henry Kincaid without any hesitation. He offered her an alternative to her sensible life, and she wasn't going to let that opportunity pass her by. Still, there were times when she wondered whether the passion she dreamed about would come. Perhaps passion took time to cultivate, Callie thought. Besides, passion fades, and then what? Callie was old enough to know that those childhood dreams of a knight in shining armor were no more than a lonely person's overactive imagination. Henry was fun. Henry was interesting. A life with Henry would be exciting and different. From where she stood, different and exciting sounded pretty good to her.

There was no question that Henry was going to live in St. Christopher, and, as sexist as her friends accused her of being, there was no question that she was going to move there with him. "I'd rather be happy in St. Christopher with him, than unhappy in New York without him," Callie had declared to her therapist.

"It's never good to base your happiness on another human being," said her grim therapist. "I see some negative, dependency issues here."

Callie had listened, but her mind was made up. At the end of the year she was going to give her law firm notice and she was going to find a job in St. Christopher. After all these years, the firm life had lost whatever allure it had for her. Working seven days a week was not her idea of how things should be. She was going to start over with a new man, a new job and a new country.

Two weeks ago Henry returned to St. Christopher to take care of some matters that concerned his family business. His family owned a textile factory in St. Christopher, and in the three months that she'd known Henry he'd made frequent trips to St. Christopher to handle the various problems that arose with the factory. This trip was longer than the last few and Callie had been surprised at how much she missed him. During their last phone call, an idea had slowly formed which shocked the practical side of her. Henry had sounded as despondent as she felt. A small, unfamiliar voice had whispered to her to go to St. Christopher. *Surprise him!* said the voice. *Not sensible*, said the voice that she was more familiar with. *He may be busy. It might be inconvenient.* The two voices raged in battle, and in the end, the stronger voice, the one that told her to get on a plane and go to St. Christopher to be with her man, won.

Callie had never done anything like this before. She was the type of person who would call her friends, even those who lived around the corner, before she dropped by. The reckless person who was getting on a plane, going to a foreign country, and showing up unannounced and unheralded was not someone Callie was familiar with. Still, it was exciting . . . scary . . . and downright foolish.

"Girl, you have a whole lot of nerve!" her travel agent Odelis declared when Callie informed her of her plan to surprise Henry. "Are you sure you want to do this? You know most men aren't big on surprises."

Although Callie assured Odelis that Henry wasn't like most men and she knew that he'd be glad to see her, she wondered whether or not Odelis was right. Odelis's words rang in her head as she sat in her first class seat on Caribbean Air. She did have a whole lot of nerve to do this. But Callie had already lived her life by the rules and although there were many who would say that a successful career with the respect of one's peers was a just reward for all that good living, Callie wasn't so sure. In her heart, she knew there was something else out there for her. She was more than good old, reliable, and sensible Callie. Besides, she reasoned—it wasn't as if she ran away to join the circus or a strip club. She was just going to surprise her fiancé. What could possibly go wrong? She settled back in her seat and took a deep breath. For once, she was not going to listen to those nagging, disquieting thoughts— thoughts that advised that caution was the better side of valor—or something like that. She was throwing caution to the wind and she felt good about it.

She glanced down at Henry's business card. The address of the family business was in Broxton, St. Christopher. Henry told her he'd be staying in different hotels around the island as he'd sold his home before coming to New York. His business often took him all over the island, he told her, and while staying at hotels was not something Henry relished, he assured her that he'd rather do that than depend on his family. Unlike her family and their clannish ways, Henry had given her the clear impression that he did not have a close relationship with his family. He'd told her that other than running the business, his family didn't have much time for each other. Callie didn't understand that concept. While her family might drive her crazy with alarming regularity, she knew that she'd be lost without their love and support. Knowing that Henry was estranged from his had only increased his appeal to her. She wanted to take care of him— to show him another side of family, the side where people supported each other.

Henry gave her the telephone number to his office and told her that was where she'd reach him if she needed him. He told her that he'd be moving around the island a lot, but his office would always be able to find him. Some of the doubt about her decision to go to Henry—the doubt that she'd felt when she encountered her family's opinion that it wasn't the best idea to surprise folks, particularly when those folks lived all the way in foreign countries—crept back insidiously into her thoughts. It really wasn't the smartest thing to jump on a plane and go to another country to find a person whose address was currently not in your possession. But, what's the absolute worst that could happen? she wondered. If for some reason she couldn't find him easily, she'd bide her time until she found a way to get to him. Callie couldn't wait to see the look in his eyes when he finally saw her.

Callie yawned brazenly and stretched her legs out in front of her as she sat in seat 3A on Caribbean Air. She'd never flown first class on a non-business trip and it felt delicious and decadent. She watched as passengers streamed onto the plane; and could see the excitement in their faces. They were all escaping, just as Callie was. She wondered if they shared her dreams of paradise, piña coladas, warm weather, golden sandy beaches, and hot tropical passion. Good Lord, she thought, I'm starting to sound like one of those romance novels my sister Penelope is always reading.

"Excuse me, is this seat taken?" A voice that could best be described as a rich, deep baritone with a distinctive Caribbean lilt, interrupted her reverie.

Callie looked up and found herself staring at a man who could easily have stepped off the pages of a *Playgirl* calendar—not that she looked at anything like that! His eyes were as dark as onyx, and his skin was the color of mahogany. Without meaning to, she found herself studying his face—the high cheekbones, full lips, and strong jawline all came together to form a very handsome man. He was smiling at her, and his smile revealed two deep dimples. For a moment, a very bad moment, Callie imagined herself touching one of those dimples. *Oh, my Lord,* she thought as she stared at him, *I'm engaged—about to be married—on my way to see my fiancé. I should not, definitely not, be thinking about running my hands over this man's face.* The word passion screamed at her and she pushed it away. Think of Henry, her mind shouted. Henry Kincaid. Your fiancé!

"Is this seat occupied?" he interrupted her

thoughts, motioning to the seat next to Callie as he repeated his question with a broad smile.

"I don't think it is," she replied, embarrassed that he had obviously caught her staring at him.

"Good." He smiled as he placed his duffel bag in the overhead compartment and sat down next to her. Callie noticed the stewardess staring at him. Apparently he had the same effect on other women as he did with her. It wasn't just his looks, Callie decided. There was something about the way he carried himself. Confident. Assured. Sexy. Sex on legs. Sex on long, lean, muscular legs or dark chocolate legs—stop it! Another treacherous thought flashed in her mind involving the long fingers that had grasped one of the magazines in the seat pocket . . . fingers which she imagined feeding her fresh fruit as they sat in a café somewhere tropical . . . stop it! Callie chided herself.

"My seat is in the front row of the cabin"—the chocolate Playgirl pinup dream smiled at her—"which ordinarily I prefer, however, I'm sitting next to the most insufferable woman and I don't think that I could spend the entire trip trapped in a seat beside her."

Arrogant, thought Callie—her attraction to him disappearing. Callie didn't like folks who talked about other people. The *Playgirl* pinup had come down quite a few notches.

"How do you know I'm any less insufferable?" asked Callie.

"I'll just have to take my chances," he replied as he leaned back in his seat.

His dimples winked again at her, as if they shared a secret together. It made her uncomfortable. His smile was almost... intimate. She decided not to reply and instead turned and looked out the airplane window. In the distance, the gray skies of Manhattan bid her a solemn good-bye.

Once again the *Playgirl* pinup's voice invaded her thoughts.

"However, if I were a gambling man... and I'm not... I'd say that you're anything *but* insufferable."

Callie turned and leveled a gaze at him. She couldn't be quite certain, but was he *flirting* with her? She realized that this was the kind of man who was used to having a lot of female attention and he obviously thought that she was one of the many females who were drawn to him. Well, she was drawn to him... just a little... but he didn't have to know. Unlike her sensible, devoted Henry, this man was probably nothing more than a player, the kind of man she spent her life avoiding—the kind of man who had women coming and going again and again and again, the kind of man who used his good looks like a wartime weapon—leaving broken hearts as he went on his merry way. *Stop it*, she chided herself. You're letting an overactive imagination run wild and free. *For all you know, this man could be a priest, a reverend, a man of the cloth.*

"In fact," he continued, sweeping his eyes over her in an almost intimate manner, "I can say without any doubt, that I'm sure I'd enjoy your company."

Well, thought Callie, there goes my priest theory. He was nothing more than a flirt. Her first instincts had been accurate.

Callie cleared her throat. "I wish I could say the same."

Her companion raised one black eyebrow and drawled, "Why don't you try me?"

Talk about the direct approach, thought Callie. Of all the nerve! Callie raised one arched eyebrow, it was time to put this player—this Lothario—in his place

"Thanks, but no thanks."

Callie turned her back to him and stared determinedly out the window, hoping that he'd get the hint. She was not interested in him, despite those dimples . . . the lilting West Indian accent . . . and the long, lean muscular chocolate legs . . . damn.

Garret Langrin shifted again in his seat. Even first class seats couldn't hold his six foot five frame comfortably. It was his own fault, he thought to himself. He had a perfectly acceptable front row seat where he could have at least stretched out his legs, providing some relief. Instead, he was sitting in a cramped third row seat with his knees bunched up in front of him just because he wanted to sit next to a woman. Well, not just any woman—a woman who from the moment she'd swept onto the airplane like an avenging angel, had captivated his interest. A woman with dark, chocolate brown skin, short curly hair, and long brown legs encased in black stiletto boots, who called to him. Looking up from the black boots to a face which literally took his breath away, he'd made up his mind there and then to get better acquainted with this woman. She was beautiful, but Garret was used to beautiful women. There was something else that had propelled him to jump out of his seat and find out who she was and where she was going. There was an air of excitement that had almost been contagious, plus the lure of her full ruby lips, and wide brown eyes had been irresistible.

He hadn't told a complete lie when he said he wanted to get away from his front seat neighbor. Nellie Sanders was one of the most annoying people he had ever met. With her incessant chatter about her brilliant and beautiful daughters, a conversation that never varied no matter where he encountered her, and her questions about his dating habits, Garret sought to avoid her whenever he could. A champion social climber who had married and divorced well and wanted her daughters to marry (and likely divorce) better, Nellie had been after him for years. He had been on the verge of telling Nellie that he was gay or had a wife in South America when he saw the woman who was now sitting next to him.

He'd watched as with the help of the stewardess, she put her various bags in different compartments over the seat. He stared at her openly, yet she didn't appear to notice him. The he heard her low, husky laugh at something the stewardess said and his fate was sealed. He waited until she was settled in her seat before he made his move. With a quick apology to an openmouthed Nellie, he'd gotten up and walked to where she was sitting. He wasn't a man who gave woman smooth pick-up lines, but he'd tried his best to show her that he was interested in the only way he knew how—the direct way. She'd shot him down quickly—landed a direct hit to his ego. And although his grandmother swore that his ego at times needed to be a little more deflated, his seat companion's absolute lack of interest in him had smarted. Garret wasn't a man who believed in love at first sight, but there was something about this woman—a feeling of instant recognition, a connection that was immediate, something he'd never experienced before. When he first saw her he knew that he had to at least attempt to meet her. He was interested in knowing her, and he only had three hours to accomplish this. Still, Garret wasn't discouraged. A lot could happen in a few hours, given the chance.

Callie woke up with a start. She was resting comfortably on the shoulder of a person she didn't know—the *Playgirl* pinup. She sat up quickly, embarrassment flooding over her.

"How long have I been doing that?" she asked, feeling the blood rush to her face. It had been a long night of packing and she hadn't slept much, but even so, taking a nap using some stranger's body part as a pillow was not something she'd ever done before.

"One hour and fifteen minutes. The stewardess wanted to wake you for breakfast, but I wouldn't let her. You were sleeping so peacefully. Besides, I rather enjoyed it."

Good Lord, he was flirting with her again! It was time to put a stop to this.

"I'm sorry," said Callie in the same voice she used when opposing counsel tried to get too familiar. "It won't happen again."

"That's too bad," he replied as his smile widened and Callie became more annoyed. Callie stared out of her window at the clouds below. She hadn't realized how tired she was. Although she often traveled on planes for business, she rarely felt comfortable enough to sleep. But here it was, she had just taken an hour and fifteen minute nap on the arm, the very muscular arm, of a stranger. What was happening to her, thought Callie. She mentally shook her head. Think about Henry, her mind shouted again. Henry Kincaid. Your fiancé!

"My name is Garret Langrin," Callie's neighbor spoke up. "I thought that since you've already slept with me, we might as well introduce ourselves. What's your name?" He seemed oblivious to Callie's reluctance to speak to him.

"Callie," she replied, instantly regretting her decision to tell him her name. She wasn't sure why she did it, just blurted out her business to a total stranger. Well, not a total stranger—at least she knew his name. Usually, when strangers asked her questions about herself, particularly male strangers, she'd give them a false name. Her favorite was Beulah Jean.

"Callie," his voice caressed her name. "That's quite lovely. It suits you."

"My mother thought so," Callie replied, refusing to take his compliment.

"Are you going to St. Christopher on business or pleasure?"

Good, thought Callie. The perfect opening. "I'm going there to meet my fiancé ."

"Really," his reply was smooth. "What a lucky man. You have to forgive me for asking you so many questions, I didn't see a ring on your finger, so I assumed you were unattached."

Callie looked down at her left hand self-consciously. Her family hadn't been happy about her no ring engagement. What was the big deal about a ring anyway? A ring was just a symbol of the love they shared. Henry had promised to get her a ring from St. Christopher, and that was fine with her.

"Well, you know what they say about assumptions," said Callie tartly. The ring comment had bothered her.

"No," Garret replied, leaning closer, "What do they say about assumptions?"

Callie sighed. "Nothing. Forget it. Really, let's just change the subject."

"If you were my fiancé, you'd be wearing my ring."

Here we go with this ring issue again. Why did the world demand that you needed a ring to prove that you were actually getting married. She'd had this same conversation with her sister Lydia right after the engagement.

"Where's the ring?" Lydia had asked immediately upon hearing the news of Callie's engagement, grabbing Callie's left hand.

"Everything happened so quickly," Callie had replied, immediately regretting sharing her good news with her sister. *"He didn't have time to get the ring."*

"Didn't have time to get a ring? If a man doesn't have time to get me an engagement ring, then I don't have time to accept his proposal."

"That's because you're materialistic. Those things don't matter to me." Callie had given in to one of her rare bouts of temper.

"I didn't say that he had to get you a big ring, Callie. I just said that he should get you a ring. Period."

The conversations with the rest of her family

went just about the same way. No one was happy for her. They were all concerned that things happened too quickly, or that she didn't have an engagement ring, or that St. Christopher really was too far away from New York, and what if she didn't like it, and the most common theme of all—how can you throw away a promising career for a man whom you've only known for three months.

"I know that I love him, and that's enough for me." Her reply sounded defensive even to her own ears, but she did not care. It was time for practical, predictable Callie to get a life, and given time, Callie was sure that her family, and her friends, would warm to the idea. Still, it would have been nice if someone, anyone, supported her decision to get married and start a new life with Henry.

Garret's voice interrupted her thoughts. "Your fiancé is a lucky man."

"We're both lucky," replied Callie, deliberately opening a magazine to put an end to any further conversation this man wanted to have with her. He made her uncomfortable and he asked too many questions.

"So, Callie, what is it that you do?"

"You don't give up, do you?" asked Callie, exasperated.

"No," replied Garret, "I'm known for my determined nature."

"Well," said Callie, returning her attention to the open magazine, with the hope that he would finally take the hint that she didn't want to talk to him, "If I were you, I'd give up. I'm a lost cause. I don't mean to be rude, but I've already told you that I'm getting married and, call me crazy, but I don't think my fiancé would appreciate another man flirting with me."

"Is that what you think I'm doing, flirting with you?"

"Oh, for heaven's sake!" Callie blurted out. Callie was used to keeping her emotions firmly in check—a good trait for a litigator—but she'd lost her cool several times with Garret Langrin. "You *know* that you've been coming on to me since you sat down next to me."

"Coming on to you?" Garret's deep voice was serious, but she could swear that he was teasing her. "Would you explain what that means? I'm not familiar American slang."

From the twinkle in his eye, she suspected that he was teasing her, but she couldn't be too sure.

"I am not talking to you," said Callie. "This conversation is finished."

The sound of a low, soft chuckle in response to her words increased her irritation. He really was the most annoying man.

"There are many folks who say that I specialize in lost causes," Garret said, after a brief moment of silence. "Just ask my grandmother."

Callie sighed. "I'd rather not."

She knew that she was being rude, but for once she didn't care. This man made her nervous. She couldn't wait to see Henry, she told herself. The first thing she'd do when she saw him was wrap her arms around him. He was her future. The man she would marry. In her mind's eye she saw herself in a beautiful white wedding dress waiting for Henry.

* * *

"Hi, Mom, It's me, Callie. I'm off to St. Christopher to see Henry. I'll call you when I get settled. Be happy for me, Mom. Love you."

Catherine Hopewell played the answering machine again and listened to her daughter's message and said out loud, "Callie has lost her mind." Although there was no one else in the house, Catherine spoke as if she expected a response. Although, she hadn't heard his voice in over twenty years, Catherine spoke to her husband Jacob every day, if for nothing but the comfort of it. He'd been more to her than her husband, he'd been an advisor, a confidant, the proverbial rock that she leaned on, clung to, touched when she needed him. Catherine wasn't going to give that up even though Jacob was now one of God's angels.

She looked up at his portrait hanging over the fireplace. The artist had done a fine job. He'd captured Jacob's perpetual easygoing expression, midnight black eyes and strong, stubborn chin. He was a handsome man, her Jacob. Even after the sickness took him, he never lost his looks or his stubbornness. Until the day he died, Catherine never thought he would allow death to claim him. Jacob was too stubborn, too strong to die. Even though the doctors all confirmed she was losing him months before, his death took her by surprise. Jacob had accepted the inevitable, as he called it. But Catherine never did. Sometimes she imagined that one day he would just wake up and step out of that portrait. What a glorious day that would be, thought Catherine. The only thing that helped ease her pain was her belief that one day she and Jacob would be reunited. She knew that she would look into those kind, dark eyes again.

Catherine sat down on her sofa and said to Jacob, "Of all our children, I always thought Callie had the most common sense. But now, here it is, she's run off to St. Christopher after a man she hardly knows." Three months wasn't long enough to know a man. Catherine had known Jacob eleven years before he finally convinced her to marry him. When Callie met Henry, she told her mother that this was going to be the man she would marry. That worried Catherine. This was the sort of romantic nonsense she would hear from her other daughters, not her practical Callie. Catherine wanted Callie to find love, but there was something about Henry Kincaid that set Catherine's teeth on edge. Callie's devotion to him caused Catherine to lose sleep at night. It was dangerous to love a man too much, and the look that Callie got in her eyes whenever she talked about Henry showed that she loved too much. She'd built her life around a person whom Catherine was very sure didn't deserve her. Callie deserved a man who was kind, devoted, strong, and sweet—she didn't deserve a man whose eyes were cold even when he declared his love for Catherine's first-born child.

Be happy for me, Mom, Callie had pleaded. Callie might be a big-time lawyer, but she was still Catherine's baby. All her big, grown daughters were her babies. They didn't know it, but she did. Even though Callie was a full-fledged responsible adult, unlike her other temperamental, dramatic daughters, she was still Catherine and Jacob's baby girl.

Jacob's picture looked down at his wife. He seemed to say, "Time to let go, Catherine." In her heart Catherine knew that she should have let go of all her children's lives a long time ago, but it was hard stepping back and watching them maneuver through life's hardships. She couldn't let go when they were children, and she was having an even harder time now that they were all grown up.

Catherine sighed and spoke to her dead husband. "All right Jacob, I'll let go . . . or at least I'll try, but I know that Henry Kincaid is no good. I just feel in my heart that he's going to hurt our baby, but I'll let go."

Catherine knew that she'd raised an independent woman and she was proud of that, even if that independence was taking her daughter down an uncharted and, she suspected, rocky road. Catherine said a quick prayer and asked the Lord to watch out for her firstborn. After that, she walked over to Jacob's picture, blew him a kiss and walked out the apartment. She was late for her choir rehearsal and if she didn't hurry, Mrs. Myers, the reverend's wife, would give away her solo to that conniving Mrs. Dean. That hussy—and she didn't use that word lightly—had been angling for a solo for some time now and if Catherine wasn't careful, it would be Mrs. Dean singing "Abide With Me," on communion Sunday.

Chapter 2

Callie fastened her seat belt. Although the stewardess had announced that the flight was in its initial descent into Queenstown, the capital of St. Christopher, all she could see outside her window was the deep blue Caribbean Sea interspersed with patches of green. The sunlight was dancing haphazardly on the waves and gave the sea a fine, almost translucent sheen of gold. Where was the land? Callie was not a nervous flier, but it concerned her that the plane was now low enough that she could see the froth of the waves below, but no land. The plane made a sudden sharp turn to the left and Callie heard the familiar metal groan of the wheels of the airplane being lowered. Where was the land? The plane was getting so close to the water that she could make out the people on the boats in the sea below them.

"Any minute now." It was as if Garret had read her thoughts. "We should be seeing the mountains."

He leaned over her shoulder and looked out the window. "Ah, yes, there they are."

When Garret sat back in his seat, Callie saw the mountains for the first time. They looked more like rolling hills, with hues of green, brown, and purple. Their simple beauty took her breath away. On the sides of the hills were houses which seemed to be part of the land, as if nature intended it to be this way. Some of the houses appeared to be spectacular, pastel colored villas with pea shaped swimming pools. Others appeared to be little more than shacks. Palm trees stood erect, and seemed to salute her arrival to a place that was to be her future home.

"Beautiful," said Garret as he looked in her direction and for a quick moment, Callie couldn't tell if he was talking about her or the lush hills below.

"Yes, it is," agreed Callie. "My new home is quite beautiful."

"So, you're going to be living here on our fair island?" asked Garret.

"Eventually," said Callie.

"Where will you be staying?"

"Broxton," said Callie, realizing that he wasn't going to stop asking her questions and it didn't matter anyway. She'd be with Henry and Garret would probably forget about her as soon as some other pretty face came his way.

"Hmm" remarked Garret. "Broxton is a very nice place."

"Is Broxton far from the airport?" asked Callie.

"About half an hour away," said Garret. Then, almost off-handedly, he asked, "Is your fiancé going to meet you at the airport? If not, my driver can take you wherever you want to go."

"Your driver?" Callie asked.

"Yes, her name is Zenna."

"You don't drive?" Callie asked, intrigued. She'd have bet her last dollar that this was the type of man who drove fast sports cars with reckless abandon. He didn't seem like the kind of person who would let someone else do the driving.

"Actually, I do drive very well, in fact."

Modesty was apparently lost on this man.

"Then why do you have a driver?"

Garret chuckled. "Actually, my driver only drives me around occasionally. She's more of an all-around assistant. Maybe you'll get to meet her sometime."

It figures that he'd have a woman driver, thought Callie. The man had hound dog written all over him.

"Thanks for the offer, but I'll be taking a taxi to Broxton."

"Your fiancé isn't coming to meet you?" Garret's tone was disapproving.

"I'm surprising him," said Callie, hoping to stop the conversation right on its tracks.

"Again," said Garret, "I have to say it, your fiancé is a lucky man."

Callie looked out the window and as the plane made its final descent, she saw that the water surrounding the island was now a brilliant emerald green.

"Have you ever been to our lovely island before?" Her companion's voice interrupted her thoughts.

"You ask a lot of questions," said Callie, turning to face Garret.

"I've been told that before," Garret answered. "I can't help it. I'm an attorney."

An attorney, thought Callie. She should have known. The habit of probing into others' lives was a hazard of her profession, and she'd been accused by her family of doing the same thing.

"I can run but I can't hide," Callie muttered to herself.

Garret smiled. "I hate to disappoint you, but there are several attorneys on the island. I just happen to be one of them."

He leaned closer to her conspiratorially. "What have you got against attorneys anyway?"

"It's a long story," Callie replied, moving away from him and turning her attention back to the scene outside the plane window.

He was silent for a moment, then said—his voice low, and she hated to admit it, sexy—"I love long stories."

"Well, I don't—so if you don't mind . . ."

Her mother would have been appalled. She could just hear her. "A lady should never be rude, Callie, and I raised you to be a lady." Her sisters would be mystified. They had no aversion to putting folks in their place if the situation warranted it, but they would have been shocked at her openly rude behavior. First, they would probably scold her for treating this handsome stranger in such a standoffish manner. Her sisters were all man crazy—even the ones who were currently involved in serious relationships—and all excelled in the art of flirtation. They would not have understood her reaction to her seat mate, the very handsome and the very curious Garret Langrin. She didn't understand her reaction to him either. It wasn't as if she wasn't used to neatly putting adversaries in their place, she usually wasn't so direct.

"I'm sorry if I've offended you," said Garret, his purposeful smile disappearing. "I do ask a lot of questions. I hope I haven't given you a wrong impression about men in St. Christopher."

The words flew out of Callie's lips before she could stop them. "The only impressions of men from St. Christopher that I'm interested in come from my fiancé."

Ouch, said a little voice in her head. That was unnecessarily sharp.

At that moment, the plane landed with a series of quick bumps and the stewardess announced cheerfully over the din of the piped-in calypso music, "Welcome to St. Christopher."

Garret watched as Callie walked across the tarmac to the main building. As soon as the plane landed, Callie had quickly gotten out of her seat, grabbed her various bags and made a hasty exit. She was the first one off the plane. He knew that he should have been insulted by her determination to put as much distance between them as possible, but he really couldn't blame her. He had come on a little strong. Usually he was a little more patient, but her continual rebuff of his attempts at polite conversation had caused him to gamble rashly. If the circumstances had been different—if she didn't have a fiancé or she hadn't made it clear that she had absolutely no interest in getting to know him—he would have liked to be the one to show her St. Christopher. Not the way the tourists saw it, behind the walls surrounding their hotel grounds, but the way that the people of his country knew the land—the rolling hillsides, the hidden beach coves, trips down the lazy rivers in the interior of the island, reggae and calypso concerts under the stars, meals at expensive restaurants and roadside shacks, trips to the island's art and history museums. There was much more to St. Christopher than the tourists saw and he wanted to be the one who introduced her to his country. But, he thought as he stood up and stretched his tall frame, that was one wish he would never have the opportunity of fulfilling. Garret collected his bags and walked down the steps of the plane. It was mid-afternoon, and the sun was at its peak. Still, even the hot, humid air gave him a sense of comfort. He'd missed this island. The nearby hills surrounding Queenstown greeted him like a familiar and faithful friend. It was good to be home.

He'd been away for three weeks, which for him was too long. Leaving St. Christopher destroyed his sense of equilibrium. Garret smiled to himself. He was more like his grandmother than he cared to admit. She always declared that her heart hurt if she stayed away from home for more than two days. As usual, business had taken him away from St. Christopher. His client, a hotel chain based in St. Christopher, had entered into a contract with a New York public relations firm for a two-year publicity campaign. The client was happy with the terms of the contract, and the attorneys for the public relations firm were fair, if not exactly decent.

The New York attorneys underestimated Garret but they didn't make that mistake for long. He gained leverage in the business deal by using his St. Christopher charm and a firm knowledge of his adversaries' weaknesses. This combination afforded him the opportunity to attain even those goals he'd once thought insurmountable. He knew that for Callie, a fiancé was an insurmountable goal and he respected that. There were too many people who didn't understand exactly what the term fidelity meant. He admired her resolve to be true to her fiancé, but he didn't have to like it.

The heat in the small immigration center was almost unbearable. Although there were many whirling ceiling fans overhead, whatever air they pushed around was too hot to bring any relief to the agents and travelers in the brightly painted waiting room. The customs agent seemed to be taking an unnecessarily long time in reviewing her passport, thought Callie.

At last, the customs agent looked at her and spoke.

"Business or pleasure?"

"Pleasure," replied Callie.

"How long will you be on the island?"

"One week," said Callie. As she responded to the official's question she noticed Garret walk through the line reserved for returning St. Christopher nationals. He looked over in her direction and grinned at her. Then, he turned and walked out of the hot room. She felt an inexplicable sense of disappointment. He seemed to have quite easily moved on, which she supposed was just fine with her because she wasn't interested, no matter how gorgeous and, she admitted grudgingly, charming he was.

"Where will you be staying?" The customs official asked, and Callie turned her gaze away from

Garret. What did she care about what he felt or did not feel about her? She would never see him again and that was just fine.

"I'll be in Broxton."

The agent stamped her passport and said with great flourish, "Welcome to St. Christopher. Enjoy your stay."

Chapter 3

Half an hour later Callie was standing outside the airport by the taxi stand. Getting her bags had proven to be an arduous and protracted experience. She'd seen Garret again—this time in the baggage area. She'd watched with undisguised envy as he got his bags and moved to the front of the line where he was quickly ushered through by two uniformed officials. Apparently Garret Langrin was someone whom folks in St. Christopher paid attention to. Looking around at the baggage area that she found herself in brought one word to Callie's mind—chaos. There were people and bags everywhere—all waiting to be inspected before they would mercifully be set free to go on their way. At least, thought Callie, with no small measure of gratitude, the baggage claim was air-conditioned. At one point she thought of calling Henry to let him know that she was on the island. She even toyed with the idea of asking him to meet her at the airport. But she had come all this way to surprise him and she was not about to ruin the surprise. She couldn't wait to see the look on his face when he saw her.

The sun beat down on her without mercy and although she wore her hat, it didn't do much good. Her now damp clothes clung to her and she could feel beads of sweat trailing down her back. The air was humid and had a sweet smell of flowers and ripe fruit. She watched as people, laden down with suitcases, rushed in different directions, either to taxis or the arms of waiting relatives. There were several women dressed in brightly colored dresses with baskets of fruit balanced on their heads, calling out the names of their various wares. A cart was parked under a tree directly across the street and an old man was shaving ice and putting it in cups filled with different flavor juices. "Snow cone! Snow cone!" he yelled. Callie was tempted to leave her spot in the line waiting for taxis to get the flavored ice. But, anxious to get going, she was not about to lose her spot.

Callie felt a light tap on her shoulder and she turned around. It was Garret.

"I thought you'd be long gone," Callie said.

"I stayed around just to make sure that you'd be okay," he replied with an easy smile.

Callie's eyes narrowed. She wasn't sure what to make of that statement. It was kind of him, but she couldn't help but think this was just another part of his attempt at flirting.

As if he read her thoughts, Garret's smile broadened. "Really, I just wanted to make sure that everything was fine with you. No ulterior motive."

Well, it was a nice gesture. Callie found herself smiling back at him.

"Thanks," she replied. "You all don't make it easy to get into this country—that's for sure. I've never seen slower immigration lines."

"We're just not as much in a hurry as you New Yorkers are," he replied.

"My driver would be happy to take you anywhere on the island you'd like to go," he said. Callie's smile disappeared and she shook her head firmly.

"That's really kind of you, but it won't be necessary."

As if to justify her words, a taxi pulled up to the curb. The taxi attendant waved to her "Where to, miss?"

"Broxton," Callie replied. She'd decided she would first go to Henry's office and if he wasn't there, she'd at least find out where he was. She'd tried to use her cell phone to call the office but she couldn't get a signal. She hoped that she'd get to Broxton before the office closed—she knew from Henry that Broxton was some distance away from Queenstown.

The cab driver got out of the taxi and helped her with her bags.

Garret opened the passenger door for Callie and she got into the backseat.

"Thanks." She smiled one more time at Garret Langrin. She wasn't ever going to see him again. It didn't hurt to be decent.

The cab driver came around to where Garret was standing. "Garret Langrin! When did you get back in town?" He slapped Garret on the back with easy familiarity.

Garret laughed. "I've just gotten back, Buick. It's good to see you, man. How's your wife doing?"

"Causing me trouble!" The taxi driver looked at Callie and said, "I see that you're in good hands, miss. Garret you always did move fast!"

"No, no—it's not like that," said Garret, still laughing. "Not that I didn't try."

"If you don't mind," said Callie, clearing her throat, "I'm anxious to be going."

"Yes, of course." Garret suddenly stopped smiling. He turned to the taxi driver. "Take the lady where she pleases, Buick. She's in a hurry. But mind you, drive carefully."

"Is Zenna coming for you?" Buick asked.

"Yes, but you know she's always late."

"I don't know how you put up with that crazy woman. Well, I guess she's easy on the eyes so that makes up for a lot."

Callie had heard enough. She should have guessed that Garret's lady driver would be good-looking. "Are we ready yet?" she asked the driver.

"You better get going, Buick," said Garret.

Finally, thought Callie, although she watched with no small amount of dissatisfaction as Garret and Buick continued their conversation a little while longer—although she couldn't hear what they were saying.

At last, the driver got in the front seat. "Where to, Miss America?"

She hardly felt like a beauty queen with her damp clothes clinging to her from the tropical heat.

"Fifty-nine Queen Elizabeth Road."

"Right away, ma'am!"

As the taxi began to pull off, Garret leaned down and said through the window, "I know we probably won't see each other again, but here's my card. If you should ever need it."

Callie took his card and before she could respond, the taxi pulled quickly away from the curb.

"Good man, that Garret," said the taxi driver.

"Is your name really Buick?" asked Callie, changing the subject.

"My name is Herbert Ignatius Simeon Cady, but folks call me Buick," he said with pride.

"How did you get from that name to Buick?"

"Well," said Buick, "ever since I was young, I wanted to drive a Buick. Took me forty years, but I finally got my Buick. Anyway, folks know about my love affair with the car and so that's how I got the name."

"What's so special about a Buick, if you don't mind me asking?"

Laughter came to Buick easily. "To tell you the truth, I don't really know. I just like how the car looks—prosperous like. I like the look of prosperity."

Callie smiled at him and their eyes met through the rearview mirror. His good nature was contagious. Glancing down at the business card which was still in her hand, she read *Garret Langrin, Attorney at Law*. There was a Queenstown address and phone number printed under his name. Callie tucked the business card in her pocket. She knew that she'd never have the need to call Garret Langrin, but it didn't hurt to be polite. Callie settled in her seat and rolled down her window more in an attempt to get some cool air. Apparently, Buick didn't believe in air-conditioning.

Buick turned on the radio and found a station playing reggae music. Callie recognized the tune as one of Bob Marley's songs. "Don't worry about a thing," Bob sang in a smooth voice that even Buick's tinny radio could not diminish, "cause every little thing will be all right." As they drove through the streets of Queenstown listening to the music of Bob Marley, Callie thought to herself, heaven must be like this. Not bad. Not bad at all.

They left Queenstown behind in a matter of minutes and were soon driving in the surrounding countryside. The narrow, winding road which served as St. Christoper's highway A-1 was bordered by the Atlantic to its east and by the lush, deep green hills to the west. Callie leaned out the window and let the wind caress her. There was something hypnotic about this country and its beauty. A beauty which like a jealous lover, did everything in its power to keep you interested, mesmerized. Her excitement grew as she contemplated the place that was going to be her new home and the man who was unknowingly waiting for her in Broxton.

A half hour later, the taxi made its way into the charming town of Broxton. Unlike the bustling capital of Queenstown, Broxton had a distinct small town feel. Like the other parts of the island that she'd seen, Broxton had pastel colored homes which flanked narrow, winding streets. The late afternoon sun had apparently kept many people inside because the streets were empty at this hour. Glancing at her watch, Callie could see that it was almost three-thirty and Henry had told her that in St. Christopher, most businesses closed by five o'clock. Henry's office would probably be open, and she prayed he was not on some other part of the island. The taxi passed through a section of town that was commercial in nature with stores, an open-air market, a bank, and other office buildings. No building appeared to be higher than two stories—a direct contrast to the tall business buildings that Callie had left behind in Queenstown. There were quite a few churches, some made of brick and limestone, which were reminiscent of an earlier time. She passed by some old men who had set up an old table and a few mismatched chairs—they were playing dominoes and laughing. There were a few other people walking leisurely to various destinations. No one appeared to be in much of a hurry.

This was Henry's home. She drank in the scenery, feeling a sense of excitement that she was here in the place that her fiancé loved so dearly. She'd heard the many stories from Henry about the colorful characters who inhabited the town, and she looked forward to meeting them all. But first she looked forward to wrapping her arms around Henry. She hoped that he'd be as happy to see her as she was to see him. Just then the words of her sister Lydia came back to her *"Not all men like surprises."*

Shrugging her sister's words away, she turned her attention back to the scenery unfolding before her. At what appeared to be the only stoplight in the town, the taxi turned down a narrow street. Callie looked up to see the street sign which read "Queen Elizabeth Road." This was where Henry's business was located.

By the time the taxi stopped in front of a gray, two-story modern building that seemed somehow incongruous with the other older, traditional West Indian structures, Callie felt her heart beat faster. In a matter of minutes she would see Henry. She was excited, but she was also a little scared. She wasn't sure why—perhaps her family's misgivings were catching up with her.

"We're here," Buick announced.

Right. She had arrived at her destination. Forcing herself to calm down, Callie opened the door and got out of the taxi.

"Would you wait for me?" she asked Buick. "At least until I make sure that my friend is in his office?"

"You mean he doesn't know you're coming?" Buick asked.

"Not exactly," Callie uttered. "It's a surprise."

"Oooooh," Buick said with a wide smile. "I'm sure it will be a most pleasant surprise."

Callie opened her purse to pay Buick.

"How much do I owe you?" she asked. "I'll pay you now . . . but if my friend isn't around, I'll probably need to check into a hotel until I can reach him."

Buick shook his head.

"There's no need for payment, miss, Mr. Garret has already taken care of that. He told me to take you to your destination and bill him."

Callie protested. "I'm sorry, I can't let you do that. I'd like to pay the fare, please."

Buick shook his head again. "Mr. Garret is a good friend of mine and I won't insult him. He wants to pay and I'm going to let him."

Callie stifled a sigh. Now was not the time to get sidetracked in some sort of macho game of manners. She was on the way to meet her future husband and if Garret Langrin wanted to pay her fare, then fine. It was a nice gesture and St. Christopher was a small enough island that she might run into him again—she could repay him or thank him then.

Closing the cab door behind her, Callie walked across the sidewalk to the front door of Kincaid Enterprises. She hesitated for a moment before opening the front door. Then, with a dramatic flourish, as if she expected Henry to be in the lobby, she opened the door and was immediately thrown into an air-conditioned haven. Indeed, the lobby of Kincaid Enterprises—the sort of wood paneled lobby that she'd seen in countless office buildings—was downright chilly. She'd expected something exotic but instead she stood on the thick burgundy carpet looking at a large oak desk, behind which was a very pretty young woman reading a magazine. There were several chairs along with a plush floral couch which dominated the room. Portraits of stern-looking men on the wall looked down at her and Callie was surprised to see that Henry was one of them. But it wasn't the Henry she knew, the laughing, charming Henry. This portrait was of a grim, unsmiling man whose cold, dark eyes seemed to mock her. Callie felt a chill come over her.

"May I help you?" The pretty lady behind the desk put down her magazine and spoke.

Callie forced a smile she didn't feel. The room intimidated her and a sense of discomfort grabbed her.

"Is Mr. Kincaid in?" Callie asked.

"Which Mr. Kincaid?" the question was asked with just a hint of exasperation.

"Mr. Henry Kincaid," Callie replied.

"Who may I say is calling?"

"His fiancé," said Callie. She wanted to wipe the sneer off the receptionist's face, and she succeeded. The woman looked as if Callie had suddenly grown three heads.

"Come again?" she asked.

"My name is Callie Hopewell," Callie replied. "I'm Henry Kincaid's fiancé."

The woman's eyes widened with surprise.

"I don't believe that Mr. Kincaid is in, but perhaps his assistant might be able to help you," the receptionist replied.

Callie watched as she picked up the telephone.

"Ramona, this is Bridgette. There's a woman here who says that she's Henry's fiancé . . . could you come down here? Thanks."

There's a woman here who says that she's Henry's fiancé.

Callie was taken aback by the woman's obvious surprise. Obviously Henry had kept their engagement a secret, at least from those with whom he worked. She could understand that. Couldn't she? Perhaps he just wanted to keep his personal life private. Perhaps.

The door opened and a thin, brown-skinned woman walked over to where Callie stood. She was dressed in a tight gray suit and black patent leather pumps with high heels. Her full lips were painted a bright red and large diamond stud earrings glinted in her ears. She was an attractive woman. Still, she was not beautiful, her looks were too cold. There was something almost sinister about the flinty stare that she directed at Callie.

Callie's sense of discomfort increased. So far her introduction to Kincaid Enterprises had not gone smoothly.

SMOOTH OPERATOR

"May I help you?" The woman she assumed was Henry's assistant spoke. Her voice was so deep that for a crazy moment Callie wondered if the woman had had a recent sex change.

Shaking those thoughts out of her head, Callie responded. "I'm looking for Henry."

"And you are?"

"His fiancé. Is Henry here or is he away on business?"

"He's not here. He's at home."

Home? Callie remembered that Henry had told her he'd sold his home because of his itinerant lifestyle. Had he bought a new home and not told her?

"Where exactly is that?" Callie asked, her patience leaving her quickly.

"As his fiancé, I'd think you'd know where Henry lived," the receptionist spoke up.

"Hush, Bridgette! Where are your manners?" Henry's assistant spoke quickly to the receptionist. Turning back to Callie, she said, "I apologize for Bridgette's behavior. Henry left the office about an hour ago and he was heading home. His address is 2903 Hibiscus Lane."

"Is that here in town?" Callie asked, feeling a little foolish. After all, Bridgette had a point. She should have known the address of her fiancé.

"Yes. If you hurry, you'll probably catch him. Henry moves around the island a lot and you never know how long he'll be in one place."

"Thank you," said Callie, feeling relief that soon she would see Henry. At least then she would get her questions answered, the first being why he told her that he was staying at different hotels if he had bought a home.

"You're welcome," said Henry's assistant, but her cold eyes spoke otherwise. Something was not right with this scenario.

Buick drove her to Hibiscus Lane. Henry's assistant, Ramona, had given excellent directions. They drove into the hills surrounding Broxton and Callie found herself gazing at the large pastel colored villas. Grand, perfectly manicured lawns with various tropical trees and brightly colored flowers only added to the already picturesque surroundings, but despite her charming surroundings, Callie felt tense.

"Up here is where the really rich folk live," he announced.

Buick's words were an understatement. While the homes in town were charming and pretty, these homes perched precariously on the sides of the hill looked as if they belonged in an episode of *Lifestyles of the Rich and Famous*. Most homes had security guards sitting out by the gates. She passed circular driveways with luxury cars parked prominently in the front of the homes. As she passed a large pink structure which looked as if it was an apartment building or a condominium, Callie asked, "Who lives there?"

"That's the Pink Hotel," said Buick. "Broxton's only hotel."

"It's beautiful," said Callie.

"That it is," agreed Buick. "I know the owner and she does a good business there. She's very particular about who she takes, though. She's partial to certain repeat guests or people who the guests have recommended the hotel to."

"Does she actually choose whom she will allow into the hotel?"

"That she does. And believe me, that's one of the nicest hotels on the island."

"Hibiscus Lane is just up the road here," Buick announced. The taxi left the paved hillside road and veered right, up a red dirt road. The houses on this road could best be described as mansions. They were not of any uniform architectural type. Their only uniform characteristic was that they were all large.

Buick stopped his taxi in front of the largest house on the road, a stark white, Mediterranean-style mansion, with deep red shutters. There was a well tended garden in front with bright tropical flowers. In front of the house an old gentleman trimmed the shrubbery. He wore a wide straw hat that obscured Callie's view of his face.

"Hey, man!" Buick called out, "is the boss home?"

The old man stopped working long enough to give a brief nod, then went back to his work.

"Looks like you're finally in luck," said Buick as he maneuvered the taxi past the wrought-iron gates.

Callie thought about what she'd say to Henry. She hoped that he had an explanation for not telling her about his house. Well, she told herself, she would keep an open mind. There was always a reasonable explanation for everything and she was sure Henry would have one. Although she was troubled that he'd hide this kind of information from her.

"Let me get your bags," said Buick. "You go ahead and give your man his surprise."

"Right," said Callie, as she forced herself to get out of the car. Her mouth was suddenly very dry.

"What's the matter?" asked Buick, who was watching her carefully. "Second thoughts?"

"No," said Callie quickly, and with more resolve than she felt. She got out of the taxi and walked up the cobblestone path that led to the front door. The sweet scent of the unfamiliar tropical flowers, along with the heat from the still unforgiving late afternoon sun, made Callie dizzy. As she made her way to the door she noticed two cars parked in front of the garage. Henry must have company. A quick movement from behind one of the first floor windows caught her eye and she could have sworn that there was someone standing there looking at her. But on closer inspection, all she saw was sheer white curtains dancing in the wind. She walked briskly to the wood front door and rang the doorbell.

The door opened instantly, as if someone were expecting her, and Callie found herself face-to-face with one of the most exquisite—there really was no other word for it—women that she had ever seen in her life. At five foot seven, Callie was considered tall for a woman. But the woman in front of her easily topped the six foot mark. She was dressed completely in white. Her dress, which came down to her ankles, was made of a thin gauzy material, which like the curtains in the house, danced about her in the breeze. She had on a shawl of the same gauzy material draped around her shoulders, which gave her the look of a fairy, or some other unearthly being. Her skin was a deep golden hue as if she had spent most of her life in the presence of the sun, and her eyes were the same gold color as her skin. Her features, if taken apart, were quite unremarkable, wide mouth, prominent chin, slightly upturned nose, large eyes. However, taken together, these features combined to create a face that would leave Madison Avenue mavens, as well as most of the men in the free world, awestruck.

"May I help you?" the apparition's clipped voice betrayed either birth or a long stay in England.

"I'm here to see Henry," said Callie.

"And whom may I say wishes to see him?"

"His fiancé," replied Callie, suddenly self-conscious.

"Ah," said the woman, not moving from the doorway, "that presents a bit of a problem."

Callie was beginning to get annoyed. She was tired. Hot. Hungry. And she wanted to see Henry.

"What kind of problem?" asked Callie. "Is he home?"

"Oh, he's very much at home," was the quick reply.

"Then, what's the problem?"

"Henry is my husband. So you see the dilemma we have here."

The words floated somewhere above Callie's head before they finally reached a place where she could comprehend their meaning. *Henry is my husband.* This had to be a joke, Callie decided. A poor attempt at humor. But this lovely woman with the perfectly arched, raised eyebrows didn't appear to be amused. Her fiancé had a wife.

Without turning her head, the woman called out, "Henry! Please come here, you have a visitor."

She was lying, thought Callie. How could Henry be married? This is the sort of drama that one of her sisters would be involved in. She was too smart to get involved with a married man. How could Henry have done this to her? Why would Henry have done this to her? But the look on the receptionist's face when Callie told her that she was Henry's fiancé, the knowledge that Henry had a house and had lied about it, the cold manner of Henry's assistant all convinced her that the woman was telling the gospel truth.

"Ah, here is my husband." The woman stepped aside, and Callie found herself facing Henry. He looked as if he'd seen a ghost, and for a fleeting moment Callie thought she saw the unmistakable look of guilt mixed with panic, but it was quickly replaced by something infinitely worse: dismissal.

"Henry, what is going on here?" asked Callie.

"Yes, Henry, what is going on here?" asked the woman, who now looked slightly amused. "This woman says she's your fiancé."

Henry's words, when they came, were harsh. "I've never seen her before in my life." Henry turned and walked back into the house. The woman remained standing in the doorway. There was a smile on her lips that didn't quite make it to her eyes.

Callie wasn't sure if it was the heat, the scent of tropical flowers, or Henry's words that made her sway, but the world around her no longer felt solid. The ground on which she stood felt as if it would open up any minute to swallow her. A wave of nausea swept over her and for one terrible moment, she thought that she was going to be sick.

"Come on, Miss America," said Buick, who had come to Callie's side. "He's not worth it."

Callie stared at Buick as if she didn't recognize him. The world had gone mad. She was in a strange place with a man named after a car and her fiancé had a wife.

Buick repeated his words. "He's not worth it."

Buick was right about that. Callie straightened her spine even as tears of humiliation and anger sprang to her eyes. She wasn't going to fall apart in front of these people. Later, she would allow herself to have the nervous breakdown that she'd earned, but she was not going to make a further spectacle of herself.

Blinking back tears, Callie followed Buick back to the waiting taxi. She was aware of the gardener who was now openly staring at her. His eyes were sad and sympathetic. She got into the backseat of the taxi and Buick closed the door behind her.

"Where to, Miss Lady?" asked Buick, as he started the taxi.

"I don't know, I really don't," was Callie's honest answer.

"Are you okay?" Buick asked.

"No."

She wasn't okay. She was hurt, humiliated, angry, and confused. There had always been a distance, a reserve that she felt whenever she was with Henry. There was always something that was slightly off, a feeling that all was not what it seemed, but she'd let her loneliness, her desire to be in a relationship, to be with a man who seemed to put her first, chase away any doubts she had about Henry. Now, she saw just how foolish she'd been and that she'd paid a high price for being a fool.

As the taxi backed out of Henry's driveway, Buick commented sadly, "I tell you, some men make me ashamed to share their gender."

Callie remained silent.

"Never you mind, Miss America," continued Buick. "The Lord says that when one door is closed, another will soon open."

Callie's thoughts turned blasphemous. Why couldn't the Lord have closed the door before she spent three thousand dollars on a first class ticket to St. Christopher?

Chapter 4

Garret stood on the balcony outside his second floor bedroom and watched as the evening sun descended over his property. His home was on the outskirts of the capital, tucked into green hills that surrounded Queenstown. He'd fallen in love with the property even before he'd built his house. The six acres that surrounded his villa insured that he'd have enough space to breathe without worrying about having neighbors too close by. He wasn't antisocial, but after spending his days in court or in offices arguing with other lawyers, he cherished the solitude, the peace of his surroundings. He'd paid an obscene amount of money for this land, and he'd spent even more on the lush tropical landscaping, complete with a garden filled with innumerable tropical plants and trees laden with fruits from the region. As much as he loved the land itself, he loved the view even more. His home afforded sweeping views of the ocean with the nearby island of Montpelier.

Ten years ago St. Christopher was a sleepy Caribbean island, but now with the development of chain hotels, villas overrun with tourists, St. Christopher had become one of the more popular Caribbean destinations. The island's lush natural beauty coupled with a stable political climate had proved to be an irresistible combination. The growth of the tourist industry, and the rapid development of the island, were seen as sure signs of progress by many, but not him. He longed for the time when there were no satellite TV dishes perched precariously on top of houses, and when traffic jams only occurred when the occasional goat or cow was crossing the road. That was the reason he bought his home in this area—it was still relatively undeveloped and retained the charm he remembered in years gone by.

He'd first come to this area as a boy, before folks discovered the benefits of living outside of the urban sprawl that Queenstown had become. Garret had grown up playing in these hills—even as a child he'd longed to escape the city. His father's business had often involved surveying land around the island, and his father had been one of the first real estate developers to see the potential in these hills. As his father had conducted his business, Garret had played with imaginary friends and slayed imaginary dragons in these hills. He'd spent countless hours looking out at the sea, dreaming of a time when he'd leave St. Christopher and his family problems behind—intent on making his own way in the world, a way that didn't involve the overbearing reach of his father.

Garret left St. Christopher for Oxford University when he turned eighteen. He'd fallen in love with

England, but his original love affair—the love he had for St. Christopher—had eventually won out, and Garret had returned, armed with a law degree and a new determination not to let his father run his life as his father had done with his mother. The pain of the death of Garret's mother when he was seven years old remained with him to this day and Garret placed the blame squarely on his father's shoulders. Although his grandmother tried to explain his mother's emotional problems and the role they played in her suicide, Garret knew it was his father's iron hand that had ultimately broken the fragile woman he knew his mother had been. After returning to St. Christopher, Garret had been able to build a successful life away from his father. Any attempt of his father to insert himself in Garret's life was been met with complete resistance from Garret. Eventually, his father had come to accept the distant relationship Garret desired.

Shaking thoughts of his father away, Garret looked out at the ocean and wondered what the delicious Callie was doing right about now. She was probably passionately making love with her fiancé. Thoughts of Callie and her fiancé weren't any more pleasant than thoughts of his father, but Garret was unable to stop thinking about her. It'd been a long time since he'd felt anything for a woman other than a mild interest. His attraction to Callie stirred something in him, something he hadn't known existed. Romantic love was a fiction. For Garret, romantic love was often a good mask for physical attraction, no more, no less. His mother had built her life on the foolish notion that this kind of love was attainable and he'd watched as his father had turned his attention from his wife and his son in his insatiable quest for financial security. He and his mother had been distant seconds to his father's devotion to his business and philandering, and while Garret had been able to deal with that reality, his mother had been crushed by it and had ultimately paid the price of her foolish notions with her life.

Still, there was something about Callie that made Garret want to believe that for some, happily ever after did exist. She intrigued him. When he watched the taxi carry her away, he felt a sense of regret that he still didn't understand. From the moment he first laid eyes on her, there had been a recognition—a sense that somehow there was a connection between them.

The sound of the evening crickets brought Garret back to his present surroundings. He sat down in one of the chairs on his veranda and waited in vain for a sense of peace to descend over him. There was no place in the world that he loved as much as his home. The white West Indian–style villa, with its blue shutters and gingerbread trim, never ceased to bring a sense of calm to him, no matter what turmoil he faced. But at this moment, nothing—not the view of the blue ocean below, not his landscaped property, not his home—eased his restless spirit. Nothing made him forget about Callie.

He could hear the sounds of his grandmother and his assistant, Zenna, on the first floor. He couldn't make out what his grandmother was saying, but he heard her laughter mixed with the laughter of Zenna. They were probably wondering about him. From the moment he'd come home, he'd barely spoken to his grandmother—he'd just given her a kiss on the cheek and mumbled something about a headache. He knew that if he didn't make an appearance soon, he'd have two worried women knocking on his door, asking questions. The wonderful scent of his grandmother's cooking caught his attention. Perhaps some of his grandmother's good food and good conversation would cheer him up. He hoped that would do the trick. It wasn't like him to be staring morosely at the world below him thinking of a woman who he hadn't known existed until this morning. It was time to end this pity party. Callie was intriguing and she presented interesting possibilities that he would have loved to explore—but it wasn't meant to be. Garret stood up just as his stomach began to rumble. He hadn't eaten anything since he'd gotten off the plane and he was hungry. It was time to join Zenna and his grandmother for dinner. He hoped that the diversion of the two people he held most dear in life would be enough to keep Callie Hopewell and what she might or might not be doing with her fiancé out of his thoughts.

The Pink Hotel stood in sharp contrast to Henry's impeccable white mansion. From a distance, the hotel looked stately and inviting; up close, however, was another story. The hotel had definitely seen better days thought Callie as she stared out of the taxi's window. The hotel's paint was peeling in several places and the shrubbery in the front yard grew wild and unattended. Several of the wooden shutters had come loose from the windows and they clattered against the building in the early evening breeze; the place had an air of benign neglect.

"Don't let the appearance fool you," said Buick

as he accurately gauged Callie's reaction to the hotel. "It's a real nice place."

"Okay," Callie replied, but she was not convinced.

"Give it a chance, now," urged Buick. "I know the owner. She'll treat you real good."

"I don't have much of a choice, do I?" asked Callie. Buick had informed her that the next flight leaving the island for New York didn't leave until the following afternoon. She was stuck on the island until tomorrow.

"Well, now, little miss, you always have a choice. You can go into Queenstown and I'll try to find you a hotel, but for my money, the Pink Hotel will suit you just fine."

Callie sighed. At this point, it didn't really matter where she spent the night. All she wanted was a place where she could bury her face in a pillow until tomorrow. She wanted to close her eyes and let oblivion overtake her. She wanted to forget. There would be time enough to deal with her humiliation, but right now she just wanted to sleep. She wanted not to have to play over in her head the look on Henry's face when he dismissed her from his life.

"So, what's it gonna be, Miss Lady?" Buick asked. "Would you like me to take you to Queenstown?"

Callie shook her head. "That's all right, Buick, this hotel will be just fine."

Callie opened the car door and got out of the taxi. Her body felt as if she had just run a marathon and lost. She was hot, her head felt light and her eyes still stung from the tears that she knew were just below the surface.

Buick got out of the taxi. "I'll get your bags."

Callie watched as Buick retrieved her suitcases from the trunk of the vehicle. For one terrible moment she thought she would burst into tears, but she wouldn't allow herself to cry over someone who could treat her as badly as Henry did. She was her mother's child, and her mother had taught her to hold her head high in times of adversity. Callie's head was anything but held high, but she would not allow herself to give in to the tears that threatened even now to fall shamelessly down her face. What a fool she'd been. She'd always prided herself on her good common sense. How many times had she watched her sisters rush headlong into disasters styled as relationships? How many times had she cautioned her friends to be wary of men who were a little too slick? Had she been that desperate to find someone to love that she'd trusted someone who never really existed?

Callie followed Buick down a cracked cobblestone path as he walked to the front door of the hotel. She could hear the sounds of laughter and general conversation within. She thought about turning back and telling Buick to find her a large hotel in Queenstown, somewhere where she could blend in with other tourists. People were generally friendly in these small inns, and all she wanted to do was find a warm, safe, anonymous place to hide.

"Come on, Miss Lady," said Buick, as if he sensed her hesitation. "This is a real nice place."

Callie forced herself to keep walking, although there was a part of her that wanted to run away. She appreciated Buick's help. He was very kind to her and she didn't take it for granted.

"I'm sure it's fine," she said. "It's been kind of a rough day, I'm sorry."

"No apologies."

Callie was certain that she'd just encountered one of those rare souls whose good humor just couldn't be dampened.

The lobby of the hotel was airy and light. There were windows everywhere and she could see the sea out of the windows just adjacent to the reception desk. The tile floors were scrubbed and shined as if polished by someone who believed cleanliness was next to godliness. Wicker chairs with brightly colored cushions were scattered around the lobby in no particular pattern, but looked comfortable and inviting. What sort of place was this that looked like a dump from the outside but once you walked through the front doors, you felt as if you had walked into someone's very neat and very orderly home? Overhead, the ceiling fan whirred dramatically and there was a cooling breeze that did small wonders for Callie's spirit. There were a few tourists sitting around, drinking and talking in the lobby, but it was obvious that the laughter and conversation she heard was coming from the back of the hotel.

There was no one at the reception desk and Callie left Buick and walked over to one of the large windows that faced the back of the hotel. She saw a patio where there was a lively game of dominoes going on. There was also a man with dreadlocks turning the dials of a stereo playing reggae music. Behind him was a very small woman, she was not over five feet and had to be less than a hundred pounds, teaching some of the guests to dance reggae. She looked as if a good breeze would blow her over, but she moved with the grace of a ballerina.

"That's the owner, Ma Ruth," said Buick, who had come to stand silently beside her.

Callie stared at the small woman, whose arms and body swayed back and forth to the music, which seemed to wind around the breeze. She was the color of ebony and Callie could not determine her age. If Callie were to guess, she would place her anywhere between the ages of thirty and sixty. She had the face of someone who had lived in her skin for some time and was quite comfortable in it.

"We might as well sit down and wait for the receptionist to get back from her dancing," said Buick.

"The receptionist is out there, too?" asked Callie.

"See that sort of large, good-looking woman in the back of Ma Ruth? The one with the bright orange dress? That's Dara, Ma Ruth's daughter. She's the receptionist. And from the looks of things, she's busy right now."

Callie shook her head. If things had been different, maybe she would have even managed a smile. The receptionist was on the patio dancing to reggae music while the guests waited to check in. What a place. At least that was one thing Henry didn't lie about—St. Christoper was a charming place.

"Look, I appreciate your help, Buick—but you don't have to baby-sit me, I'm sure you have other places to go."

"You tryin' to get rid of me?" Buick asked, with an easy smile.

"No," Callie replied, remembering Buick's conversation with Garret Langrin about his wife. "I just feel bad that you're here with me when you could be home with your wife."

"Believe me, my wife is probably out and about," said Buick. "But even if she's home, she'll just have to wait until I see that you're all settled in."

His kindness almost brought her to tears. The lump in her throat prevented her from responding, but when she was quite sure that she could speak without crying, she looked at him and said, "Thank you."

Chapter 5

Callie lay on the bed in her hotel room and said out loud, "I will not cry. I will not shed even one tear. He's not worth it." She repeated the phrase out loud, like a mantra, until her eyes grew heavy and sleep started to finally catch up with her exhausted body. Checking in had been a blessedly quick affair once the receptionist came back from her reggae dance session. Buick had refused to leave until both he and Dara had taken her up to her room and deposited her inside. Even then, he hesitated until Dara told him to leave her in peace.

"Dara has my phone number," Buick said, before he left the room. "If you need anything, just have her call me. I'll come get you in the morning."

Callie had thanked him and then sent him on his way. By the time he left, night had fallen.

Dara had seemed equally hesitant to leave. "If you need company, just come on downstairs. There's going to be a reggae party in the courtyard—not that you look like you're in the mood for a party."

Callie shook her head. "I'll be fine here."

"I'll send you up some food in a little while," Dara said. "I'll have the cook prepare you something special."

Callie knew there was no way she could force any food down her throat the way she was feeling, still, she thanked Dara. She knew that Buick told her about what had happened. The look of pity in Dara's eyes was confirmed by her words.

"Don't let that man get the best of you," Dara said. "Men like that, eventually they get just what's coming to them."

When Dara and Buick finally left the room, Callie sank into the bed fully clothed and pulled the covers over her head.

Outside she could hear the sounds of laughter, conversation and reggae music. Under different circumstances, very different circumstances, this might have been a very enjoyable place. But now all she could think of was getting as far away from this beautiful island as possible. Dara promised to take care of the changes to her flight arrangements. "Leave everything to me," she'd said, in a voice that sounded as if she would burst into song momentarily, "I'll take care of it for you, don't worry."

Callie had been relieved to not have the responsibility of changing tickets and giving explanations. It was going to be difficult enough explaining to her mother, her sisters, her friends, her secretary, her hairdresser, and her travel agent. Well, she thought, as sleep finally began to descend, there's time enough for that tomorrow. Right now I just want to forget that this day ever happened.

* * *

From the lively conversation and laughter coming from his kitchen, Garret knew his grandmother was in a good mood. His stomach rumbled again as he smelled his favorite dish, escoveitched fried fish, plantains, and rice and peas. His grandmother loved to cook, almost as much as she loved to meddle in his life. He supposed he shouldn't complain too much. At forty-two, it was nice to have a grandmother who was still around, despite her predisposition to stick her delicate nose into his business.

"We're in the kitchen!" his grandmother called out as she heard his footsteps. "I hope that you're hungry!"

Garret stopped in his progress to the kitchen to look through the mail which had been sorted in three piles by his efficient housekeeper. There was one pile for emergencies, one pile for things that could wait and the last pile was the "don't bother" pile. There was one letter in the emergency pile. He frowned as he recognized his father's handwriting. *Now, what does he want,* thought Garret as he picked it up.

It was probably another attempt by his father to get close. He put the letter back in the pile, unopened. It was a little too late for his father's attempts at reconciliation.

"Garret, your fish is going to get cold!" His grandmother called out to him from the kitchen.

"And if you don't get here soon, I'll be eating your piece," Zenna called out.

He would deal with his father's letter later. Garret walked to the kitchen with quick, sure strides. When he entered his kitchen he saw Zenna sitting at the kitchen table, already devouring her food.

His grandmother was standing by the stove turning over pieces of seasoned fish so they would be crisp, but not burned.

Garret walked over and gave his grandmother a kiss on the cheek. Eighty-two years old and she was still the most beautiful woman he had ever laid eyes on. His grandmother shared Garret's dark complexion, as well as his eyes. The rest of her was a mix of her eclectic African, Chinese, Indian, and Scottish background. Her long hair had now turned completely white. She refused to dye her hair and instead wore it braided in its natural state, with the braid twisted into a bun and secured at the nape of her neck with a butterfly clip. She was a short woman, but she carried herself as if she were ten feet tall. Her legendary beauty, a trait her late daughter had shared with her, was undiminished despite her age.

Garret smiled as he took in his grandmother's outfit. Dreama Beckford was a woman who believed in her own sense of style. Garret would often tease her that octogenarians shouldn't wear high heels, but Dreama's legs still looked good and she believed, even now, in showing them to their full advantage. His grandmother was dressed in a bright orange dress with splashes of every color in the rainbow and then some thrown in strategic places over the dress. It looked as if it were an orange canvas with different colors of paint thrown on it for good measure. She had on gold pumps and sheer red pantyhose which covered legs that retained their shapeliness and spoke of his grandmother's passion for ballet. Over this dress, his grandmother had on a pink apron covered with white ruffles. She was a sight to behold.

Dreama Beckford had raised him from the time his mother, Mariah, had died. Even though his mother passed away when he was seven years old, by the time Garret had memories of her, she'd become a frail, loving, but somewhat distant figure and Dreama had become his surrogate mother. He remembered times when she'd lock herself in her room for days, only opening the door when his father would arrive home exasperated, or Dreama would cajole her out of her moods. Dreama had always been there for Garret, even when his parents weren't, and there were times when he noticed a certain fragility that wasn't previously there, and his heart would tighten with fear. He couldn't imagine a life without his grandmother. She was the one constant in his life.

"I was wonderin' when you were going to come on down and join us for dinner." Dreama inclined her cheek towards her grandson and he dutifully kissed it again. She smelled like French perfume mixed with peppermints.

Zenna stopped eating long enough to say, "He was mighty quiet on the ride home from the airport."

"Hmph!" his grandmother declared as Garret sat down at the table in the kitchen. "There's only one thing that makes a man act like that—and that's a woman!"

Zenna chuckled. "I was thinking the same thing, but I wasn't as brave as you to bring up the subject."

"So," said his grandmother, staring directly at him. "Who's the lady in question?"

They were bloodhounds, Garret thought, shaking his head. That's what they were, or they simply knew him so well that they could read him like a book.

"I don't know what you're talking about," said Garret as he began eating his grandmother's fish. "This is delicious."

Although Garret's home had a formal dining room, on most nights his grandmother preferred eating in the large kitchen. The kitchen table was made of blue and white Mediterranean tiles and was located in the back of the kitchen by a large window overlooking Garret's backyard and terrace. His grandmother loved looking out the window at the tropical foliage and the occasional mountain goats and other four-legged creatures that ventured uninvited into his backyard.

"Don't lie to me," his grandmother said as she sat down next to him. "You know ever since you were a boy in short pants I could tell when you weren't telling me the truth."

He looked over at Zenna.

"Can't you help me out?" he asked. "Don't you have any new boyfriend stories to tell?"

"Not me," said Zenna. "I've sworn off men. I'm heading for a convent."

"I'm waiting, Garret." His grandmother was as determined as a dog who wouldn't let go of a delicious bone.

Garret knew when it was time to accept defeat.

"Okay," he said, putting his fork down in surrender. "I met a woman. I liked her. She didn't like me. End of story."

His grandmother's eyebrows raised in disbelief. "But who wouldn't like you? You're perfect!"

Garret grinned at his grandmother. "The lady in question didn't think so."

Zenna sucked her teeth. "She must be blind! If you weren't almost a relative and my boss, you'd make me rethink my vow to give up on men."

Garret grinned at her. "Thank you."

"Well, who is this woman?" asked Zenna. "What's she like? She must be very beautiful for you to be interested."

"She is beautiful," replied Garret. "And I like her spirit. She's feisty like you, Gram. I think you'd approve of her."

"Hmm," said his grandmother. "I haven't been too impressed with the women you've brought across my threshold recently."

Actually, thought Garret, it was his threshold, but he had the good sense not to correct her.

"She has the kindest eyes I've ever seen," said Garret.

"Did you meet some kind of American sex goddess?" Zenna asked.

His grandmother's response was quick. "This is a Christian house, Zenna. No need for talk like that."

"Thank you," replied Garret.

"But she does have a point," his grandmother asked, "is she good in bed?"

"Gram!" Garret choked on his lemonade. "What kind of talk is that . . . you just said it's a Christian house and all that!"

"It was just a thought," said his grandmother. "I mean, you're a good-looking young man and if you're anything like my Nestor, God rest his soul . . ."

"That's enough!" Garret struggled to refrain from laughing. "I have no idea if she's good in bed. I've never slept with her."

"You've never slept with her and you're mooning over her?" Zenna asked.

"I am NOT mooning over her!" said Garret.

"Yes, you are," said his grandmother. "Maybe she's the one—you know, I just had a dream about that the other day . . ."

"Oh, Lord, not the dreams again," said Zenna.

Garret's grandmother was known for her dreams. She would insist that all her dreams came true, but Garret suspected that she would simply interpret her dream to fit conveniently into whatever situation she found herself in.

"I dreamt that I had to make a long white wedding dress and I just knew it was for your wife!"

"Grandmother, please, can we just drop the subject?"

"I tell you it's my dream . . . there's going to be a wedding in this family!"

"There's not going to be a wedding," Garret replied, trying to calm his grandmother down. Although she disapproved of every woman Garret had ever been with, dating back to his teenage years, she still wanted him to get married and give her great grandchildren to fuss over. "She's getting married to someone else."

His grandmother whipped her head around. "If she's getting married to someone else, what the devil is she doing with you?"

"She's not with me—" Garret tried to explain.

His grandmother cut him off. "Garret, how many times have I told you not to mess with these loose women!"

"I haven't messed with her!"

His grandmother continued as if he hadn't spoken.

"I taught you to have more sense than that! A cheating woman will bring you on a road where only the devil travels!"

Garret had long ago stopped trying to make sense of his grandmother's sayings.

"Could you help me out on this one?" Garret asked Zenna.

Zenna smiled at him. "No one told you to sleep with a woman who's engaged to another man, and if you had to sleep with her, why'd you go and fall in love with her!"

"I didn't sleep with her," said Garret, but his words were lost as his grandmother lectured him on the evils of women with loose morals.

Chapter 6

The knock on her door awoke Callie from a dreamless sleep. She opened her eyes to a darkened room. There was a warm breeze coming through her open window and with it came the scent of the sea and unfamiliar tropical flowers. The sound of crickets and other sounds of nature which Callie could not identify competed with the sound of a steel band which sounded as if it were playing just below her window. She could hear laughter and the clinking of glasses. She blinked her eyes and tried to get her bearings. Where was she? Then she remembered.

The knocking continued, becoming louder and more insistent. Callie got out of the bed and turned on the lamp on the bedside table. Her eyes hurt from the light and she had a throbbing headache. She looked at the LED numbers on the alarm clock at her bedside and saw that it was ten o'clock in the evening. She remembered that Dara had promised to bring her up some food, but that was hours ago.

Callie walked over to the door. When she opened it she found herself staring at Henry. She moved quickly to slam the door shut but her reflexes weren't fast enough.

Henry moved into the open doorway and held it with one hand.

"Callie, let me explain, please." There was an urgency to his words, and Callie almost believed for a moment that he was sincere, but she knew better. Recent events had shown otherwise.

In spite of her determination not to speak to him, her curiosity got the better of her. "How did you find me?"

"News around here travels fast, someone from the hotel works with my gardener and mentioned something about a new guest. I figured it was you."

She'd heard enough.

"Go away, Henry," said Callie in what she hoped would be a calm and determined voice, though she knew that it sounded as weak as she felt. A look close to pity crossed Henry's eyes. At least he had the decency to look as if he felt bad for hurting her, Callie noted with a small amount of satisfaction.

"Callie, I was trying to protect you," he said, his eyes never leaving her face. He seemed nervous. "Your coming here was not a good idea."

The nerve of this man, Callie thought.

"Tell me something I don't already know."

"My wife is a very dangerous woman," said Henry, his voice urgent. "Believe me when I tell you that you need to leave."

"Don't worry, Henry. I'm leaving tomorrow.

Neither you nor your wife have to ever worry about seeing me again."

"Callie, there's something I want to give you," said Henry, his voice urgent.

"There's nothing on earth that I want from you, Henry," Callie replied, surprised at how steady her voice was. She refused to let Henry see the anger and hurt his betrayal caused.

"Callie, please take this," Henry said, holding out an open, black velvet jewelry box containing a large sapphire solitaire surrounded by small diamonds.

Callie was speechless. Henry had lost his mind. Everything he'd said to her about loving her and wanting to be with her was a lie, yet he was now handing her something that looked suspiciously like an engagement ring.

"What is this, Henry?" she asked.

"It's the ring that I bought for you. I want you to have it."

Callie was unable to keep her voice under control. "What is *wrong* with you? You lie to me, allow me to make a complete fool of myself, and now you want to give me a ring? You're already married to someone!"

"I want you to have this," Henry replied. "I want you to know that I meant every word I said to you about wanting us to be together. I fully intended to follow through on all of our plans. This ring is the proof of that, Callie. I'm not a bad person."

"Whether or not you're a devil or a saint, you're not the man I thought you were. I don't want your ring and I don't want you. Please leave."

"Callie, I . . ."

"Save it," Callie replied. "There's nothing you

can say to me to change my mind. I'm leaving this island tomorrow. You won't hear from me again."

"I'm sorry, Callie."

"I don't want to hear any more of your lies, Henry. Just go away," Callie replied.

He acted as if she hadn't spoken. "I thought that maybe we had a future . . ."

"So you lied to me, pretended that you loved me, asked me to marry you when all the time you had a wife here in St. Christopher?"

"It's complicated," Henry replied.

"Yes, I suppose it is. Living a double life can tend to lead to complications. Leave me alone, Henry," she said, not bothering to hide the anger she felt.

He flinched as if she had hit him, and his hands dropped helplessly to his sides. He said, "I deserve that."

"Yes," agreed Callie, "you do."

Then, without any further words, Callie closed the door in his face.

Garret listened to Buick's story while he tried to keep his anger under control. He'd been surprised by Buick's visit. Although he had known him a long time, and had done some business for him years ago, Buick had never come to his house. When he opened the door to find him standing on his doorstep, he knew that someone was in trouble. Buick got to the point of his visit quickly. "Miss America is in trouble."

When Buick finally finished talking, Garret stood up and walked over to the window in his living room. He looked out at the lights of Queenstown glistening below him in the night. He had to calm down. The rage he felt when he heard Buick's words frightened him. He was a man who was used to keeping his emotions in check, and he was unfamiliar with this lack of control. He believed if he saw Callie's fiancé, he could very easily do him serious bodily harm. How could any man treat a woman, particularly this woman, like that? What type of man treated another human being so callously? Thoughts of his father came quickly to mind, but he pushed them aside. The person who needed his attention now was Callie. He knew firsthand what betrayal felt like, he had his father to thank for that, and he knew exactly how she was feeling.

"What can I do?" Garret asked Buick. "She doesn't know me that well, and what she knows, she doesn't like."

"Listen, mon," Buick replied. "This ain't no time for playing the fool, pardon my directness. I saw the way you were lookin' at the lady. However long you've known her, it's obvious that you have some kind of feelings for her—oh, don't bother tellin' me that what I see ain't so. All I know is that if I looked at a woman the way I seen you lookin' at her, and I know that woman is in trouble, you wouldn't have to tell me twice what to do. I would be right there with her."

"She won't want to talk with me," said Garret. "I'm sure that I'm just about the last person she wants to see."

"Maybe," agreed Buick with a shrug. When he didn't say anything further, Garret ran a hand down his face. He opened his mouth to say Lord knew what, then closed it again.

"I hardly know what to say," said Garret, feeling completely out of his element. Callie Hopewell was not going to be happy to see him. "I'm probably the last person she wants to see tonight."

"Maybe," Buick replied, "but the lady needs someone and she doesn't know anyone else on the island."

"What makes you so sure about this?" asked Garret.

"Just call it intuition, or call it a hunch—I think you should go and check on her."

"Oh, hell," said Garret, crossing the living room with quick strides and grabbing his jacket from where he had earlier draped it across a chair. "Where is she now?"

Buick said a silent prayer of thanks. "She's staying at the Pink Hotel in Broxton. Do you want me to take you there?"

"No," said Garret, already on his way out. "I know where it is."

The walls were closing in around her. Callie couldn't stand being in the hotel room another minute. She had to get out. Take a walk. Go to the pool. She wanted to get away—feel the night air on her face. She felt the tears running down the sides of her face, and she wiped at them angrily. Seeing Henry had dissolved her intention not to cry. She wasn't crying for him, but for the fool he'd made of her. Damn him! She took a deep breath and opened the door. There was no one in the hallway, and she was grateful. There was a part of her that had feared Henry would be waiting in the hallway, ready to continue with his wild stories. She said a silent prayer of thanks he'd apparently gotten the message that she didn't want to see him again.

She walked quickly down the hallway and to the stairs that led to the ground floor. It was now almost midnight, and the only person in the lobby was a man at the reception desk whose head was bent over a book, too engrossed to notice her. The desk was at the opposite end of the lobby from the stairs, and Callie opened the door located just beyond the foot of the stairs. She walked down a short corridor and pulled a glass door open, which led to the pool area. There was no one there. The revelers had all turned in, and once again, Callie felt grateful. The last thing she wanted was for anyone, even strangers, to talk to her.

She walked past the pool to the surrounding grassy area, just beyond the patio. There was a solitary white beach chair which had her name written on it. She sat down in darkness and let the tears which she had tried without success to keep away, fall down her face.

Something was wrong with Callie. Something terrible had happened. Catherine Hopewell sat in her bed and looked at the clock on the far wall. Two o'clock in the morning, and she couldn't sleep. Her left eye had started twitching about an hour ago. Although the world, as well as most of Harlem, knew she was a God-fearing woman who didn't believe in superstition, the only time her left eye twitched was when one of her children was in trouble. She had telephoned the four daughters that she could reach, and all were physically all right, even though at least two of them had muttered about the late-hour call. That left Callie. Catherine had no idea where her eldest child was, only that she was somewhere in St. Christopher with a man who Catherine could not bring herself to trust. It wasn't that there was anything particularly wrong with Henry Kincaid, as Catherine saw it, there just wasn't anything particularly right with him. He was a little too glib, a little too easy with that flattering tongue of his. Besides, he had a way of not looking at you when he talked to you. No, indeed, Catherine definitely did not trust him.

None of her sisters knew where Callie was staying. Apparently, she had kept them all in the dark. Not that Catherine blamed her daughter. No one had acted overjoyed at Callie's news that she was engaged and about to run off to an island that no one in their family had even visited.

Too soon, was the general consensus. Too fast. Catherine had seen the hurt in Callie's eyes, and she had been immediately sorry to have been so forthcoming about her distrust of Callie's fiancé. But Catherine always tried to be honest with her daughters. She never wanted any of her children to doubt her word. Now her words just might have pushed her daughter away at a time when she was certain, just as sure as her left eye continued twitching, that she was in trouble.

She picked up the telephone receiver on the nightstand and started dialing. After two rings, the one daughter who she knew would condone her crazy schemes, answered the telephone.

"Mama, this better not be you," said the sleepy voice on the other end of the telephone line.

"Who else would it be, Phoebe?" her mother calmly replied. "Anybody else call you at two o'clock in the morning?"

"No, but I keep hoping that Sidney Poitier might be up late wondering when he can come see me."

"Sidney Poitier is old," replied Catherine, annoyed that Phoebe was breaking her train of thought with this nonsense.

"He might be old," replied Phoebe. "But he's still *fine*."

Catherine decided that it was time to get to the point. "My left eye is twitching. I think Callie's in trouble."

Any other daughter would have told her to go back to bed. Even Callie. But Phoebe, her youngest child, the child she had when the doctors said that there would be no more, responded, "What're you going to do?"

"Any idea where she might be?"

"Other than sleeping in the arms of a man she thinks she loves on a tropical island, no—I really couldn't say."

That was more information than Catherine cared to know.

"Do you still have the keys to Callie's apartment?" asked Catherine, turning her thoughts to more immediate matters.

"Yes," Phoebe replied. Phoebe was the official caretaker of Callie's plants whenever she went on her business trips.

"Can you meet me over there in the next half an hour?"

"I'll be there," replied Phoebe without hesitation.

Catherine felt relieved for the first time since her left eye started twitching. "I knew I could count on you, Phoebe."

Chapter 7

Callie felt someone's hands shaking her awake. She'd fallen asleep on the pool chair somewhere in between feeling sorry for herself for being such a fool and being angry with herself for being the same fool. She opened her eyes to find herself staring at the face of proprietor of the Pink Hotel, Ma Ruth.

"You gave me quite a scare, child," said Ma Ruth. "I couldn't sleep tonight, so I thought I would come down to the pool for a swim. It's how I keep up my good figure, really. Anyway, imagine when I look over and see you lying in that chair. I thought you were a duppy for sure."

Callie sat up. Her body ached, although she wasn't sure if the chair was the culprit, or recent circumstances had just taken their toll.

"What on earth is a duppy?" Callie asked, not knowing if she wanted to hear the answer.

"A ghost," said Ma Ruth with a flourish. "A haunt.

That's what we folks here in St. Christoper call ghosts. Duppy."

"Well," said Callie, "I'm sorry for the scare. As you can see, I'm very much alive."

"Yes," replied Ma Ruth, staring at her, hard. "I can see that."

Callie felt embarrassed. What must this woman think, seeing her sleeping in a pool chair in the middle of the night.

"Why don't I walk you back to your room," said Ma Ruth.

"That's all right," replied Callie, when she found her voice. "I don't want to trouble you—I'm sure you want to get back to the pool."

"No trouble at all," said Ma Ruth, in the same tone Callie's mother used when the word no was not an option.

The two women walked silently past the pool and through the open sliding glass doors that led to the hotel lobby. The lobby was still deserted, except for the man sitting at the front desk whose head was now nodding in his sleep.

As they reached the stairs that led to the second floor, Ma Ruth turned and said, "I don't know you at all, but I can tell that things aren't going too well for you."

Callie didn't reply. Ma Ruth was accurate in her succinct assessment of the situation.

"I can say this," said Ma Ruth as they climbed the stairs, "things have a way of working out."

Callie remained silent. She was precariously close to crying and she had no desire for Ma Ruth to witness her complete humiliation. She just wanted to get to her room, lie in the bed and hope for the blessed release of a dreamless sleep. Then, she would leave the island tomorrow and put the whole ordeal behind her.

Ma Ruth, apparently sensing her mood, fell silent. When they reached the top of the stairs they walked down the hallway to Callie's room. Callie noticed that the door to her hotel room was ajar. She did not remember leaving it open, but in the state she was in when she left the hotel room, it wouldn't have surprised her. Her heart started hammering in her chest. Did Henry come back? Had he forced the door open? She couldn't face Henry. Not now. Not ever. She did not want to see him. She'd had enough humiliation for a lifetime, and then some.

"I'll go in there with you, child."

"Thank you," Callie whispered. She knew that she was being weak. She knew she should politely refuse the offer; instead she walked to her room quickly, with Ma Ruth on her heels. If Henry was there, she was sure that Ma Ruth's presence would aid in his swift departure.

Callie reached the room first. It was completely dark. She felt the wall for the switch, and then she turned on the light. The room was completely in order, as she had left it, but there was someone in her bed. It was Henry. Her first thought was that he'd fallen asleep, but why on earth would he have come back to her room? Then, she noticed a growing dark stain on the white sheets where he lay. His eyes were open, but even from where she stood by the doorway, Callie could tell that Henry's eyes no longer saw her. He was dead.

Callie heard Ma Ruth whisper, "Sweet Jesus," and then everything else fell silent, as her world faded to black.

* * *

Garret heard the commotion as soon as he entered the hotel lobby. He heard the sound of a woman yelling and saw the man at the front desk sprint towards the stairs. Garret followed close behind him. Only disaster caused a person to shriek the way this woman had done. *Callie.* His instincts told him that whatever had happened involved Callie. The tightness in his throat convinced him that he was right.

He got to the room at the end of the hall almost at the same time as the man whom he was following. A small crowd of people had gathered outside the door, and Garret pushed his way through, as if propelled by force. Once inside, he saw what made the woman who was kneeling on the ground, shriek. Then, his attention was drawn back to the kneeling woman. She was kneeling over Callie.

His throat constricted, and for a moment he struggled to breathe. *Calm down. Calm down. Calm down.* But the words had no effect on him. Instead, he walked quickly over to where she lay on the ground, her head cradled in the woman's lap.

He watched the soft rise and fall of Callie's chest. *"Thank God,"* he whispered fiercely. *"Thank God."*

"What happened to her?" asked Garret, his voice harsh.

"Fainted clean away, poor child."

Garret's only thought was to get Callie out of this room, away from the blood, away from the prying eyes of strangers. Away.

"Let me have her," said Garret, willing his voice to not sound hard, and frightened.

"Who are you?" asked the woman holding Callie.

"My name is Garret Langrin. I'm a lawyer in

Queenstown. I met Callie on an airplane this morning," replied Garret, keeping his voice calm. "Now, please let me take her out of here."

The woman didn't reply, but she offered no resistance when Garret lifted Callie up and walked out of the room. The crowd by the doorway parted like the Red Sea, and Garret walked as quickly out of the room as his burden allowed.

The woman who had been keeping vigil over Callie walked beside Garret, almost running to keep up with him.

"My room is at the other end of the hall," she said. "We can take her there."

"Get me some smelling salts, or something strong," Garret ordered without breaking stride.

The woman turned and talked to someone else who had been following them. "Dara, you heard the man. Hurry!" Then, she opened the door to her room and watched as Garret lay Callie down on the bed.

The woman then stuck a bottle of perfume in Garret's hands.

"What the hell is this?" he asked.

"It's perfume," she explained, "expensive stuff, I might add, and there's no need to use profanity with me. Open the bottle and let her smell it."

It was one of the craziest things that Garret had heard to date, but he was a desperate man, willing to try anything. Anything to get her to wake up. He opened the perfume and waved the bottle under Callie's nose.

"Callie," he said softly, "wake up. Wake up. Come on, Callie. Wake up."

He didn't know how long he sat there, urging Callie to come back to him, but after what seemed to him a time somewhere close to an eternity, he watched her dark lashes flutter, and then her eyes opened and looked directly into his.

She looked at him for a second as if she didn't recognize him, then her eyes widened in surprise.

"Garret Langrin," she said, her voice surprisingly strong for one who had just come out of unconsciousness. "What're you doing here?"

Then, as memory came back completely, he watched as she covered her face with her hands and started to cry. Without any hesitation, Garret sat on the bed next to her and held her while she let loose her soft, keening sobs.

She looked around the room, "Where're Dara and Ma Ruth?"

"If you mean the two ladies who were here when I carried you in, they've gone to deal with the guests—who I understand are quite upset."

She sat up in the bed. She wanted to leave the room, but where could she go? Going back to her hotel room was out of the question. She would never go there again. Never. She would go to the airport and wait there until the next plane left for New York.

"I've got to go," she said. "I've got to get out of here."

"Fine," replied Garret. "I'll take you wherever you need to go."

She tried to get out of bed, but the room seemed to close in. It was as if the air started slowly leaving the room. She couldn't breathe. Panic seized her, as she started gasping for breath.

Garret was quick. He sat next to her on the side of the bed and forced her to take deep breaths. "Just breathe, Callie. Nice and easy. Take it slow. Take it easy."

His words were soft and insistent, as if he were willing her to breathe. Willing her to get over her panic. "You can do it, Callie. Just take it easy."

She listened to the rhythm of his words, and soon, whatever it was that had gotten hold of her, passed. That had never happened to her before, but she had never seen a murder victim before, either. In the past few hours she had been through a lot of firsts, and none of them appeared to be good.

Callie took a deep breath. "Thank you."

She didn't look at him. She was embarrassed at

losing control in front of him, and she didn't want to see any pity in his eyes.

"It was your fiancé, wasn't it?" asked Garret, his voice still soft.

Callie nodded her head. "Yes."

He didn't say anything else; instead, he pulled her to him with one arm and let her lean on him.

In the midst of the most unlikely circumstances, she felt comforted, even as her mind rebelled at the thought of depending on anyone for comfort. *Desperate times* she told herself. *Besides, I'm not depending on him. Not really. I'm just feeling a little weak, and when I feel better . . .*

A knock on the door interrupted her thoughts. Callie raised her head as Ma Ruth opened the door to the room.

"How is she?" Ma Ruth asked Garret, even though she was staring directly at Callie.

"I'm fine," she answered.

"You don't look so fine to me," Ma Ruth replied, "but I have someone here who needs to see you. Inspector Mobray—he's the long arm of the law here in Broxton. I told him this wasn't exactly a good time, but you know how these policemen are . . ."

"Tell him that she'll talk to him in the morning. She's in no condition to talk to him now." Garret's voice was hard and brooked no disagreement.

The door opened wider, and a short balding man in crisp khakis and a white oxford shirt, that looked as if someone had spent a lot of time ironing it, walked past Ma Ruth into the room. Callie's first thought was how could anyone appear so starched and unwrinkled at such an early hour in the morning.

"She already conveyed that message to me," the policeman said with a tight smile, "but unfortunately, someone was murdered in this lady's bed and I need to ask questions. I know it's a bad time, but there never really is a good time when someone is murdered, now is there?"

The inspector strode across the room and stood in front of Callie and Garret. "Miss Hopewell, I'm sorry to bother you at this time, but there are a few questions I have to ask."

"Can't this wait, Mobray? Surely even you can see that this woman is in no condition to talk."

Did Garret know everybody on this island?

"Ah, Langrin," replied the inspector. "I didn't expect to find you here. You give a new meaning to the words 'ambulance chaser.'"

Apparently, there was no love lost between the two men.

"I'm not about to tell you what you give a new name to," Garret replied. "In any event, my client is not talking to you."

"Your client?" Inspector Mobray and Callie spoke at the same time.

"Is this man your attorney?" asked Inspector Mobray.

"No," replied Callie.

"Yes," replied Garret.

"Well, now I'm confused," said the inspector.

Callie turned to Garret. "I know that you're trying to help me, but if he wants to ask me a few questions, I'd rather just answer them and be done with it."

"Callie," Garret's voice was low and urgent. "You're an attorney. I don't need to tell you how unwise it is to talk to a policeman under these circumstances. My God, you might be a suspect in this case. If he wants to arrest you, let him. If not, don't speak to him."

"A suspect?" The thought was so preposterous that at any other time Callie would have burst into laughter. "I hardly think you have to worry about *that*."

"It appears that the lady would like to speak to me," Inspector Mobray cut in.

"What do you want to know?" asked Callie.

Ma Ruth, who was still in the room during the conversation, spoke. "Maybe you should listen to the attorney, child. He knows what he's doing. He's one of the best on the island. Anyone who gets in trouble on this island knows about Garret Langrin. He's the best."

"I am also an attorney," Callie replied calmly. "There's no need to worry. I don't know anything about this anyway, so the quicker the inspector asks his questions, the better for me. I want this behind me."

"You're a wise woman," said the inspector. There was, however, something about the way he looked at her that brought to mind a circling buzzard. A voice inside her head urged her to be cautious. It was foolish to talk to him if an attorney was advising her not to do that, but she wanted to answer every question this man asked so that she'd be free to get on a plane and leave St. Christopher and the bad memories it now held behind.

For the next hour, Callie calmly answered the inspector's questions. She told the inspector how she met Henry. She told the inspector how Henry had deceived her. She told the inspector about Henry's visit to her room, and she told him about finding him lying on her bed. When she got to the part about finding Henry dead in her room, her voice faltered, but she quickly regained her composure.

When she finished speaking, the inspector asked, "So you didn't know that he was married? That seems rather far-fetched, if you don't mind my saying so."

She did mind. She knew that she looked like a perfect idiot, but it was the truth. She had no idea that Henry had a wife in St. Christopher.

"I don't know . . ." Callie felt foolish answering this question. "The phone number in St. Christoper that I had, no one else answered but him . . . it was a cell phone I think, but I'm not sure . . . In retrospect, I was foolish. Very foolish to trust him."

"Foolish enough to kill him?" Inspector Mobray's question startled her. Could he really think that she could be capable of murder?

Garret muttered a curse under his breath.

"You talking craziness!" said Ma Ruth, hot in her defense of Callie. "The girl was with me when she found him. She didn't kill that man, any more than I did."

Callie was not a violent woman, but her palms itched as she fought the urge to slap the inspector. She took a deep breath and forced herself to remain calm.

"I did not kill Henry, Inspector Mobray," said Callie. "I was angry, hurt, and a lot of other things, but there's nothing is this world to make me kill another human being, no matter how badly he may have treated me."

The inspector stood up. "May I have your passport, please."

"My passport?" Callie was confused.

"Well, the investigation into this murder is anything but complete and something tells me that you and I are going to be talking again. In any event, while the investigation is continuing, I'll need to have you close by. I'm sure we'll wrap this up in a few days. We'll probably have a suspect by then."

Callie turned and looked at Garret. She was grateful that he didn't utter the words, "I told you so," but his expression was grim.

"Can he do this?" Callie asked Garret. "Can he keep me from leaving the country?"

Garret nodded his head. "I'm afraid so," he replied. "Since there is a pending investigation, he can keep you in the country for two weeks without charges, after that he has to either charge you or let you go."

"Two weeks!" Callie stared at Garret and the inspector as if they had both lost their minds. "I can't stay here for two weeks."

Inspector Mobray replied, "Where is your passport, ma'am?"

"Mobray, you know this lady ain't got nothing to do with the killing!" said Ma Ruth.

But Callie knew when she was defeated.

"My passport is my hotel room—in my purse..."

"I'll get it for you, dear," said Ma Ruth. "You don't have to go back there."

"Thank you," replied Callie. She wondered if they had removed the body yet. She shook her head at the thought that the person who was once Henry had now become "the body."

"Will you be staying here at the Pink Hotel?"

Callie shook her head. There was no way she

could stay here in Broxton, at the place where Henry was murdered.

"She's staying with me," replied Garret.

Once again, Callie looked at him. She wanted to stay at a hotel, somewhere in Queenstown, but she didn't know where to go and at this point she was too tired to go looking for another hotel. Garret Langrin's house would have to do for now.

"You know the address, Mobray," said Garret.

The inspector gave Garret a small smile, then he turned to Callie and said, "I'm sorry that you had to go through this, but I was only doing my job."

"Is that what you call what you just did?" Garret asked in a mild tone.

"Good night, Miss Hopewell," said the inspector. He left the room without any further comment.

"I found it!"

Catherine Hopewell's voice was triumphant, but it wasn't difficult to find Henry Kincaid's number. It was attached to the front of Callie's refrigerator by a heart-shaped magnet. She expected Henry's number would be tucked away somewhere discreetly. Callie was well-known for guarding her privacy from her family's prying eyes. This was unlike Callie, and her mother took the fact that the paper was conveniently placed on the refrigerator as a sign her daughter indeed needed help, or more specifically, help from her mother.

"It's a sign," said Catherine to her daughter Phoebe. "Finding his number so quickly is a sign."

"A sign of what?" asked Phoebe, who had already raided Callie's cookie box, and was nibbling one of Callie's oatmeal raisin cookies. One of Callie's many talents was that she was an excellent chef. She didn't cook often, but when she did, as with everything else, she excelled at it. Phoebe, who thrived on frozen diet dinners, thought briefly about the unfairness of life.

"A sign that your sister is in trouble, and a sign that she needs our help."

"You got all this from finding Henry's number on the refrigerator?" Phoebe asked. She worked hard to keep her tone neutral. She didn't want to offend her mother. Her mother was easily offended.

"Yes, indeed!" declared Catherine Hopewell. "It's a sign, I tell you."

"Mama," said Phoebe, now working on the second cookie, "a lot of people put phone numbers on their refrigerator."

"Not Callie," said Catherine, her voice firm in her conviction that she knew her daughter better than anyone else living. "She would have tucked it away somewhere. It's a sign. My baby needs me."

Phoebe wasn't about to argue with her mother. Catherine Hopewell's mind was made up, and Phoebe knew that only a note from Jesus would convince her to change her mind once it was set in a particular direction. She did, however, try to reason with her mother.

"Maybe we should wait to call in the morning, Mama. After all, it is three o' clock in the morning."

"I don't care what time it is," replied Catherine Hopewell. "Callie needs me. My left eye hasn't twitched this much since you broke your leg on that foolish jet skiing accident last year."

"OK, Mama," said Phoebe. "Let's call Henry Kincaid."

"Go get me that cordless telephone Callie has in the living room," replied Catherine Hopewell.

As Phoebe left the kitchen, she could hear her mother fussing about Callie. "I don't know why Callie doesn't have a telephone in her kitchen like most normal people. And I don't know why she ran off to St. Christopher after some man she thinks she's in love with. I thought she had more sense than that."

Phoebe couldn't suppress her smile. Her mother might be worried about Callie, but that didn't stop her from fussing over her. Some things never changed.

Chapter 9

Ma Ruth was worried. She stared at Callie and Garret with a deep frown.

"There's a reporter here," she said. "How they found out about what happened to Henry Kincaid is beyond me, but I think you two should leave before he starts asking you questions."

"I don't want to speak to anybody," replied Callie with a calmness that surprised her. Her voice betrayed nothing of the turmoil she was feeling. All evidence of her earlier breakdown had disappeared, along with any trace of her tears. The public Callie was back. Cool head and steady hands. Someone had once told her that she thrived in times of upheaval. She could always been counted on not to fall apart. It was an integral part of her makeup.

Callie sat on Ma Ruth's bed and regarded the grim faces of Ma Ruth and Garret Langrin. Ma Ruth was enamored with the color pink, judging from the pink walls, pink shag carpet, pink curtains and hot pink, bordering on fuchsia, bedspread. *What in the world am I doing here,* she thought, *and how did things get to be so awful?* Yesterday, she was planning a life with someone she obviously didn't know, and today that person was... gone. She had always been in charge of her own life, her own destiny, or so she thought.

"You don't have to worry about that reporter, I'll run anybody off who tries to mess with you!"

Callie's mind flashed on the probable headline: *"Lovelorn lawyer rushes to St. Christopher to find her fiancé is already married,"* and *"Fiancé turns up dead in lovelorn lawyer's bed."* Her life had turned into a soap opera. A bad soap opera. She'd wanted excitement, but not this much excitement.

"Callie, now would be a good time to leave the hotel," said Garret.

"I need to get my suitcases..."

"I'll send your things on to Garret's house," said Ma Ruth. "They'll be there by morning light."

"Believe me," said Garret, "we need to get going. If you stay here or at any other hotel, you're only going to be hounded by reporters. I can protect you if you're at my home."

She knew he was right. She couldn't run to a hotel. She'd be hounded by reporters, and that was the last thing she wanted. She'd spent her life hiding from people's scrutiny. She'd hidden behind the facade of lawyer, dutiful daughter, and she'd carefully chosen clothes, makeup, and anything else that would help her blend into a crowd. She felt more comfortable blending in. Now, she was about to be the subject of a tawdry love triangle, and she was certain that the sleepy island of

St. Christopher would be fixated on the story of the lovelorn tourist who murdered her cheating boyfriend.

"When can we leave?" asked Callie.

Garret's smile betrayed his relief. "There's no time like the present."

"The thing is," said Callie, hesitating as she saw her life being directed by someone else, "I really hate running. I feel like I'm running away."

"Sometimes," said Ma Ruth, her eyes focused on some distant memory, "the best thing to do is to run like hell."

Catherine Hopewell hung up her daughter's telephone with a frown.

"I don't like this," she said. "I don't like this one bit. No one is answering the telephone."

"Mama, its not even daybreak, maybe the guy's asleep, or maybe he isn't even there."

Catherine's internal alarm bells were ringing loudly now. She didn't want to scare Phoebe, but now she was frightened. The fact that no one was there to answer the telephone probably had a reasonable explanation, but Catherine would bet her AT&T stock and her entire portfolio that something was wrong, and whatever it was involved her firstborn.

"Why don't we just call Henry Kincaid in the morning," Phoebe suggested.

"Yes," said Catherine, her mind already formulating a plan B. "We'll call him in the morning."

* * *

Garret drove his car away from the Pink Hotel as if demons were chasing him. Beside him, Callie sat staring silently out of the window.

The midnight blue sky had thin flashes of pale pink signaling the approaching dawn.

As they left the hotel, they'd seen the police cars, the TV station trucks, and a crowd of people standing in front of the hotel. They'd also seen the ambulance that was going to be used to transport the body of Callie's fiancé to the morgue.

He'd watched as Callie wavered for a moment when she stared at the ambulance. He saw her tremble and he'd instinctively reached out to take her hand, but he'd decided against that course of action. Somehow he knew Callie would misinterpret his gesture as one of pity, when it was anything but that. He just wanted to hold her, to reassure her that in spite of everything, she was going to get through this. There was a core of strength inside her he'd recognized immediately. He'd seen that same strength in his grandmother. The momentary panic he'd seen in her eyes as she looked at the ambulance quickly disappeared and gave way to a look of determination.

"Let's get out of here," she said.

He was in agreement with that particular sentiment. If he never saw the Pink Hotel again that would be just fine with him.

Garret turned on the radio to one of St. Christopher's three radio stations and the only one that was on for twenty-four hours. This station played jazz at night, and Garret wanted to hear the calming sounds of music. He wanted to think. Callie was in trouble, more trouble than she suspected.

Garret was certain that right now Mobray was

formulating a theory in which Callie was the prime suspect in Henry Kincaid's murder. He'd heard of the Kincaid family. They were a family whose power (it was whispered) derived originally from illegal drug trafficking, but no one had been ever able to prove that the Kincaids' now-flourishing business empire had its roots in the drug trade. The few people who had claimed they had information about the Kincaids' illegal activities had either turned up dead or had disappeared from the island. This was not a family one wanted to mess with, and Garret knew it would be in Mobray's best interest to tidily wrap this case up by presenting the killer for justice.

Garret also knew that anyone fingered as the killer wouldn't make it to trial. They'd be killed long before trial, just like the other people who'd crossed the Kincaids. He'd met Henry Kincaid a few years ago at a party and he'd come away from the meeting singularly unimpressed. Henry Kincaid was a little too smooth and a little too disingenuous, Garret had decided. He'd also watched as Henry had openly scoped out the women in the room, even though his wife had been planted permanently at his side during the entire party. Garret's father had been a philanderer and Garret had no respect for men who cheated on their wives. He'd seen first-hand the toll that kind of behavior took on the family.

When Callie told him about her fiancé, he never had any idea that she was talking about Henry Kincaid. He could have warned her about him if he'd known. Still, he suspected that a woman like Callie loved deeply and wouldn't have listened to him about his misgivings concerning her fiancé.

He let the music of Billie Holliday singing "Don't

Explain" wash over him. He loved Billie's raspy, raw, soul filled voice. It reminded him of his mother, who loved Billie Holliday and would play her records often. *"Hush now, don't explain..."* Billie's voice rose and quavered as if she were singing just for him. In his mind's eye he could see his mother dancing by herself in the living room at the old house, dancing to Billie's music. He hadn't thought about his mother in a while, and tonight, for some reason, the thoughts of his mother didn't bring the typical searing pain—only a wistfulness, a longing for something he would never have again

Callie's voice broke into his thoughts. "I thought you had a driver."

"I do. But Zenna doesn't drive me everywhere I go. Usually she just picks me up from the airport. Zenna's more of an all-around assistant."

"I see," Callie replied. Then, changing the subject she said, "I never did thank you for being my knight in shining armor."

He looked over and smiled. "No need to thank me."

"Yes, there is," Callie replied. "You've been very kind to me..."

Her voice wavered as if she were going to cry.

"It's okay, Callie." Garret took one hand from the steering wheel and placed it over her hand, which was shaking. He squeezed her hand and held it tight until the shaking stopped.

"Is it?" Callie asked, when she'd regained her composure. "Is it ever going to okay?"

"Absolutely," said Garret, keeping his voice strong. "You've just got to believe."

"I believed in Henry," Callie said quietly. "I got my heart broken and now he's dead."

Garret placed his hand back on the steering wheel as he navigated a steep curve in the road. The sky was getting lighter, and dawn was about to make its appearance.

"You're not responsible for Henry getting killed," said Garret.

"How do you know that?" Callie asked. "The inspector thinks I killed him. Why don't you?"

"Because the inspector is a fool," said Garret, "and I'm not. I'm a very good judge of character and I know that you couldn't have killed Henry any more than you could sprout wings and fly away."

"I'm scared, Garret," admitted Callie.

"I know," Garret replied. "But you're going to get through this just fine."

"You sound like an optimist," said Callie.

"I've been accused of worse," Garret said with an easy smile.

For the briefest moment, Callie was tempted to return that smile. Shaking her head at what she could only guess was a case of tropical madness, or bad nerves, Callie focused her attention on her current predicament. The words of her mother came back to her as she sat in silence, listening to Billie Holliday sing the blues: "Be careful what you wish for. You just might get it." She'd wanted excitement. She'd wanted an escape from her dull, predictable life. Well, after last night she'd had as much excitement as she would ever want, but something told her that the excitement she'd experienced was just the beginning.

They reached Garret's house just as the sun made its early morning appearance. Callie had finally given in to exhaustion and slept until the car pulled into the driveway. Her sleep had been troubled with disjointed dreams—dreams about Henry, dreams about death, dreams about dark skies. She was still tired when she awoke, and her mind still carried images of Henry lying dead in her hotel room, images she tried to shake.

"Are you hungry?" Garret asked as he turned the car engine off.

Callie shook her head. The thought of food left her feeling vaguely ill. "I think it's going to be a good long while before the thought of food appeals to me."

Garret laughed. "My grandmother will change your mind quickly."

Callie turned to him. "You live with your grandmother?"

"Yes," he replied, "and my assistant Zenna also lives with me."

A feeling of awkwardness gripped Callie. How was he going to explain to his family who she was and why she was here?

"Listen, I don't want to cause you and your family any trouble," said Callie. "I mean, isn't there a hotel somewhere I can stay?"

"Going to a hotel isn't the best idea right now," said Garret. "You'd never get any peace. You can stay here in my guest house, and nobody will bother you—except my grandmother, but that will only be to fuss over you."

"Guest house?"

Callie focused on her surroundings for the first time and her breath caught in her throat. Garret's house was stunning. A large white West Indian mansion with blue shutters was surrounded by the most colorful garden she'd ever seen. Her eyes swept down to the view and she forgot to breathe for a moment—the sight of Queenstown surrounded by the bright blue ocean was breathtaking.

"This is where you live?" asked Callie. "It looks like something you'd see on a postcard."

"Thank you," replied Garret. "You'll be staying in the guest house up the hill."

Callie looked in the direction Garret was pointing and saw a charming cottage about a hundred yards away from the main house. The guest house was built in the same traditional West Indian style, white with bright blue shutters—a smaller version of Garret's home.

"It's very beautiful," Callie said, when she got her voice back.

"And private," said Garret. "There's a guardhouse that we passed just as we entered the gates to the property—you were sleeping, so you didn't see it. We have two permanent guards—Gavin is our day security guard, and Ray has night duty. Both are licensed to carry firearms and are trained in martial arts. No reporter will get past them."

Callie looked at him and asked, "Why do you need armed guards?"

Garret's smile almost distracted her from the seriousness of his reply. "At the risk of sounding immodest, I am a very successful lawyer and I've made some pretty powerful enemies. The guards are more of a precautionary measure. Besides, I travel a lot and I want to make sure my grandmother is safe."

Callie sighed. What had she gotten herself into? After everything she'd been through with Henry, she wasn't about to trust another person . . . or to be more specific, another man. She didn't know anything about Garret Langrin. Still, she had no choice. She was in a foreign country without her passport. She was also a suspect in a murder. She could see why the inspector focused on her—after all, she did have a motive to kill. She'd also had the opportunity. The time she'd spent sleeping outside the hotel by the pool—no one could vouch that she'd been there the whole time.

"Come on," said Garret. "I'll take you to the guest house. You can meet my grandmother and Zenna later after you've had some time to rest."

Callie couldn't suppress a tired smile. "Are you trying to say that I look like hell?"

"You just look tired," Garret replied. "Beautiful, but tired."

Once again, there was something about the words, something about how he looked at her when he said those words, that made Callie distinctly uncomfortable.

Callie decided to move the conversation in another direction. "Is there anyone else who lives here—besides your grandmother and Zenna?"

"Well, our housekeeper Winsome sometimes sleeps over—but that's only when she and her husband have had a fight, which, come to think of it, happens frequently."

Callie watched as Garret got out of the car and went around to her side to open the door. He held out his hand to her and despite everything she'd been through, or perhaps because of it, when she took his hand, she felt a wave of familiarity—a sense that somehow, in some way, they shared a common history and that their destinies had now become intertwined.

Feeling distinctly uncomfortable with her foolish thoughts, Callie got out of the car and followed Garret to the cottage.

Zenna, Winsome, and Dreama looked out the window of Dreama's bedroom at the scene unfolding below. From the time the cab driver had burst into their house babbling about someone who needed help and Garret had rushed out looking as if someone had punched him in the gut, Dreama had been worried. She'd awakened Zenna and Winsome—who'd had another fight with Brother Africa, as her husband Stan now insisted that he be called—and they'd chatted until the early hours of the morning. They were used to Garret dealing with his clients at all sorts of crazy hours, but Dreama was convinced that whatever was going on had something to do with the American lady her grandson was interested in. The ladies had all fallen asleep on Dreama's king size bed, only to be awakened by the sound of Garret's car coming up the diveway.

They'd watched as Garret sat talking to the lady in the car and then walked with her up the driveway to the guest house. Dreama knew her grandson wasn't expecting any company because he usually informed her before he brought guests over. Even though this was her grandson's home, he always acted as if she were the lady of the house. The woman was beautiful—tall, slim, and brown-skinned. They'd glimpsed high cheekbones, big eyes and a full mouth. She was wearing blue jeans and a long, light blue sweater.

"Look how he's looking at the gal," said Winsome. "Brother Africa never looked at me like that."

"Lord, give Brother Africa a rest," said Zenna. "This is an entirely different situation—although you have a point."

"But isn't this woman engaged to someone else?" asked Winsome, who'd heard the entire story of Garret's new love interest.

"I don't know," said Dreama. "It's all confusing to me. First Garret goes to America on a business trip as sane as ever and now it looks like he's come back crazy."

"Or in love," said Zenna.

"It's the same thing," Winsome chimed in.

"That's not what you said when you first met Brother Africa," said Zenna with a laugh.

Winsome sucked her teeth—the universal way of folks from St. Christopher show displeasure. "I was as blind as the singer Stevie Wonder when I met that man. If only I had known..."

Dreama cut in. "Hush, Winsome, you know that you'll be back banging headboards with your husband soon enough. You two will be married until God calls one of you home. Now, I wonder if maybe my grandson has finally found someone he can bang headboards with..."

"Miss Dreama!" Zenna called out, clearly scandalized. "What kind of a way is that to talk—and you're a lady over eighty!"

"I'm eighty-two and I'm not dead. It wasn't so long ago that I was banging headboards with my own husband!"

The ladies stopped talking as they watched Garret open the door to the guest house. He leaned down as if he were going to kiss the American lady, but it seemed that he had simply said something to her. But there was an undeniable closeness between the two and Dreama wondered if at last her grandson had found a chance for his own happiness. Since the day his mother took her own life, Dreama had watched as her grandson shut out the rest of the world. Despite his successes, she knew he was not happy. She longed for the child who had wept inconsolably at his mother's grave to finally find peace, to find happiness.

Maybe this was the one, Dreama thought. Just maybe.

Callie sank gratefully into the plush, cream sofa in the living room area of the guest house. She was tired, but not too tired to drink in the comfort of her surroundings—the pale blue walls were a direct contrast to the deep blue of the ceramic tile floor. There were windows everywhere, it seemed, and the lush tropical scenery just outside the house seemed to be an extension of the home. The living room was comfortably furnished, with the couch and other wooden chairs and an ottoman covered in a blue and beige seashell print. There was an antique grandfather clock in the corner of the room and a mahogany reading table in the center of the room. On the walls were various framed antique maps of other Caribbean islands.

"I trust you'll be comfortable here." Garret Langrin's words broke through Callie's thoughts.

Callie looked over to where Garret stood, across the room by one of the large windows that framed the mountains in the background.

Callie managed a weak smile. "I'll be fine."

"Would you like me to give you the house tour now, though you look like you could use some sleep."

The tiredness Callie felt seeped into her bones and she wanted nothing more than to sink into the oblivion of sleep, but she feared she wouldn't be able to close her eyes without seeing Henry. She felt her heart start hammering in her chest and a feeling of panic washed over her. Henry was dead. Murdered. She was a suspect in Henry's death. Her passport had been confiscated from her. She was in a house, albeit a charming one, that belonged to a stranger. She was stuck on an island for at least two weeks, or maybe more. She felt the walls start to close in around her.

As a child, she'd had panic attacks. Only her mother had known the truth about the times when she'd lose her breath as if someone had wrapped their hands around her throat and had started to squeeze. Her mother had taken her to a therapist and, in time, the panic attacks had gone away—only appearing occasionally in the past few years. When the feeling of panic had threatened to overwhelm her, she'd learned to close her eyes and breathe deeply until a feeling of calm would come over her. But she knew that the panic that now gripped her would not be chased away by deep breathing. The room became unbearably hot and she began to feel nauseous.

She closed her eyes and forced herself to breathe, but her breaths came out in shallow gasps. She began to tremble.

Almost instantly, she felt a cold glass in her hands and she opened her eyes.

"Drink this," Garret ordered.

She obeyed him without thinking, and soon the cold water that he'd given her calmed her.

Garret sat next to her. "You're tired."

Callie nodded. "Maybe I do need to lie down. I'll take the tour later," she managed weakly.

Garret stood up and held out his hand. "I'll show you the bedroom."

Callie took his hand and stood up. She felt a sudden urge to burst into tears.

Garret held her hand and gave it a reassuring squeeze. He kept holding her hand as they walked to a room adjoining the living room. The bedroom had the same deep blue tile on the floor and, like the living room, it also had large windows that looked out towards the mountains. There was a mahogany four-poster bed in the center of the room with decorative carvings of palm trees on the posts. In the corner was a mahogany dresser with two rattan chairs by the window. A lamp sat on top of a wood bedside table.

When they entered the bedroom, Callie let go of Garret's hand. Garret Langrin was the kind of man who would be easy to lean on. The manner in which he'd come to rescue her as if he were the cavalry and she was a damsel in distress did not sit right with her. The one and only time she'd depended on a man had led her into this mess and had possibly cost him his life.

There was a part of her, a big part of her that wondered if Henry's murder was connected to his relationship with her. He'd been worried about his wife. The one genuine emotion he'd exhibited was fear when Callie last saw him alive. Could his wife have killed him? Callie knew that if she was in the position that Henry's wife was in, she wouldn't resort to murder—but who knew what anger could propel a person to do? Betrayal was certainly a motive in many crimes of passion.

As if he could read her thoughts, Garret Langrin's deep voice cut through her thoughts.

"You need to lie down and sleep. Running things over in your mind when you're tired and upset is not going to do you any good."

Garret walked over to the bed and turned it down.

"Try to get some sleep," he said. "I'll be working from home today, so when you wake up, you can either walk over to the main house or you can pick up the telephone and hit thirty-three—that'll connect you to the telephone in the house. Would you like me to send over some food for you?"

Callie shook her head. The thought of food made her nauseous.

"Okay," said Garret. He seemed hesitant to leave her.

"I'll be okay," Callie said, although she wondered if she'd ever be all right after this experience. Shaking away all thoughts of self-pity, Callie spoke in a stronger voice. "Thanks," she said. "I appreciate your help."

Garret's grin lit up his face. "Glad to be of assistance."

There was an awkward moment of silence between them, as the same feeling came over Callie—something she couldn't explain—a bell of recognition—a sense of the familiar. She was comfortable with him and she had no reason to be. She trusted him. He was solid and familiar. Still, she known him for only a short time, and in light of her current circumstances, her ease with Garret

Langrin made no sense. She was just tired, that was all. She'd been through a lot and her mind was playing tricks on her.

"Well, then . . ." said Garret. "I guess I'll go. Remember, if you need anything—anything at all—I'm just in the main house."

"Thank you," Callie repeated.

"You're sure you're not hungry?" Garret asked.

Callie smiled. "Quite sure. Thanks, anyway."

Garret walked over to the open doorway, but before he left, he turned around and said, "You'll be safe here, Callie."

Somewhere, deep inside her, in a place that she did not know existed, she felt a sense of calm. She believed him. For the time being, she'd be safe at Garret Langrin's house. But, there would come a time when she was going to have to leave the protection she found in his home, and what would happen then? Forcing herself not to think about the frightening possibilities that lay ahead, she lay down on the bed and to her surprise, in a few minutes she found herself drifting off to sleep. Still, right before she fell asleep, a disturbing thought appeared—did St. Christopher have the death penalty?

Josephine Kincaid sat in the funeral director's office beside her father. The office was stuffy, despite the open windows that brought in the bright St. Christopher sunshine. It was small and cramped—the desk untidy with papers, and files strewn around, giving the appearance of chaos. The funeral director was a friend of her father's which was why he'd agreed to see them on such short notice. Charles Battenmount was the premier funeral director of the area. His Battenmount Funeral Homes serviced the more well-heeled members of St. Christopher society. Typically, one of Charles' many assistant funeral directors would handle matters—Charles now was in semi-retirement, spending most of his time chasing golf balls at different exclusive golf courses around the world. But as a favor to Josephine's father, and in recognition of the powerful Kincaid name, Charles had opted to deal with this matter personally—even if it meant postponing a trip to Florida that he'd scheduled for later this week.

Josephine was dressed completely in black, as befitted a widow. Her black suit clung to her curves and the wide-brim black hat that she wore completed the picture of the grieving widow. She hated the color black. It did nothing for her pale complexion, but now was not the time to be concerned about that. She'd be wearing black for at least six months as St. Christopher tradition mandated. She was going to play the part of unhappy widow, even if it killed her.

Beside her, her father sat silently, occasionally reaching over and patting her hand. It was the first time Josephine had seen him look his seventy years. She knew her father didn't care for Henry, so his grief and shock at his murder had come as a surprise to her. Her father had not been one to show his emotions, but several times that morning she'd seen him wiping tears from his eyes.

Josephine had called him immediately, as soon as the police had telephoned her about Henry's murder. Her father had always been her rock—the one person in the world who she could depend on. God knew that she could never depend on her husband.

She'd never intended to marry Henry Kincaid—he'd been a conquest whom she'd grown bored with long before he'd proposed. But her father had urged her to make the union. The Kincaids were a powerful bunch, and their power and connections would be good for her, or so her father had convinced her. So, she'd married Henry, knowing how weak he was. In her mind, she'd marry him, spend his money, divorce him, get more money, and then move on with her life. Although Josephine's family was wealthy, she'd always believed that one could never be too rich.

She never fooled herself that Henry had ever loved her. What she and Henry shared was passion—no more, no less. They each lived separate lives, with separate lovers—understanding the need to be discreet. Josephine believed in attraction, lust, not love. Both she and her sister, Esme, had seen what love had done firsthand and they'd suffered for it. Their mother had left them all—her father, her sister and Josephine, for love. Josephine's mother had fallen in love with another man and she hadn't let her marriage or her children stand in her way. She'd run away with a man who worked for Josephine's father. Six months later, both she and her lover had died in a car crash. Josephine didn't love Henry, nor did he love her. He'd married her because her father had even more money than the Kincaids. Her father's business—building upscale hotels throughout the Caribbean, had made the family a fortune. Henry had shrewdly decided that an alliance between the families could benefit his family.

Henry had always adhered to her request that he be discreet—until Callie Hopewell had showed up at her doorstep. Henry had tried to explain that he'd fallen in love with Callie. He hadn't intended to, he'd told her, but there it was. He was in love with the woman who'd shown up at their front door. He knew Josephine would never let him divorce her to marry Callie without putting up a fight—a fight that would be ugly and would only hurt the Kincaid family name. So, he'd told Josephine that he was prepared to let Callie walk out of his life. Henry knew love didn't pay the bills and he knew that, financially, he stood more to lose than Josephine did. He was not prepared for the fight that he knew Josephine would put up and he'd told her that.

She'd won—in the end, Josephine got what she wanted. Henry told her he wasn't going to leave. But she knew it was only a matter of time before Henry packed his bags. He wasn't faithful to her, and Josephine knew that even if he found Callie again, he wouldn't be faithful to Callie either. He was a weak man. Unlike her father, who let her mother walk out on him without looking back, Henry was not a man who could thrive on adversity. He also was not a man who would stand up to his family and his family would never have stood for Henry leaving the marriage. They, too, had benefitted from Josephine's and Henry's marriage as Josephine's father had been very generous to the Kincaids over the years. The contacts in the banks and in the building industry from Josephine's father had lined the pockets of the Kincaids with millions of dollars. Henry was not about to walk out on that.

The funeral director Charles Battenmount cleared his throat. He was a man whose looks had improved with age. As a younger man, he'd been considered something of an island Lothario, whose long-suffering wife finally left him after years of philandering. Josephine remembered that in past years, she had personally discovered the rumors of Charles's lovemaking prowess were actually merited. Their mating, she couldn't call it anything else, happened infrequently and at odd times—during an afternoon lawn party, after a funeral of a St. Christopher dignitary, during a chance meeting in a restaurant. Charles's passion had intrigued Josephine—but Charles was a friend of her father's and his fear that Josephine's father would discover that his good friend and his daughter were intimately acquainted had eventually won over his lust. It was just as well, Josephine thought. In recent years, Charles had actually become predictable and dull.

Still, Josephine couldn't help noticing the strong brown jaw, full lips, wide dark eyes, and salt and pepper hair. His hairline was receding slightly, and there were a few more laugh lines in the corners of his eyes, but otherwise, Josephine noticed a firm body underneath the dark blue suit. She remembered times when her hands had roamed freely down that body.

As if he could read her thoughts, Charles nervously cleared his throat again.

"I've spoken to the police," said Charles. "And they won't be releasing the body until an autopsy can be done."

"How soon will that happen?" William Hawthorne, Josephine's father, asked.

"Don't really know," Charles replied, sneaking a look at Josephine.

"This is just dreadful!" William Hawthorne did not bother to hide his agitation.

"Daddy, it's going to be all right." Josephine turned her attention to her father. She'd never seen him so out of control—not even when her mother had left him.

"It's just . . . I can't believe that this sort of thing would ever happen on our island."

"There have been murders before," Josephine gently reminded him.

"True," William Hawthorne agreed, "but I never thought that anything like this would happen to our family . . . to you . . . Josephine, you shouldn't be here. Let me handle this for you."

"Daddy, I'm fine, really. What happened to Henry is terrible, but I'm going to get through this," said Josephine. "Our family will get through this."

"Yes, yes—that's true, but having the coroner hold up the . . . the body is only going to drag this process out and make things tougher for you."

"The coroner is backed up these days—but they should be able to get to it by tomorrow," said the funeral director.

"Can't they do it today?" William asked. "The sooner we get this behind us, the better."

Charles stared at him for a moment without speaking, then he said, "I could see if I could put some pressure on them—but this is a murder, William. The coroner needs the chief magistrate to sign off on the autopsy, and according to the coroner's office, the chief magistrate is away today at a conference in Jamaica."

"Damned nuisance! It's bad enough that Henry

was murdered, but now he can't even be allowed to rest in peace!" William blurted out.

Josephine turned and looked at her father. "What difference does it make, Daddy? Tomorrow is soon enough. We have enough to keep us busy today..."

William leaned over and squeezed his daughter's hand. "I just want this to be over with. I know how difficult it must be for you."

Charles looked over at Josephine but said nothing.

Actually, thought Josephine, it wasn't that difficult at all. She was free of Henry Kincaid and she didn't have to go through the drama of divorce. She was sorry he was dead, but there was nothing she could do to bring him back. Josephine knew she was being cold, but after hating Henry Kincaid for nine of the ten years of their marriage, she couldn't bring herself to mourn his death.

Josephine sighed. "It's difficult, Daddy, but I have you here to help me. I'll get through this."

Once again, Charles stared at Josephine without saying anything.

"Charles," said William Hawthorne, "I want you to take care of everything. Pick out the coffin, the flowers, whatever. Take care of the funeral program. I don't want Josephine to have to deal with any of that. Just send me the bill."

"Any price range I should be aware of?" Charles asked mildly.

William waved his hand in the air as if dismissing a bothersome employee. "I don't care what you choose or how much it costs. Just make sure it's tasteful, for Josephine's sake. Poor Henry—what a rotten way to go."

"I assume that Henry will be buried in the

Kincaid family plot?" Charles asked, clearing his throat.

"That's what they want," said William, "but it should be up to Josephine. She's his wife."

Widow, thought Josephine, trying hard to suppress the glee. She was finally free of Henry Kincaid.

"William," said Charles Battenmount, "I know this is trying for you. Let me handle everything and you just take Josephine home."

William narrowed his eyes. "I'm fine. It's my daughter you should be worried about. She just lost her husband."

"Daddy, let me handle this," said Josephine. "I need to do this alone. I can handle it. You go home and I'll call you as soon as I finish with my business with Charles."

William stood up and said, "Take care of this for me, Charles, and send me the bill. Josephine, I don't think that you should be alone."

Josephine looked up at her father and said, "You go ahead, Daddy. There're a few things I need to talk to Charles about . . . in relation to the funeral. I'll send for a car to pick me up when I'm ready to leave."

"Are you sure?" William asked. "I'm sure that Charles can handle all this without you having to deal with this unpleasantness."

"It's okay, Daddy," said Josephine. "I need to do this."

William Hawthorne bent down and kissed his daughter on the cheek. "If you need me, just give me a call."

"Thank you, Daddy," said Josephine as she watched her father leave Charles's office after saying his good-byes.

SMOOTH OPERATOR

After the door was closed, Josephine took off her hat.

"It's been a long time, baby," she said, with a knowing smile. "So, how's the funeral business?"

"Busy," he replied nervously.

"Good for you," she said with a seductive chuckle that clearly showed that the funeral business was the last thing on her mind.

"Josephine..."

"I'm happy for you, Charles."

Charles fidgeted nervously in his seat, then clumsily distributed his weight.

"When I found out about Henry, I told Daddy to give you the business."

"Josephine..."

"I've always liked how you *handled* your business, Charles."

Charles understood the invitation immediately.

Josephine stood up and walked over to the desk. With one swift motion she pushed all of the papers and files to the floor.

"Tell you're secretary that you're going to be busy for the next hour—to hold all calls."

"Josephine, this isn't the right time..." said Charles, but Josephine knew that he wanted her.

"Yes, it is," said Josephine as she began unbuttoning her black Chanel suit jacket, giving Charles an unencumbered view of her black lace bra.

Charles cleared his throat. "Josephine, for God's sake..."

She walked over to where Charles sat and leaned over him, whispering in his ear.

"Are you sure you want me to go, Charles?"

Josephine lightly ran her tongue along his earlobe, and Charles felt himself weaken. She was a bad habit—but God help him, he wanted her. Right now. Right here. In his office. Even as they planned her husband's funeral.

Charles picked up his telephone and said to his secretary. "Hold my calls... I have some important business I need to discuss with Mrs. Kincaid."

He placed the telephone receiver back in the cradle.

Josephine smiled as she sat on his lap, moving her hands quickly to unbuckle his belt.

"I've missed you, Charles."

"Josephine, for heaven's sake, you've just lost your husband... this isn't right."

She stopped unbuckling his belt long enough to take off her jacket.

"No, it isn't right." she smiled. "It's downright improper."

Sleep came to Callie, but along with it came disjointed dreams of death and the Caribbean Sea. She dreamt of Henry. She dreamt of the sea. She dreamt of her dead father who reached out to her, telling her to hold onto his hand, even as a turbulent blue sea threatened to swallow her. She dreamt of a laughing woman, a woman whose laughter was drowned out by rain. She dreamt of palm trees uprooted, rings rolling down the side of the hill and the sound of the rushing sea filled her ears. She fought in her sleep, fought to get away from the sea, from Henry, from the laughing woman. She fought to reach out to her father's hand which was just beyond her reach. "Hold on, Callie!" he shouted. "Hold on, girl!"

Callie awoke with a start. The sun was streaming in and she was drenched in sweat. She hadn't bothered to put on any pajamas, choosing to sleep in her clothes. Her heart hammered in her chest as the images of her dreams came back at her. Since her father's death, he'd always come to her in dreams when she was in trouble. Whatever challenge she faced, she dreamed of her father. Even now, so many years after death had stolen him from the family, she could still remember his touch, his kindness, the way his eyes would light up whenever he saw any of his women—his wife and his daughters. There were times when she would close her eyes and try to remember his voice, deep, rich, and loving. She had never missed him more than she did at this moment.

Her search for someone like her father had led her into Henry's arms, but Henry was nothing like her father. Her father would have cut off his right hand before he betrayed her mother. Her father believed in old-fashioned concepts like honor, fidelity, trust. After he died, she'd imagined that one day she would meet a man like him—a man who would love her unconditionally. A man who wouldn't ask her to change to fit into his concepts of what he thought a woman should be, or how a woman should be. A man with whom she could share her life. A man who would serenade her, just as her father would serenade her mother with songs from Motown. Before Henry had come into her life, she'd given up hope that this would ever happen, but Henry had given her hope—false hope—that she would meet a man as strong, loving, and wonderful as her father. Now, she saw that her search for this elusive thing called love had led her into something that could ultimately cost her—her freedom.

"I miss you, Daddy," she whispered.

Then, she closed her eyes, and let the sounds of the tropics—the birdcalls, the crickets, the rustling of bushes in the wind—lull her back to sleep.

Chapter 10

"How long will she be staying?" Garret's grandmother did not beat around the bush.

Garret remained in his seat on the back patio overlooking the pool and the gardens. His grandmother sat next to him. When he'd returned home, he'd found Zenna, Winsome, and his grandmother waiting for him. One look at his face had sent both Zenna and Winsome scurrying out of the room, but his grandmother remained.

"Let's go outside and talk," he'd told her, and they'd gone out to the patio where Garret prepared to answer what he knew would be an onslaught of questions from his grandmother.

"I don't know how long she'll be here," Garret replied. "I know that she'll be here for a few days at least."

"Is this the woman you met yesterday?" his grandmother asked.

Garret nodded his head. "It is."

"Is she in some kind of trouble?"

Garret should not have been surprised by the question. His grandmother always seemed to know things, even before they were revealed to her. Still, Garret was taken aback by her question. How had she known?

"Yes," replied Garret. "She's in trouble."

"Are you mixed up with her trouble?"

"No, I'm not."

"Then why are you helping her?"

Garret took a look around his property. Once again, the sight of the grounds—the lush greenness, the sloping hill that led to the sea—brought him a sense of peace. Even in the middle of what he suspected was going to be a tough fight on behalf of Callie Hopewell—he knew that he was not going to let her go through this fight alone—he had a sense that at least for this moment, things were going to work out. He just wasn't sure how to go about it but he was going to find a way.

"Why are you helping this woman?" Garret's grandmother repeated her question.

"I don't really know how to answer that," Garret replied. True, he was attracted to Callie Hopewell. But there was something else that he couldn't explain. From the moment he first saw her on the airplane, Callie had pulled at a place inside him that he couldn't understand.

"Hmm," said his grandmother. "I hope she knows how lucky she is to have you in her corner."

Garret smiled. "I'm not so sure she'd consider herself lucky right now. Her fiancé was murdered last night and she's a suspect."

"Is she your client?" his grandmother asked.

"Not yet," said Garret. "I'm hoping that the police will realize that she had absolutely nothing to do with Henry Kincaid's murder."

"Henry Kincaid was her fiancé! I thought he was married."

Garret sighed. "It's a long story."

"Are you sure that this woman isn't mixed up in Henry's murder?"

"Absolutely sure," Garret replied.

"That's good, because the Kincaids are a powerful and nasty bunch. I hope for her sake she doesn't have to tangle with them."

As usual his grandmother had accurately assessed and summed up the situation.

All of Catherine Hopewell's alarms were going off, loudly. Something was wrong. Something was more than wrong. She spent half the night and most of the morning dialing Henry Kincaid's telephone number, and no one had answered.

"Maybe he's gone somewhere with Callie," Phoebe had suggested in an attempt to ease the worry from her mother's eyes. It didn't work.

Catherine Hopewell placed the telephone receiver back into its cradle. "I'm going to St. Christopher to find my daughter."

"Mama, be reasonable," said Phoebe. Like her sisters she would usually go along with her mother's crazy schemes, but jetting off to a foreign land to rescue someone who might not want to be rescued, was taking things too far. "Why don't we wait a few more hours? I'm sure Callie will get in touch with us by this evening. She knows how you are. She'll call you."

"I'm going to St. Christopher," Catherine Hopewell repeated. "Are you coming with me?"

"Mama, I have a job. People are depending on me. I can't just call up my boss and tell him I'm going off to a Caribbean island."

"Then I'll go there without you."

"Mama, be reasonable. Let's just wait for a few hours. If we don't hear from her, then we can go to St. Christopher."

"I'm going. With or without you."

Phoebe knew when she was beaten. "All right, Mama, I'll go with you. I can't have you running around in a foreign land by yourself."

"I'm perfectly capable of taking care of myself, Phoebe Andrea Hopewell."

Whenever her mother called people by their entire name, that usually signaled that she was not happy.

Phoebe sighed. "I know you can take care of yourself, Mama. But I'd just feel better if I was there to help you."

I'll be damned, thought Phoebe. *The woman is good. She has me begging her to do something absolutely crazy and something she wants me to do. The CIA should know about her. Hell, the CIA, and the FBI.*

"Well, thanks for the offer, Phoebe. I think I'll take you up on it. Let me call the airline, maybe we can get a flight out tonight."

Chapter 11

There was someone in the room with her. As she opened her eyes after a fitful sleep, Callie was aware she was not alone. Her eyes widened in alarm and she sat up in the bed quickly.

"I didn't mean to startle you."

Callie looked over to see a tall, slim, brown-skinned woman with flaming red dreadlocks sitting in a chair across the room.

"Who are you?" Callie asked, when she calmed herself enough to get the words out. She'd been through a lot in the past twenty-four hours and there was nothing like finding a dead body in a hotel room to leave a person spooked, at the very least.

The woman smiled at her. "I'm Zenna."

Callie could see that this woman was very beautiful. Model beautiful. Tall, thin, and gorgeous. She was the kind of woman who wore her confidence around her as if it were another article of clothing—the kind of woman who men tended to fall quickly and irrevocably in love with. She was wearing a loose-fitting white cotton shirt tucked into black jeans that looked as if they were painted on her athletic body. Callie watched as she pulled a hand through her red dreadlocks, which tumbled around her shoulders. Her eyes, which were as dark as midnight, stared at Callie with open curiosity.

"I guess you're wondering why I'm here," Zenna said, still smiling.

Callie's instincts told her that this woman meant her no harm, but as recent events had shown her, sometimes instincts were not to be trusted.

"You might say that," Callie replied, pulling the covers closer.

"Well, I'm very close to Garret—although technically he's my employer—he's the closest thing that I have to family," said Zenna. "I don't think Garret's ever brought a woman home to stay—mind you, he's had more than his share of female company—but he usually meets them on their own turf."

Callie waited for her to get to the point.

"I just wanted to meet the woman who Garret's mooning over," said Zenna.

Callie shook her head quickly. "You've got it all wrong," said Callie. "He's helping me on a . . . professional basis, that's all. There's nothing going on here and he certainly has no designs on me."

"Really?" Zenna raised one skeptical eyebrow. "You're a client, you say?"

"Well, not exactly . . ." Callie found herself stammering. "I might be needing some legal help and Mr. Langrin has offered to help me."

Zenna shifted in her chair as if she were trying to get more comfortable.

"I've known Garret for a very long time and this is the first time he's let any of his clients stay in the guest house."

Callie cleared her throat. "It's complicated."

She didn't want to explain anything to this woman, but she didn't want to be rude, either. She was a guest of Garret Langrin's and it was obvious that this Zenna felt she had some vested interest in her relationship with Garret. A sudden thought emerged—the relationship between Zenna and Garret must be of a romantic nature. This woman thought that she was a rival!

"Listen," said Callie. "You don't have to be concerned at all. There's nothing going on between him and me. He's offered to help me in a . . . situation. I just arrived on the island and I might need some legal help. That's all. Really. Any claim you have on him . . . well, put it this way. I'm not interested and neither is he."

The last thing Callie needed was yet another woman who believed that she was moving in on her guy. It was bad enough Henry's wife probably thought she was some home wrecker—maybe murderer—but she didn't need Zenna to think she had any interest in Garret Langrin. As grateful as she was for Garret's help, she would be just as happy to put him, this island, and the terrible things that had happened, firmly behind her.

Zenna threw back her head and laughed. "You think Garret and I are together?"

"I wasn't sure," said Callie, wishing Zenna would leave, but having been bred by a mother who stressed good manners, she refrained from asking her to leave her alone. "It's just, you seemed very interested in Garret and myself."

"That, I am," said Zenna when her laughter subsided. "Very interested, in point of fact. But I'm not in love with Garret. True, he is a very, very handsome man and he's just about the most honorable, kind person I've ever met. I owe him a great deal. If it weren't for Garret, I'd probably be dead. But Garret is like a brother to me. He is my very best friend and let's say I have a vested interest in his happiness. I just wanted to meet you."

"I think you've gotten the wrong impression here . . . about Garret and myself."

"Have I?" Zenna asked.

"Yes," replied Callie. Her patience was now wearing thin—notwithstanding her mother's admonition about good manners, Callie wanted to get up, take a hot shower and figure out how to get out of the mess she was now firmly in. "I don't mean to be rude . . ."

"Say no more!" Zenna stood up. "I've been the rude one, barging in here like this. My curiosity got the better of me. I'm sure that you have things to attend to . . . I'll take my leave now."

She sounded like a proper English governess who spoke in a lilting, West Indian accent.

"I do have some things that I need to deal with . . ." said Callie.

"Well, I'll see you around. By the way, what's your name? Garret hasn't told me that yet. Ever since he got home this morning, he's been in his office at the house behind closed doors. Whatever trouble you're in—he's dealing with it."

Whatever trouble you're in. Oh, Lord. The reality of

just how much trouble she was in came flooding back.

"My name is Callie. Callie Hopewell."

"Well, I'm Zenna Wexford. I'm Garret's chauffeur, assistant, confidante and friend. And I love him dearly."

Callie stared at Zenna as she stood by the doorway to her room. Her declaration of her feelings for Garret was heartfelt.

Zenna hesitated for a moment, then she said, "Garret is a good man, Callie. Don't hurt him."

Zenna turned around and walked out before Callie had a chance to respond. Pulling the covers off, she swung unsteady legs to the floor. The past events had taken a toll on her emotionally and physically. She pushed Zenna's strange warning out of her head. There was no danger of hurting Garret Langrin. In about two weeks, if all went well, she would never see Garret Langrin or this island again.

The funeral director, Charles Battenmount, wiped the taste of Josephine Kincaid off his lips. Even for Josephine, this went beyond callous. He'd always known that despite her outward beauty, Josephine was a cold, calculating number. But he'd thought that she'd have some respect for the dead, especially when the recently departed was her own husband. Shaking his head, he surveyed the mess that they'd made. The evidence of their recent "lovemaking" was apparent in the papers strewn on the floor, his own rumpled clothing, and the lipstick that he'd just wiped off his face. He was ashamed of himself. He'd thought that his ill-advised attraction to Josephine had ended, but somehow she'd managed to heat things up again—with very little effort on her part.

Of course, the passion they'd always had between them had wiped out all common sense—not to mention any sense of decency—clean out of his head for about an hour or so. After it was over, he felt dirty. He felt used. It was always the same way with Josephine.

He'd lusted after her while she was still a teenager, but it wasn't until shortly after her eighteenth birthday when she cornered him at a family picnic—where they'd escaped for fifteen minutes of unbelievable pleasure in his family boathouse—that he'd given in to his attraction. He was a friend of her fathers, but that didn't stop him from becoming involved with her. Involved might have been a more charitable term for what he had with Josephine. It was just sex, no strings attached. She came, she took . . . and she came again, then she left. It might be months, and at times, years between their encounters, but there was something about her—despite his revulsion for the person she was—that kept him coming back.

After they'd made love, he'd watched as she dressed, putting herself together so effectively and efficiently that no one would guess that the recent widow was doing anything other than grieving for the loss of her husband.

"We shouldn't have done that," Charles had told her.

"Why not?" Josephine had smiled. "We're both consenting adults. And neither of us are attached . . . at least not anymore."

"That's cold, Josephine," Charles had replied, thinking about Henry Kincaid. True, Henry wasn't one of his favorite people. He was a little too taken with himself, just as all the other Kincaids were—but the dead, even the ones who he didn't care for when they were living, deserved some respect. The fact that he'd just engaged in a pretty heavy sexual encounter with the recently departed's wife wasn't lost on him. What he did was wrong, but Charles reasoned, at least he had the good grace to feel bad about it. Josephine, on the other hand, felt no remorse.

"After the funeral, we'll have to do this again," said Josephine with a slow smile when she'd finished dressing.

"No." Charles shook his head. "I don't think that would be a good idea."

"Don't be a prude, Charles," said Josephine. "It's not an attractive trait. You and I both know that there'll be a next time."

"No, Josephine—that's it. This is where I get off the train. Good God, woman, your husband hasn't been dead for twenty-four hours yet!"

"I'm sorry he's dead, but there's nothing I can do about that," she said with childlike reasoning.

"Are you?" Charles had asked before he had a chance to stop the words from coming out. "Sorry he's dead?"

Josephine stopped smoothing out her skirt and looked at him. When he saw the coldness in her eyes, he flinched.

"That wasn't very nice," Josephine said slowly.

Charles felt a chill race up his spine. It was all he could do not to run to the obeah woman two doors away to buy some holy water and sprinkle it all over himself. Looking at Josephine was like looking at the devil.

"You almost make me regret the past hour," Josephine said, her lips stretching into a tight smile. "Almost."

Charles just wanted to get the hell away from her.

"I'm sorry," he said automatically. Josephine Kincaid was not a woman whom he wanted to have on his bad side. God knew what she was capable of. "This whole thing is very upsetting. I mean Henry being murdered . . ."

"Yes," said Josephine. "It's very upsetting. I can understand how it would shake you a bit. I forgive you, Charles. You know I can't stay angry at you too long anyway."

She'd walked over and kissed him, but as soon as she'd walked out of his office he'd wiped his mouth. He had just kissed a serpent.

As soon as Kincaid's funeral was over, he was going to get the hell off the island and as far away from Josephine Kincaid as his checkbook could manage. He'd been thinking about taking a trip to visit an ex-girlfriend who'd relocated to Venezuela. He picked up the telephone receiver. It was time to give her a call.

Chapter 12

The hot afternoon sun of St. Christopher greeted Callie when she opened the front door of Garret's guest house. She'd slept for a few fitful hours, but after the visit from Garret's protective friend Zenna, Callie found that sleep was impossible. There were too many thoughts going through her mind. She needed to call her family to let them know what was going on, but first she needed to figure out how she was going to get herself out of this mess. She didn't want to call them about her problems until she at least had a possibility of a solution in mind. A brisk shower and a change of clothes had given her back some of her natural optimism—but not much. Somehow, she'd get out of this predicament, but she had no idea how she was going to accomplish this feat.

Closing the door behind her, she walked down the path towards Garret's house. She'd called him to let him know she was coming to talk to him and he was waiting for her by his open front door. He'd changed his clothes and was now wearing blue jeans with a light blue T-shirt. Although the casual look suited him, Garret was a man who appeared to be equally at ease in a suit or in jeans. Henry had never worn jeans. For him, jeans were "common"—business suits were his norm, although for the times when he went casual, his usual mode of dress was crisply ironed tan khaki pants and a white oxford shirt with black penny loafers to complete the picture. Secretly, Callie thought Henry was a snob, but she'd convinced herself that she could make him change. Shaking her head, she wondered at just how foolish she'd been—thinking that she could make another person change.

She heard a rustling sound coming from the second floor of Garret's house and looked up to see three faces in a window. Almost as quickly as she saw the three women, the window closed and the curtains were drawn. She smiled to herself. She was not the only one who had curious family members. Obviously, Garret had a similar family although, Callie was convinced, no one had a family quite so dramatic, or crazy, as hers.

"It's good to see you smiling," said Garret as she walked in front of him.

A feeling of guilt swept over her. What on earth was she smiling about? Henry was dead. She was a suspect in his murder. Her passport had been taken from her and she was now staying at the house of a stranger—even if a handsome stranger. Though it didn't really matter if Garret Langrin looked like a movie star or a candidate for plastic surgery—his looks didn't enter into the equation. She needed to focus on her predicament.

"I hope I didn't get you at a bad time . . ." Callie faltered, suddenly unsure of herself. Asking someone—especially a stranger—for help was a strange notion to her. But she without a doubt needed Garret Langrin's help. He was the only person she knew on this island. She remembered how short she'd been with him yesterday when she'd met him on the airplane. What a difference twenty-four hours made. The same person she'd rebuffed yesterday was the very person she was going to beg for help.

"Don't worry about it," Garret replied. "I was just going over some correspondence in my study. Are you hungry?"

"I'm starved," Callie replied. Her appetite had returned hours ago.

"Good." Garret grinned. "My grandmother made us some food for lunch."

Callie followed Garret through the open door and stepped into the marble foyer. Looking around at her surroundings, she forced her mouth not to drop open. Garret's home was spectacular. There were no other words to describe it. Just beyond the marble foyer a large living room surrounded by floor to ceiling windows stretched out in front of her. The windows framed a backdrop of brightly colored tropical foliage surrounding a breathtaking infinity pool with sparkling blue water.

She walked into the living room and decided that if she ever got out of this mess and won the lottery, she would hire Garret's interior decorator. Everything from the gleaming hardwood floors, the soaring ceilings, and the antique mahogany chairs to the West Indian art that graced the walls, the

African statues, and pictures of family members, appealed to her. It was as if someone had asked her what her dream house would look like and then designed it.

"Who is your interior decorator?" asked Callie when she found her voice.

Garret laughed. "You're looking at him."

"You did this?"

Garret nodded his head. "Don't act so surprised."

"It's just that I assumed . . ." She didn't finish her sentence.

"That a woman decorated my house?" Garret asked.

Callie cleared her throat. She didn't bother to lie. "Yes."

"Why, Miss Hopewell, that's downright sexist."

"Not to mention idiotic," Callie admitted.

"Your words, not mine," said Garret. "But if it's any consolation, no one believes that I did this on my own. They all assume that I had help. *Female* help."

"Well, I guess it's natural to think that maybe a girlfriend helped you," said Callie.

"There is no girlfriend, Callie."

Suddenly, the mood changed. The light banter they'd just engaged in was gone. The way he spoke those words was as if he were making a declaration. She turned to where Garret stood across the room, looking at her.

Callie decided that it was time to change the subject. She found it hard to believe that a man as attractive, and obviously as wealthy, as Garret, didn't have a horde of women at his beck and call—not that it should matter to her either way. She pushed those thoughts out of her mind.

"Which way is the kitchen?" Callie asked.

"Right this way," Garret replied.

Callie followed Garret through the living room to the adjoining dining room. The dining room was as spectacular as the living room. High ceilings, with a large crystal chandelier, framed an antique mahogany dining room table which glistened as if it had just been polished. On the table was a feast of various Caribbean dishes—rice and peas, stewed chicken, plantains, a fruit platter, codfish dumplings and pitchers of different kinds of juices. Callie felt her stomach rumble with hunger.

"Were you expecting an army?" Callie asked.

Garret pulled out a chair for Callie to sit. "My grandmother does everything in excess," he said mildly. "Just ask Zenna."

"I've met Zenna," said Callie as she watched Garret sit in the seat at the head of the table.

"I'm afraid to ask how you met her."

"She came by to talk with me," said Callie. "She's very protective of you."

Garret laughed, "Okay, what did Miss Zenna ask you?"

"She wanted to know my intentions," Callie replied.

"Your intentions?" Garret repeated the words slowly, almost as if he were issuing her an invitation.

The room suddenly became very warm, despite the cool air flowing from the air conditioner.

Callie suddenly found it very hard to concentrate.

"Yes, my intentions. I assured her that my intentions towards you are completely honorable."

Garret's smile was wide. "That's a shame."

"Well," said Callie, changing the subject, "let's not let all this good food go to waste."

Chapter 13

Inspector Mobray sat in the living room of the widow Josephine Kincaid as the thought came to mind that he'd encountered murderers and other sociopaths who weren't as cold as she. Although she pretended to be the grieving widow, complete with the occasional tearful outburst, Mobray could see through her act. Her eyes gave her away. Eyes that were full of malice. His instincts told him that Callie was involved in the murder of Henry Kincaid. He knew that jealousy and betrayal were often emotions that led to dangerous behavior. She wouldn't be the first wronged woman who decided to get revenge, but the evil he saw in Josephine was missing in Callie.

Callie's grief had been real. There was no acting there. But was Callie simply showing remorse because she'd murdered Henry?

As if reading his thoughts, Josephine Kincaid shifted on the plush, white sofa and sighed impatiently. "I don't know why you're asking me all these questions, it's that little tramp Callie Hopewell who you should be talking to!"

Mobray cleared his throat. "I've spoken to Ms. Hopewell already and I intend to speak with her again, but I do need some more information from you about your husband's movements last night—I'm sorry that I have to ask these questions so soon after—er..."

"His murder!" Josephine spat out the words. "You regret that you have to ask me these questions about my husband's murder, but you've got a job to do, isn't that right, Inspector Mobray?"

"Something like that," Mobray replied. "I know this is probably the worst possible time to talk about this, but I'm sure that you'd like to catch whomever is responsible, and that's why I'm asking you these questions."

"I told you who's responsible!" Josephine snapped. "Callie Hopewell killed my husband and while you're wasting time sitting here with me, you could be talking with her—preferably in the confinement of a jail cell!"

The raised voices that came from the foyer outside the living room prevented Mobray from answering. The door to the living room opened and in walked a younger and even more beautiful version of Josephine. Mobray recognized Josephine's sister Esme Hawthorne. Esme was a former Miss St. Christopher and she'd parlayed her good looks into a successful real estate business. Many of the high-end properties on St. Christopher were sold by Esme. Her pretty face graced billboards around the island and she was frequently seen on television in her many commercials.

Esme stalked into the living room followed by her father, William Hawthorne. Mobray had met William on various occasions, and while he was impressed with William's business successes, like his daughter Josephine, William could be bitterly cold at times.

Esme stood in front of Josephine, her hands clasped in front of her as if in prayer. "Josephine, what on earth is going on! What is this about Henry being murdered? Why didn't anyone call me!"

"Esme, for God's sake, pull yourself together!" William Hawthorne's deep bass voice filled the room.

"Yes, Esme," Josephine said calmly, "pull yourself together. The police are here to ask me questions, then I'll talk to you!"

This was odd, Mobray thought. Henry was killed last night, and no one in Josephine's family had informed her sister.

"The hell with that!" Esme's voice raised, and cracked. "Why didn't someone tell me that Henry had been hurt?"

"The word is murdered," said Josephine, "and pardon me, but I was in the midst of dealing with the fact that my husband had just been killed."

"Esme, we thought you'd left the island for business in Jamaica yesterday." William tried to reason with his youngest daughter.

He stood next to her, looking back and forth between his two warring offspring.

"I was in Jamaica," Esme hissed, "but I came back last night! I was only there for a few hours."

"Esme, spare me the drama!" said Josephine. "I don't need it right now. May I remind you that it was my husband who was murdered last night."

Inspector Mobray watched in fascination as Esme crumpled to the floor, her loose, white cotton dress billowing around her. Esme let out a wail that came from somewhere deep inside of her. The tears, the grief, the disbelief—all the emotions Mobray expected from Josephine, Henry's wife, came pouring out of her sister, Esme.

William knelt down beside his youngest daughter and wrapped his arms around her.

Josephine stood up, her voice tight.

"Inspector Mobray, as you can see, this isn't the right time for this discussion. I'll be glad to talk with you—but our family has suffered a terrible loss."

Mobray knew he could have pushed it, but he suspected he wasn't going to get much more information from Josephine Kincaid. She'd already told him they had an argument about his affair with Callie Hopewell, and Henry had left the house after the argument shortly after eight o'clock that evening. Josephine had remained at home in her room until she'd learned her husband had been murdered. The night watchman at their house had verified Henry had left at the time that Josephine stated. For now, Josephine Kincaid was in the clear. But for Mobray, Josephine's story was a little too clear cut. She'd freely admitted that she'd argued with her husband. Most people would argue if they found out their spouse was unfaithful. But Mobray suspected that she hadn't told him the full story about what happened between her and Henry last night. However, he knew he wasn't going to get that information today.

Mobray stood up. "Of course, Mrs. Kincaid. I

understand. I apologize for the intrusion. I'll see myself out."

Catherine Hopewell slowly counted to ten in her head before she asked the attendant at the counter of Caribbean Air, "What do you mean the flight is cancelled?"

"I'm sorry, ma'am," the woman said nervously, as if she thought Catherine would do her bodily harm. "The aircraft has some technical difficulties."

"Technical difficulties!" Catherine lost the battle to hide her exasperation. "This flight was supposed to have left hours ago, and now, after we've waited all afternoon and well into the evening, I might add, you're cancelling the flight!"

A mutinous murmur rose in the crowd that had assembled by the Caribbean Air counter. The flight attendant looked around nervously for backup.

Phoebe spoke up. "Ma, would you rather find out that the plane had problems when it's in the air?"

The flight attendant looked at her with deep gratitude.

Catherine sighed. Phoebe was right. Catherine was a nervous flyer and it was only her strong sense that her firstborn was in trouble that would get her on an airplane. It had been seven years since she'd last taken a flight, and the experience had been so awful she'd vowed that short of a life and death emergency, she wasn't about to go anywhere she couldn't drive or take a train. Like Aretha Franklin, Catherine Hopewell was not born to fly.

"When is the next flight?" Catherine asked.

"Well, there's a connecting flight that leaves for Miami tonight, but the seats on the Miami to St. Christopher leg are all taken."

"Then what good is it!" Catherine asked.

"Ma, remember you're a church woman," Phoebe whispered. "Please don't go off on this woman and embarrass me!"

Catherine sighed again. "Is there a flight tomorrow?"

"Yes," said the attendant. "There's one that leaves tomorrow at eight and it connects through Puerto Rico. You'll be in St. Christopher by two in the afternoon."

"Good," said Catherine, accepting that her attempts to get to Callie would have to be postponed for a day.

"Have you tried Callie's cell number again?" Catherine asked Phoebe.

"Yes, Ma," Phoebe replied. "I can't get through. I keep getting the same message that she's out of the service area."

"Damn cell phones!" said Catherine.

"Ma!" said Phoebe, scandalized. "Remember that you're a church woman. Church women don't talk like that!"

"Don't lecture me, Phoebe Hopewell," said Catherine. "I go to church regularly, that's true—but I think that after everything we've been through today, the good Lord will forgive me."

Chapter 14

Garret sat in his study and watched as the beautiful woman in front of him paced back and forth in front of his antique oak desk. His study was a sanctuary where even his grandmother rarely ventured. This was the place he went when he needed to work, or unwind, or solve a difficult problem. The wood paneled room was comfortable and comforting to him. The late nineteenth-century oak kneehole desk had belonged to his grandfather and it was his favorite piece of furniture in the room. All of the furniture were antiques—the set of four walnut balloon-back chairs with carved pierce splats and overstuffed seats upholstered in dark green velvet were both exquisite and comfortable—a rare combination.

He'd personally selected all the antiques in the study—the mahogany bookshelves with dentil cornice glazed doors were filled with his favorite books; the Victorian rosewood drop-dial wall clock with its decorative carvings was an acquisition from one of his many trips to England for business, the mahogany inlaid sofa in the corner of the room was a recent acquisition and a perfect complement to all of the other pieces in his study. He found it odd that it wasn't strange for him to have Callie in his private study. In fact, it was as natural to have her in the room with him as if she'd been coming here often.

Garret watched as she walked to the corner of the room, throwing herself on the sofa. *Careful,* Garret cautioned himself. *Keep your feelings for the lady in check.* Right now the very beautiful, the very desirable Callie was in deep, deep trouble and he needed to keep his wits about him if he was going to be able to help her get out of this mess.

"Tell me again, did Henry seem frightened when you last saw him?" Garret asked.

After the meal they'd shared, Garret and Callie had come to his study to brainstorm. They'd spent the past several hours talking about the events of last night. It had been difficult for Callie—Garret could see the pain shadowed in her eyes, but he'd seen something else, also. He'd seen a determination on her part to get to the bottom of what happened. Callie could have easily played the victim. She had every right, every reason to fall apart, but he'd watched as she held her emotions in control and discussed some tough subjects—including her fiancé's betrayal—with a cool detachment he knew she didn't feel.

Callie sighed. "He seemed upset, but I'm not sure if he was scared. He'd warned me about his wife. He seemed nervous when he talked about her."

"Well, she certainly had the motive," said Garret, "but did she have the opportunity?"

He saw a fresh wave of pain cross Callie's face and he cursed himself for being insensitive. He was talking about the woman who was married to the man she'd intended to marry.

"Do you think Henry's wife is involved?" Callie asked.

"It's a possibility," Garret replied.

He looked out the window and saw dusk was fast giving way to evening. There was a lot to do tomorrow. They'd decided to go back to Broxton to do their own investigation. Garret suggested to Callie that she should lie low and let him do the legwork, but she'd shot down his idea with alarming speed.

"It's my neck that's on the line," she'd replied, "and I'm going to be right there with you when you go back to Broxton."

"It might be awkward for you," Garret warned her. He'd hidden the afternoon newspapers from her because the story of Henry's death and her possible involvement had been splashed on the front page. St. Christopher was a small island and Callie was now a person of some notoriety. Garret could tell that Callie was strong, but he wasn't sure whether or not she was strong enough to deal with the negative scrutiny that was going to follow her until her name was cleared.

"You're right," Callie had replied. "It'll probably be awkward, but not as awkward as ending up in prison for a crime I didn't commit."

She had a point there. A very good point. Garret conceded gracefully. "We'll go to Broxton after breakfast tomorrow," he told her, and in return he'd been granted a beautiful smile.

"Thanks for seeing things my way," she'd replied.

"As if I had a choice."

"True, but thanks for making it easy for me."

Looking over at her, sitting on the sofa with one shapely, bare brown leg crossing the other, Garret found it hard to concentrate on exactly what Callie was saying. The simple light blue sundress she wore was as sexy to him as a Victoria's Secret negligee. It had been a while since he'd been intimate with anyone, but that didn't explain the shot of lust that raged through his body when he looked at those legs, and the dainty feet in the strappy, impractical sandals that she wore.

A brisk knock on the door saved Garret from any further dangerous thoughts.

"Come in," Garret called out, tearing his eyes away from Callie Hopewell.

Garret's grandmother opened the door and walked into the room. Turning to face Callie, who'd risen from the sofa when Dreama had come into the study, she held out her hand and said, "I'm Dreama Beckford, Garret's grandmother. You must be the infamous Callie Hopewell—I've been hearing about you on the television news."

Garret shook his head. He wasn't surprised that his grandmother would use the direct approach. Sometimes he wondered whether or not his grandmother had ever met a thought she didn't care to share with the rest of the world. She was a kind woman, a loving and a strong woman. There was no one in the world who Garret loved more than his grandmother. But there were times when the words that came out of her mouth would make him cringe.

If Callie was taken aback by his grandmother's words, she didn't show it. Instead, she fixed a smile on her face and shook his grandmother's hand vigorously.

"I'm Callie Hopewell," she replied in that husky voice Garret knew he'd never get tired of hearing. "What are they saying about me on the news?"

Dreama sat down on the sofa and Callie sat beside her.

"Well, they say you're implicated in the murder of Henry Kincaid."

"Is that all they're saying?" Callie asked.

Garret spoke up quickly. "Those news reporters are trying to drum up interest in this story. Nothing too dramatic happens on our island, so they're bound to sensationalize things."

"I think the facts are sensational enough without anyone having to exaggerate them," said Dreama, fixing a direct stare on Callie. "There's a word for women who sleep with other women's husbands."

"I've heard that word before," said Callie, "and believe me, if I'd known that Henry was married, I never would have had anything to do with him. I certainly wouldn't have shown up at his house. Mrs. Beckford, my mother raised me to respect marriage vows—whether they be my own vows or those of someone else. I feel humiliated and disgusted that I trusted Henry, but I didn't kill him."

Dreama smiled at Callie. "I'm glad to hear that." She patted Callie's hand. "You wouldn't be the first woman to be taken in by a double-timing man, may God rest his unfaithful soul."

"Gram, could we possibly talk about something else?" Garret asked. Trying to get his grandmother off a subject was like trying to get the wind to change direction.

Callie smiled at him, and once again he felt that hot flash of attraction. Staying around her and maintaining his focus was going to be very hard.

"It's okay, Garret. Your grandmother is right about everything she says. If anything, I appreciate her giving me the chance to explain what really happened. Most people wouldn't have been so generous or open-minded."

Dreama Beckford looked over at her grandson and said, "I like this woman, Garret."

So do I, thought Garret. *God help me, so do I.*

Callie waited until her mother finished asking all of her questions about her current predicament. Night had fallen in St. Christopher and a loud symphony of crickets outside the window of Garret's guest house kept her company. She'd waited until nighttime to call her mother. She knew that she should've called earlier in the day, but it had taken most of the day to get the nerve to call and tell her that her fiancé was not only married to someone else, but had been murdered and she was the chief suspect in his murder. Callie sat on one of the couches in the guest house living room and waited patiently while her mother grilled her with questions about Henry.

"I knew something was wrong!" her mother

wailed. "My left eye has been twitching all day, and then we couldn't get a flight to St. Christopher, but we'll be there tomorrow."

"Mom, please—it's not that bad, really. I can handle this."

Her mother's voice rose an octave. "*Not that bad! You've got one foot in prison and the other foot on a slippery banana peel! What are you waiting for—a guilty verdict! Trust me, Callie. This is bad. This is very bad.*"

It wasn't that Callie didn't agree with her mother. She knew the full extent of the trouble she was now facing, but she didn't want to drag her mother into this mess. She'd gotten herself into this, and she was going to have to get herself out. Besides, there was nothing her mother could do for her, other than put in a prayer that the Lord would get her out of this situation.

"Mom, right now I need you to stay in New York. There might be things that I need you to do for me there."

"Like what?" her mother replied. "Water your plants? Pick up your mail? What could possibly be more important than coming down there to help my firstborn child?"

Callie's eyes watered. There was a part of her that wanted her mother to come and wrap her arms around her. When she was a child, Callie would always bring her troubles to her mother, and her mother's kind words, wise counsel, and warm kisses would chase the troubles away. Now that she was an adult, things were different. She needed a lot more than her mother could give her right now.

"Mom, I just don't want you to be dragged into this."

"As if you have a choice," her mother replied. "You're my daughter. I'll be down there tomorrow."

"No." The dutiful daughter who always said yes, decided to say no.

"What do you mean?" Callie's mother asked, as if she'd never heard the word no before.

"I mean, please don't come down to St. Christopher," said Callie, trying to be as gentle as she could. "Not yet, anyway. Mom, I need you. I always need you. But right now I need you to be in New York. The family is going to freak out when they find out what's going on and you need to be there with them right now. I'm in good hands. I have a lawyer. I have a place to stay. Right now I'm considered a person of interest, but I haven't been charged with anything. For all I know, I might get my passport back tomorrow and then I can get off this island. I think you should wait until something definitive happens."

There was a moment of silence while her mother digested her words.

"But I don't want you to be alone down there." Callie's mother was weakening, but she hadn't given up the fight completely.

"I'm not alone. I told you that I have a lawyer, and I'm staying at his place."

"I don't like it," Callie's mother responded. "Who is this lawyer and why are you staying at his house? For all you know he can be some Caribbean gigolo who's just after your money... or worse, your body!"

Callie laughed. "I can't say if he's a gigolo, but I know that he's not after my money. He seems to be fairly well off. And if it'll make you feel any better—I'm staying in his guest house. He lives with his grandmother, so I don't think that he's going to be making the moves on me anytime soon."

"How do you know he's a good lawyer?" her mother asked. "How do you know anything about this man? Do you trust him?"

These were all good questions, and Callie didn't have an answer for any of them.

"Mom, I'm just going on faith here. If he's not a good lawyer, then I'll get another. As for trusting him—I don't know him. I haven't been the most reliable person when it comes to judging folks. Look at what happened with Henry..."

"Don't you go blame yourself for what happened to that no-good, two-timing—"

"Mom, please—Henry's dead."

"Yes, he is, and I'm sorry for that. But that doesn't change the fact that he was a low-down, dirty... well, if I wasn't a church-going woman I'd say more, but you get the general idea!"

"Yes, Mom. I do. I get the general idea. Henry did some terrible things to me but he didn't deserve to be murdered."

"True," Callie's mother agreed. "But you didn't deserve to have him lie to you the way he did."

"Nothing we can do about it now, Mom," said Callie, wishing that they could change the subject. She didn't want to think about Henry. She didn't want to think about his lifeless body any more than she wanted to think about his betrayal.

Her mother sighed. "You're right about Henry and you're right about me not coming down there tomorrow. I'll wait to see how things go... but if you need me, you'll let me know, Callie—won't you?"

"Mom, I always need you," Callie replied.

There was a catch in her mother's voice.

"You're my firstborn Callie. I love all my children equally—but there's a bond between a mother and her first child . . . I just don't want you down there trying to be strong all by yourself when you know you've got backup. You've got me, and you've got your sisters."

"I know that, Mom."

"You'll call me every day?" her mother asked.

"Every night I'll give you a full report, Mom."

"Well," said Callie's mother, "you have one week. If this thing isn't resolved in a week, I'm coming down there."

"That's fine, Mom. Hopefully I'll be back home long before then."

There was a knock on the front door and Callie looked out the window to see Garret bathed in the light from the front porch.

"Mom, I have to go . . ."

"Who's coming by at this late hour?" Her mother asked.

"It's the lawyer who's helping me."

Callie glanced at the clock. It was almost nine P.M.

"Mom, please. He's here to help me."

"I don't know, Callie. He probably knows how vulnerable you are and he might try to take advantage."

"I've got to go, Mom. Don't worry about me."

Callie heard another of her mother's deep sighs.

"You might as well ask me not to breathe."
"I love you, Mom. I'll call you tomorrow."
"Be careful, Callie," her mother cautioned.
"I will, I promise, but now I have to go."

Chapter 15

Garret felt slightly foolish when Callie opened the door. He hadn't intended to come over to the guest house. In fact, after their last brainstorming session, he'd walked her to the guest house and said good night. But as he sat in his study reading through some background news articles about Henry Kincaid and the Kincaid family his associate Maxim sent to him, he'd found it difficult to concentrate. He wanted to make sure Callie was all right. He thought about everything she'd been through and although she'd handled herself with a lot more courage and fortitude than he would have displayed if he'd been facing the same circumstances, he still wanted to make sure that she was all right.

"Is everything okay?" Callie asked.

She'd changed into a pale blue silk pajama set, with a darker blue robe of the same material. She pulled the robe around her and tied the belt firmly as she stood in the open door. Her face was devoid of any makeup and although she looked tired, his felt his physical attraction to her deepen. He wanted to scoop her in his arms and hold her and protect her. He knew Callie Hopewell was the last woman who thought that she needed anyone to protect her, even in her current circumstances. But he couldn't help it. From the time he'd first laid eyes on her, he'd felt an almost irresistible need to be connected to her. He'd never experienced that kind of feeling before and he wasn't sure if he liked it. He was a man who liked to be in sound control of his emotions.

Garret cleared his throat. "Everything's fine. I was just checking on you."

Callie stepped aside and Garret walked past her. She smelled vaguely of lemons and baby powder. Garret forced himself to keep his focus on the matter at hand.

"I'm fine," Callie said, with a tired smile. "Really . . . under the circumstances."

Callie sat down on one of the couches in the living room of the guest house. Garret watched as she crossed her legs, revealing her bare brown feet. Another surge of pure attraction jolted him. It was all he could do to keep from grabbing her right there and then and making a complete fool of himself.

He cleared his throat again. "May I sit down?" he asked. "I won't stay long, I promise."

"Of course," said Callie.

Garret sat on one of the chairs across the room from her. He didn't trust himself to sit any closer.

After a moment of awkward silence, Garret spoke. "I've been thinking that we need to look into

Henry's background. I know a very good private investigator who can help us."

"That's a good idea," Callie answered.

"Is there anything you remember Henry telling you that might shed some light on who would want to do this to him?"

Callie shook her head. "Other than the obvious people—his wife and me—I don't know anyone who had anything against Henry. He didn't know too many people in New York—at least, that's what he told me. He actually had the nerve to tell me he was antisocial. As we both found out, I really didn't know my fiancé very well."

"I'm sorry you had to go through this," said Garret.

"Don't be," said Callie. "I'm going to be fine."

She looked so sad, Garret was tempted to forget his earlier determination to be noble and sweep her into his arms. He wanted to taste those full lips until she was breathless, until she forgot about Henry and all the ugliness surrounding his death. He wanted to kiss her until he was the only man she thought about.

"We're going to be leaving for Broxton early tomorrow." Garret changed the subject.

Callie nodded her head.

"You probably need to get some sleep. It's going to be a long day tomorrow."

"You sound like my mother," Callie said. "Are you sure you guys have never met?"

Garret stood up. "Your mother sounds like a wise woman."

Callie laughed. "She'd agree with you."

She stood up and walked to the door with Garret.

He was acutely aware of Callie's closeness. He felt an intimacy with her that was natural, a sense of familiarity, although he didn't understand it—after all, he hadn't known her for very long—the feeling pleased and scared him at the same time. He resolved to make himself a stiff drink when he went back to his home.

"Well, good night," said Callie.

"Good night, Callie," Garret replied as he stepped outside into the warm night air.

He turned to walk away, but Callie called to him.

"Garret, wait . . ."

Garret turned around and faced her. She was only a few steps away and he felt whatever self-control he possessed slip perilously away. She stood in her silk pajamas, framed by the doorway like some exquisite portrait. Unable to stop himself, his eyes slid over her lush body. Some men preferred slender woman, but he was a man who had always appreciated a woman with curves, and the silk pajamas and dressing gown left very little to his imagination.

"I just wanted to thank you," said Callie. "I . . . I don't know what I would have done if you hadn't been here to help me. I appreciate your letting me stay here, and your helping me clear my name."

Garret smiled. He wanted to tell her that the pleasure was all his, but instead he said, "You're welcome."

"I've learned that there are some very terrible people in this world," Callie continued, "but I've also learned that there are some very kind ones also. Thanks for being in the 'kind' group."

He stared at her for a moment. She seemed so vulnerable standing there in the doorway. He could only imagine the fear that she was facing. Still, there was something else he saw when he looked at Callie Hopewell. He saw a quiet strength in her. She might be down, but she most definitely was not out. Callie Hopewell was a fighter. She wasn't going to lie down and let what happened to her signal defeat.

"I'll see you tomorrow," said Garret, as he turned and made his way back to the main house.

Callie greeted the next day with a sense of purpose she hadn't felt the previous day. She'd slept well, and that helped. She'd awakened to sunlight streaming through her open bedroom window, and in spite of her current circumstances she felt cautiously optimistic. She was not a woman who liked to play the victim. Whatever happened to her was bad, but what happened to Henry was far worse. There was someone on the island who'd killed Henry and landed her in the prime position to take the blame. She was not going to waste time feeling sorry for herself. She wasn't the first person who'd been made a fool of. Her pride was hurt, but she'd make it through this, hopefully outside of a prison cell.

She'd eaten a big breakfast with Garret and they'd set off for Broxton at breakneck speed. It was just about ten o'clock in the morning when Garret's sleek black Mercedes pulled into the driveway of the Pink Hotel. Memories of the last time she'd been at the hotel came flooding back and, for a moment, all of the strength she'd been feeling slipped away. Instead, a vision of Henry lying dead in her hotel room floated towards her. *Get yourself together,* she sternly told herself. *You can't fall apart right now.*

"Are you okay?" Garret asked. "I know this has got to be tough on you."

Callie forced herself to take a deep, steadying breath.

"I'm fine," she replied. "Let's get on with this."

"I called Ma Ruth," said Garret. "She's expecting us. She says that she has some information that might help us."

Ma Ruth was waiting for them inside her small office just off the lobby.

"Come in, child!" Ma Ruth said, after giving Callie a tight hug.

Callie sat on a white whicker chair with a pink cushion. Garret sat on the other chair and Ma Ruth sat behind her desk. The office was cheerful and cluttered. Family pictures vied for space with reams of papers and folders. There was a vase filled with hibiscus flowers and the air smelled of Ma Ruth's strong perfume.

"Thank you for seeing us," Callie said.

Ma Ruth raised one thin, brown hand in the air. "Stop right there. You've had a *raw* deal, my girl . . . and when I say raw, I mean just that. I pride myself on being a good judge of character, and I can tell that you have a kind heart. I'm going to help you in any way that I can."

"Thank you," said Callie, not trusting herself to say anything more before she started bawling like a baby.

"Ma Ruth, you said you have news for us?" Garret asked.

Ma Ruth nodded her head vigorously. "Indeed, I do, Mr. Langrin. Indeed, I do. I've heard some information that might be helpful."

Ma Ruth hesitated, then she said, "It appears that the late Henry Kincaid wasn't making time only with you, Callie . . . but he was making time with another woman, a woman who ended up losing her life over that no-good man. Apparently this woman killed herself over this fool."

Callie felt her heart sink. Not that it should matter, not that anything else she found out about Henry should hurt her, but this hurt. What a fool she'd been to trust this man. What would drive a woman to take her life over a man? No matter how tough things got, Callie couldn't imagine thinking that suicide was an option.

"Tell us what you know," Garret said, his voice grim.

Thank God that he was focused, thought Callie. All she wanted to do was run and hide, forget that she'd ever met Henry, forget that she'd ever come to this island. *Damn you, Henry Kincaid,* she silently raged. *Damn you.*

Ma Ruth looked quickly at Callie and then looked away. "I heard that Henry was fooling around with a woman named Reynalda. Reynalda Chin."

Garret's voice was sharp. "Kincaid was mixed up with that mess?"

Ma Ruth nodded.

"What mess?" Callie asked.

Garret turned to her. "Reynalda Chin was married to one of the island's wealthiest businessmen, Max Chin. He owns a bunch of hotels here. My father has done work for him on occasion. In any event, about a year ago his wife was found dead. A drug overdose. She took her own life. Max was devastated. The last time I saw him, I didn't recognize the man. He'd lost weight. Looked like he was twenty years older. It was a really tough break. How does Henry Kincaid fit in with all of this?"

Ma Ruth sighed. "He was having an affair with Reynalda. Henry had convinced the poor woman to leave her husband. He told her that he would leave his wife."

Callie felt the blood rushing to her head. For the second time in her life she felt as if she were going to pass out. She made herself take a deep, steadying breath. Now was not the time to fall apart.

"Are you okay?" Garret asked. He was looking at her, his eyes intense.

Callie took another deep breath. *Be calm,* she told herself.

"Maybe I should get her some water," Ma Ruth said. "This warm tropical air can really get to folks who aren't used to it."

Callie shook her head.

"No, please. I'm fine. Really."

Neither Garret nor Ma Ruth looked convinced, but Ma Ruth continued speaking.

"Reynalda was a sweet girl. I knew her mother years ago," said Ma Ruth. "Anyway, apparently she got involved with Henry and they had this thing going on for some time. He convinced the woman to leave her husband, but then when it came time for him to leave his wife, well, I guess he had a change of heart. Reynalda took it pretty hard. She took an overdose of pills, poor girl, all because of Henry Kincaid."

"I'd heard about what happened to Reynalda," said Garret. "But I didn't realize that Henry was involved. The story I heard was that her husband was overbearing . . . I'd heard tales that there was physical abuse and that was the reason she took her life."

Ma Ruth sighed. "No one can know for sure why someone does a terrible thing like that, but one thing is certain. Max Chin blamed Henry for his wife's suicide. In fact, the word is that was the reason for Henry's departure to the States. His family wanted Henry out of the country for his own good. Max was very vocal about his threats to hurt Henry."

"Couldn't the Kincaid family protect Henry?" Callie asked. "From what I was told, his family has a lot of influence down here."

"That's true," said Ma Ruth. "They are a powerful and nasty bunch, but Max Chin is just as powerful and he was crazy about his wife. He took her death hard. Henry's family thought it best that Henry leave the country until all of this blew over."

"How did you find all this out?" Garret asked. "I have a private investigator on the case and I would bet my last dollar that he hasn't found this out yet."

Ma Ruth smiled. "You would win the bet, I'm sure. Listen, this is a small island, and Broxton is a small community. Everybody knows everybody else's business. I'd heard rumors about Reynalda being involved with Henry, but I just found out the rest of this stuff last night. The night watchman, Kendall, has a cousin who works at one of Max Chin's hotels. His cousin told him about Max and his vendetta against Henry Kincaid. The cousin heard about Henry's murder here at the hotel and called with the information."

Callie let out a deep breath that she didn't realize she'd been holding.

"Why aren't the police looking into Max Chin?" Callie asked.

"We don't know whether or not they know anything about this," Garret replied. "Although for all we know, they might be exploring this angle."

"Well, according to the news reports, I'm the main suspect," said Callie.

"Rubbish," said Ma Ruth. "Those news people smell a juicy story. They don't have no respect for the truth!"

"Well, at least we have a new angle to explore," said Garret. "We're going to pay this Max Chin a visit."

"Be careful of him," said Ma Ruth. "He's a rather tough character. I wouldn't want to tangle with him if I were you."

Garret's voice was grim. "He might be tough, but I'm tougher. Callie has a lot on the line, and I'm not going to leave any stone unturned, as they say. Callie didn't do this but she's got the attention of the St. Christopher Police Department."

Ma Ruth raised her eyebrows. "I know you're tough, Mr. Langrin. But I have to warn you. Max Chin is not a man to play with."

Garret stood up. "Neither am I, Ma Ruth, and please call me Garret."

"Where can we find this Max Chin?" Callie asked.

"His offices are in downtown Broxton," said Garret.

"Thank you, Ma Ruth," said Callie. This was the

first lead that they had and like Garret, she was determined to follow it.

"No need for thanks, Callie," Ma Ruth replied. "You got a raw deal with that Henry Kincaid, but I know that you're no killer. Although if ever there was a man who needed killing . . . well, that's another story, I guess. Besides, vengeance is mine says the Lord."

"It looks like someone got impatient with the Lord's timetable and decided to take matters into his own hands," said Garret.

Or her hands, Callie thought. She couldn't shake the feeling that somehow Josephine Kincaid was involved in her husband's murder.

Chapter 16

Max Chin was not happy to see them. After keeping them waiting in the reception area of his office, Max Chin's secretary reluctantly let them in.

"What is this about?" Max got straight to the point.

"Mr. Chin, my name is Garret Langrin and I'm here with my client, Callie Hopewell. We'd like to ask you a few questions about Henry Kincaid."

Max Chin was a man who looked like he'd be at home on a football field. He was at least six feet four and close to three hundred pounds. With a thick black moustache and almond-shaped eyes that harkened to his Asian ancestry, Max was a striking figure. He was dressed entirely in black—a black suit and black cotton shirt.

"I know who you are," said Max to Garret. "And your client is all over the news. I have to say that it is a pleasure to meet the woman responsible for Henry Kincaid's death."

"I'm not responsible for Henry's death," said Callie.

"So you say," Max replied. "What questions do you want to ask? I'm extremely busy and the subject of Henry Kincaid, quite frankly, does not interest me."

"May we sit down?" Garret asked. "We won't take up a lot of your time."

Max Chin sat down behind his large oak desk and waved in the general direction of the chairs in front of the desk.

"The only reason I'm talking to you, Mr. Langrin, is that I know and respect your father. Go ahead, sit down, but don't make yourselves too comfortable."

As a litigator Callie had met her share of ill-mannered, rude people—but Max Chin was in a class all by himself.

"Your father certainly wouldn't have barged in like this at my place of business," Max Chin continued speaking to Garret. "Especially after it was made clear that this was not a good time for me."

Callie watched as a muscle in Garret's jaw tightened. Max had clearly hit an emotional chord.

Garret sat down slowly. For a moment he said nothing. Then, he replied, "It's true that my father and I have little similarity, but that isn't why I'm here, Mr. Chin. I'm here to find out everything I can to help my client. She's been accused of something she didn't do."

"Sit down, Miss Hopewell," said Max Chin. "Or is it Mrs.?"

Callie ignored the question and sat down. She resisted the urge to tell him exactly where he and his impertinent question could go. Instead, she settled for glaring at him silently.

"Mr. Chin, as I understand—you believe that Henry Kincaid had something to do with your wife's suicide," said Garret.

"You really aren't like your father, are you?" Max Chin's voice was low and deadly. "Your father would have never asked me a question like that. What I believe is none of your damn business. Now, if you're finished, I'd like you both to leave."

Callie spoke up. She understood that underneath the harsh words was a deep level of pain. The man had lost his wife and it didn't matter that she had betrayed him. He still loved her. Callie could see it in his eyes.

"Mr. Chin, we're sorry to bring up such a painful subject," she said. "I know what it's like to lose someone you love. I know what it's like to be betrayed, to be lied to, to find out that everything you believed in was a lie. It hurts. It hurts like hell. Sometimes you feel like you can't even breathe, it hurts so much. I know that feeling all too well and believe me, if there were any other way to get the information we're looking for without causing you any more pain, I would do it. I'm accused of something I didn't do, something I *would never* do—but I might lose everything if I don't find the person who did this. I know that Henry lied to your wife. He lied to me, too. But I didn't kill him."

Max Chin's voice was sharp. "Are you suggesting that I had something to do with Henry's murder!"

"No," Callie replied. "I'm not suggesting that. What I do know is that you have information that might help me fill in the blanks. Please, I need your help."

Max took a deep breath and Callie watched in horror as his shoulders started to shake as he began sobbing. She looked at Garret who shrugged his shoulders silently as Max Chin wept. Garret clearly had no idea how to proceed and while Callie wanted to go to him and give him some sort of comfort, she didn't know what to do. They waited silently until Max's sobs subsided.

Wiping his eyes with the black handkerchief in his breast pocket, Max said quietly, "I hope he rots in hell."

Callie didn't respond. She was certain, however, that there were others who shared Max's sentiments.

"Reynalda was a good woman," said Max. "I loved her from the time she was a young girl, barely in her teens. I was ten years older than she and I waited for her—I waited for her to feel the way I felt about her. There was never any other woman for me except Reynalda. Even now, there'll never be anyone else who can take her place. *Never!* Henry Kincaid didn't give a damn about her. She was a beautiful prize, that's all she was to him—a plaything, something that he used and discarded. I'm to blame. I left her alone too much, trying to build this business. All this was for her, but she didn't understand that. She got caught up with Henry Kincaid and now she's dead."

"Do you blame Henry for her death?" Garret asked.

"Of course I do!" Max Chin snapped. "Reynalda would never have taken her own life if he hadn't messed with her head!"

"We heard that Henry left the island because he was afraid of you," said Callie. "I apologize for having to ask you this question but did you ever threaten him?"

Max stared at Callie long and hard before he answered.

"I might have threatened the son of a bitch," he replied.

"What was the exact nature of the threat?" Garret asked. "Did you threaten to kill him?"

Max stood up.

"Show's over," he said. "My secretary will see you two out. Miss Hopewell, I'm sorry about your predicament, but there's nothing I can tell you that will help you. I'm sorry."

"So what do we do now?" Callie asked as they sat in Garret's car.

"We're going to meet with Ransom," Garret replied. "My investigator."

Callie smiled. "Is that his real name?"

Garret nodded his head. "I think it's a great name for a private investigator."

Garret Langrin had a sense of humor. Callie watched as Garret shifted gears and eased the Mercedes out of the parking space. There was something downright sensual about the way he wrapped his hands around the stick shift and maneuvered it. An explicit scene involving Garret's hands and her body flashed through her mind. A bolt of heat surged through her as she imagined exactly how those hands would feel. . . .

"Are you all right?" Garret asked.

Callie cleared her throat. She was mortified. If he only knew what she'd just been thinking about.

"I'm fine," she replied. "This is just a little overwhelming."

"Listen, do you want me to take you back home before I go to Ransom's office? " Garret asked. "This has got to be tough on you. You've been through a lot, and I suspect that you're going to hear some more disturbing things about Henry . . . things that are going to hurt."

Callie pushed all thoughts of Garret's roving hands out of her mind. She was facing the fight of her life and she needed to keep her wits about her.

"I'm fine," Callie repeated. "I appreciate all of your help, but I can't let you do this alone. It's my life that's on the line and I can't sit by and let someone else do the heavy lifting."

"I understand that," said Garret. "If I were in your position, I'd feel the same way."

The drive to Ransom's office took about a half hour. His office was located in the second floor of an old warehouse in what appeared to be the rough side of Queenstown. There were a couple of old men sitting on overturned crates in front of the warehouse, drinking from a rum bottle.

"Hey, Garret," one of the old men called out. "Who de the pretty lady?"

"She's a friend," Garret replied as they walked up the stairs to the entrance of the warehouse.

"Well, me hope you let this one stick around," the other man spoke up after taking a considerable swig from the bottle of rum. "Me like the looks of her."

SMOOTH OPERATOR 187

Callie heard Garret mutter a curse under his breath.

Apparently Garret was used to the company of many women. It made sense. He was handsome and rich. He was charming. He appeared to be the total package, but her relationship with Henry had taught her that appearances meant nothing.

"Alexander, where are your manners, man?" Garret asked.

"Me don't mean no harm, Garret," the old man quickly apologized. "Me antennae tells me that this one is a keeper. De others, well . . ."

"Alexander, shut your old trap!" Alexander's companion entered the fray.

Garret took Callie's arm and quickly ushered her through the front door of the warehouse.

When they were inside, Callie turned to Garret and said, "How do you know those men?"

Garret released her arm from his light grip. "Believe me, you don't want to know."

They walked up the narrow stairs that led to the second floor of the warehouse. The thin film that covered just about every surface of the warehouse got on the light blue linen dress that Callie was wearing.

"Garret you have to pay this man more money," said Callie. "At least enough that he can afford to get someone in here to clean this place up."

Garret laughed. "Don't be fooled. Ransom probably has more money in the bank than I do."

Callie had a strong feeling that Garret was exaggerating, but if this man had some money in the bank, it would serve him well to get a cleaning company in here fast. When they got to the second floor, Callie followed Garret down a dark, narrow hallway and knocked quickly on a door marked *Ransom Miller, Investigator.*

The door was opened by a short, thin man who was completely bald. He was dressed in an African dashiki and black pants. His small dark eyes surveyed her with interest before he commanded, "Come in!"

They entered Ransom's office, which was as different from its outside surroundings as night from day. The office was a suite with two rooms and a small reception area. The floors were gleaming hardwood that looked as if they'd just been waxed and polished. The walls were a cream-colored stucco with various paintings of tropical landscapes. The antique furniture in the office rivaled the furniture in Garret's home in its beauty. The atmosphere in the investigator's office could best be described as cozy.

"Please, come into my office," said Ransom. "Can I get you guys any tea or coffee?"

Garret accepted the offer of a cup of tea, while Callie declined. She was busy marveling at Ransom's office. His office had the same antique mahogany furniture as Garret's, but it was filled with pictures of various family members.

"I've never seen a private investigator's office quite like this," said Callie. The few times she'd used private investigators for her cases, they'd had nondescript offices in nondescript office buildings. They certainly never had offices that looked as if they belonged on the pages of *Architectural Digest,* located in an old warehouse.

"Yes, Ransom has an interesting way of doing things," Garret replied neutrally.

Ransom entered the office and gave Garret his tea. Then he sat behind his massive, mahogany desk.

"I've had some time to do a little digging into Henry Kincaid's past," said Ransom. "By the way, I'm sorry about your loss, Ms. Hopewell. I understand that at one time you were friends with Mr. Kincaid."

Callie felt a sadness creep over her. What Henry did to her and to his wife had been cruel, but he didn't deserve to die.

"Thank you for your kind words," said Callie.

Garret cleared his throat. "What did you find out about Kincaid, Ransom?"

"Some of the things are . . . rather indelicate," said Ransom, looking at Callie. "Ms. Hopewell, if you'd prefer not to hear this . . ."

"Mr. Miller, Henry is dead and I'm the main suspect in his death. Whatever you know, please tell me. I can handle it, and Mr. Miller, please call me Callie."

"In that case," the private investigator replied, "call me Ransom."

Garret cleared his throat again.

Ransom continued speaking. "My sources tell me that Reynalda Chin wasn't the only woman who Kincaid was fooling around with. There was someone else, although we're not quite sure who the person is yet. Apparently, Reynalda found out about the other woman and that's why the poor woman took her life. I spoke with Reynalda's mother myself yesterday to follow up on that lead, and she confirmed that Reynalda had been devastated when she found out that there was someone else. She found out that while he was cheating on his wife with her, he was cheating on her with someone else. What goes around comes around, I always say... but Reynalda took it hard."

"We spoke with Max Chin this morning," said Garret.

"You spoke with him?" Ransom asked. "You all are some brave, but if you don't mind me saying it, foolish people. Max Chin is a nasty character. He threatened Henry after Reynalda died. Several people heard about Max's threat, and shortly after Reynalda's funeral, Henry went to New York. I also learned that Kincaid owed some very bad people a lot of money. He was heavy into gambling, but apparently he had difficulty covering his bets."

"Henry gambled?" Callie was surprised. "The only gambling I ever saw Henry do was when he bought his weekly lottery tickets."

"He was doing a lot more than playing the lottery," said Ransom.

"Who loaned him the money?" Garret asked.

"I'm not sure about that," said Ransom. "But I understand the folks he owed the money to were not exactly upright, law-abiding citizens, if you get my drift."

"Could these people be the ones who killed Henry?" Callie asked.

"I don't know," Ransom replied. "But money is as good a reason to kill as sex, pardon me for being so blunt, Callie."

Callie smiled. "Ransom, in my other life, I'm a New York lawyer. I've heard worse."

"How soon can you find out who these folks are?" Garret asked.

"Give me to the end of this week," said Ransom. "I should know by then. I just started looking into this yesterday."

Chapter 17

Six hours later Garret was sitting with Callie at one of his favorite restaurants on the island. *Tati Marie* was a creole restaurant in the small seaside town of Old Harbor. The food was consistently exquisite, the service impeccable and the oceanfront view unparalleled. On special occasions Garret would take Zenna and his grandmother to the restaurant, but he'd never taken any of the women he dated there. The owner, Emile Robert, was a Haitian expatriate who was a close friend of Garrets. Many times he would come and speak to Emile about difficult cases. In addition to owning one of the best restaurants on St. Christopher, Emile was also an attorney who still practiced law occasionally.

Garret hadn't intended on going to the restaurant, but after a day of following leads that didn't lead anywhere, he'd thought that both he and Callie could use some cheering up. They'd tried to speak with Reynalda Chin's mother, but she'd refused to speak to them. After telling them that Max had called her and warned her not to talk to them, she'd politely but firmly shut the door in their faces. They'd gone back to Broxton to see if they could find the night watchman at the Pink Hotel, but he'd called off sick for the coming evening and when they'd gone to his home, no one had answered the door—although Garret could have sworn he'd seen someone looking through the window. Garret couldn't blame folks for not wanting to get involved. Henry Kincaid's murder was big news on the island, and the murderer was still on the loose. In fact, judging by the recent news media coverage, an indictment for murder against Callie was imminent. It didn't surprise him that people might choose to give her a wide berth.

Night had fallen and the symphony of St. Christopher's crickets filled the air. Emile had given them a corner seat on the restaurant's patio. At first, Callie had been reluctant to go to the restaurant. She'd wanted to go back to the guest house but Garret had seen how discouraged she'd looked and he thought that *Tati Marie* would be a welcome diversion. He could only imagine the hell she was going through—finding out the truth about Henry, finding him after he was murdered, and then being accused of his murder. She was holding up pretty well under the circumstances, but the strain was starting to show in her eyes.

It was just past seven o'clock and the restaurant was starting to get crowded. The tables in the restaurant were covered in white tablecloths with white flickering votive candles. There was a musician playing classical guitar on the inside of the restaurant and the effect of the music and the candlelight was romantic. Looking around, Garret could see various couples. Maybe this wasn't the right place to take Callie. He'd never realized that this place was so romantic. For him, *Tati Marie* was about the food and his friendship with Emile. It wasn't until he brought Callie to this place that he realized there probably was no more romantic restaurant on the island.

For Garret, romance had always been a vague notion, something that happened to other people. He'd been with his share of women, but there was no one whom he'd ever been in love with. He just didn't understand the concept. He'd seen what love had done to his mother. Like Reynalda, love had caused his mother to lose her life. This was not an emotion that Garret cared to be acquainted with. Look at what love had done to Callie. Still, looking at Callie with her face framed by the soft candlelight, he could understand the lure and the need to have someone to love.

He watched as Callie studied the menu, her expression intense. She was a beautiful woman, but it wasn't just her beauty that intrigued him. There was something in her spirit, a sense that he had finally met someone who had a strength of character that rivaled her outward beauty. He admired the way she handled herself, even in the midst of everything she was going through—she hadn't lost her temper or her composure. At times, he saw the fear and the grief shadowed in her eyes, both emotions that he was familiar with. He was seven years old when he lost his mother and he'd never gotten over the pain of that loss.

He still remembered as if it were yesterday the time his father and grandfather had come home to tell him that his mother had died. At the time his grandmother had explained that his mother had died from a broken heart. It wasn't until he was a teenager that he learned the truth. His mother had let depression overtake her after his father's serial philandering. The official cause of death was pneumonia, but the family knew that his mother, already fragile, had lost the will to live after living with a man who did not know how to love her. Soon after his mother's death, he'd lost his father also. His father had thrown himself even more into his work and his grandmother had taken over the task of raising him. Sometimes he'd try to remember his mother's voice. Although she'd spent a lot of time in various mental health institutions during his childhood, she'd still made an effort to be there for him as much as she could.

When her depression would hit, she would spend days in her room, crying, despondent. His father would make an occasional appearance but he was too busy climbing the ladder of success to deal with a depressed woman and a scared child. Thank God for his grandmother, or Garret would not have known anything about stability and family life. His grandmother had always been there for him. She was there when he cried, when he couldn't understand what was happening to his mother. She was there for him the final time when they took his mother away.

"What are you thinking about?" Callie's voice broke through his sad thoughts.

Garret told her the truth. "My mother."

Callie stared directly into his eyes. "You look very sad."

Garret nodded his head. "Thinking about her makes me sad."

"I'm sorry," said Callie. "When I lost my dad, I thought that I was going to lie down and die. I thought that I would never be able to live in a world where he no longer existed. I think the only thing that kept me going was that I knew my mother and my sisters needed me. If it weren't for them, I don't know what I would have done."

"I know what you mean. My mother died a long time ago, but I still miss her. Sometimes it just comes over me."

"What was she like?" Callie asked.

Garret stared at her. No other woman had asked him about his mother. The other women who he'd dated hadn't seen beyond the cool, in-control facade that he wore. No one, except Zenna and his grandmother, had ever recognized the pain that was behind the facade. He wasn't sure if he wanted to let Callie into this private place, this place where the pain that accompanied the loss of his mother, was hidden.

"She was an amazing woman," said Garret. "Only she never realized just how amazing she was. She was an accomplished pianist. She'd gotten a scholarship to study at the Julliard School of Music in New York but by that time she'd met my father and she was pregnant with me. I remember sitting outside the window of the music room in my house, just sitting there and listening to my mother play the piano for hours. Her favorite composer was Chopin. I still get sad whenever I hear any of his works because it reminds me so much of my mother."

Garret looked over at Callie. She sat there silently,

listening to him. She didn't try to give him any tired platitudes about time healing his pain. The pain that he felt from the loss of his mother would never be healed. It might be dulled, but it was still there, underneath it all.

"She suffered from depression, and her choice of a husband didn't help her depression. My father didn't understand her, and he retreated from her and from me."

Callie sighed. "My parents were extraordinarily close. They loved each other so much that we weren't sure whether or not my mother would make it without my dad. The first few years were the hardest for her, but in time, she was able to accept that he was really gone. For the longest time, she would still set out a plate at the dinner table for him. I comfort myself by thinking about my dad being in heaven. He loved to talk and he loved his crazy family. He was surrounded by women all day, and while most men might have complained, or at least wished for a son . . . he was happy with what God had given him. Sometimes I imagine him in heaven, telling everyone stories about his girls. Maybe your mom has met my dad up there."

Garret stared at her. A bell of recognition went off somewhere deep inside him. Just a few minutes ago, he'd thought that he could never fall in love with anyone. But looking at the woman sitting in front of him, the only woman outside of his family whom he could talk about his mother with, he decided that if he could fall in love, this would be the woman he'd fall in love with. Still, he didn't believe in love.

"Have you decided what you want to eat?" Garret asked. "Everything here is good."

SMOOTH OPERATOR 199

Callie smiled ruefully at him. She knew that Garret wanted to change the subject.

"I'd welcome any recommendations," said Callie. "I'm suddenly feeling very hungry."

Josephine Kincaid walked over to the mahogany table in her living room and poured herself another drink—a rum and coke—light on the coke, heavy on the rum. Placing the rum bottle back on the table, she took a long drink.

Then, she turned to her sister Esme and said, "Tell me, how long had you been sleeping with my husband."

Esme was sitting on the worn, brown leather sofa, sipping her drink of choice, rum with ice—heavy on the rum, light on the ice. It was Esme's third drink of the evening.

Josephine watched as Esme put the drink down on the leather ottoman in front of the sofa and calmly replied, "Three years."

It wasn't that Josephine had ever really cared for Henry. She knew about Henry's dalliances. She knew about the Reynalda Chin incident. She'd had several of her own dalliances. She was a practical woman. She'd married a man who was weak, a man who was incapable of honesty, incapable of fidelity, incapable of doing the right thing. She'd made her peace with this long ago. But the confirmation of her suspicion about her sister and her husband hit her hard. There had always been a competition between the two women, as far back as Josephine could remember. As the younger sister, Esme always wanted what Josephine had—dolls, dresses, men—it made no difference.

"You bitch," Josephine said quietly.

Esme looked over at her and replied, "You never gave a damn about Henry. You were very clear about that. He knew it. I knew it. Hell, all of the St. Christopher knew it. So, why would you care that he tried to find something in me that you obviously didn't have?"

Josephine had always thought of herself as a person who kept her emotions firmly under control. Whatever actions she took, whether it was sleeping around on her husband, planning a party, plotting revenge on someone who'd done her wrong—all of those actions were done deliberately. But what happened next surprised her.

Josephine did not recognize the woman who walked over and slapped Esme on the face. She'd never laid a hand on her sister in anger, even though at times, it was tempting. She'd never let Esme's taunts get the best of her, but this time, she couldn't control the surge of anger that gripped her and would not let go. She wanted to hurt Esme. She raised her hand to slap Esme again, but this time Esme caught her raised arm.

"If you hit me again, I will kill you," Esme said calmly as she let go of Josephine's arm.

Josephine saw that Esme's bottom lip had split open and was bleeding. She felt a vague sense of satisfaction that she'd hurt her sister, almost as much as her sister had hurt her. She'd long ago known that Esme was a selfish, uncaring and at times cruel person. Josephine also knew that she shared the same attributes with her sister. But she'd believed that there was honor among thieves. There was a line that Josephine had always believed that even Esme wouldn't cross, and although Josephine knew that Esme coveted all of the men she'd been with, she never believed Esme would stoop so low as to try to hook up with any of Josephine's men.

She'd noticed a closeness between Esme and Henry and she'd questioned both of them about her suspicions that they were having an affair. Both parties had denied any inappropriate behavior. Still, there was always a small, gnawing feeling, deep inside, that made her uncomfortable whenever she saw the two of them together. At times, she'd shaken off these feelings by convincing herself that they both knew how crazy she was and they wouldn't risk the wrath that would come down on both their heads if they had an affair with each other. But Esme's reaction after Henry's death had opened Josephine's eyes. Esme had cried the tears of a woman who'd lost her lover.

Josephine took a step back from her sister. The rage that had enveloped her refused to let go. For one terrible moment, she imagined herself picking up a knife and stabbing her sister until she lay bloody and inert on the immaculate beige carpet in the living room. She wanted to kill her.

"How could you have done this?" Josephine asked, her voice hoarse with fury. "How could you have slept with my husband?"

"I didn't think you cared," Esme replied. "I honestly didn't think you gave a damn about Henry."

Josephine took a deep breath, and tried to steady herself. "He was still my husband, Esme. Some things . . . some things you just don't do."

"Josephine, you've been cheating on Henry

since before you got married. I was there the night before your wedding, remember? I was the one who found you with Max Chin."

Josephine felt the bile in her stomach rise to her throat. She was going to be sick. Her sister slept with her husband and knowing Esme, she'd done this purely out of spite.

"Get out," Josephine whispered to her sister. "I never want to see you again."

"So, are you falling in love?" Dreama got right to the point.

She was sitting in the kitchen with Zenna and Garret. It was just before midnight, and no one in the group was interested in getting any sleep. Garret had come home from his dinner with Callie agitated. His thoughts about the delectable Miss Hopewell were keeping him from focusing on anything else, like saving her pretty neck. He'd tried to go to his office to review notes he'd taken about her case. He'd wanted to come up with a more coherent strategy, but all he could think about was . . . well, her full ruby lips curving into a smile, her long brown legs, the small mole at the base of her neck. Good God, what was happening to him?

He almost never talked about his mother to anyone, yet he'd opened up and told Callie about that painful subject. It seemed almost natural to him to talk about personal details of his life. In spite of the trying day they'd spent chasing down leads, Garret had been able to get Callie to relax and enjoy the meal. He'd been pleased to see that she was a woman who enjoyed her food. Most of the women he knew were too concerned about their figures and only ate sparingly. Callie devoured her own food, and then ate her entire dessert and half of his. Watching Callie eat was a sensual experience. Her moans of appreciation after each course threatened to shatter his self-control, and when she licked her fingers after her chocolate flambe dessert had gotten a little messy, his mind went straight into the gutter and it took a supreme effort not to grab her right there and then and do what he'd been wanting to do almost from the moment he'd first laid eyes on her—kiss her.

He'd gotten her to laugh while sharing stories with her about crazy cases and clients he'd encountered during his law practice. He'd watched as her face changed as the laughter reached her eyes. It was easy talking to Callie. Garret had often found that when he went on dates with women, he was the one who monopolized the conversation, but it was different with Callie. He found himself intrigued as she told him about her life with her sisters, her law practice, her college summers which she spent building schools in West Africa, the various colorful characters she sang with in her church choir. When the meal was over, Garret found that he was reluctant to leave the restaurant. He didn't want their conversation to end. Callie's relaxed mood had continued on the drive home. They'd talked easily and listened to jazz music on the radio. When they got back to Garret's house, he'd walked Callie to the guest house and said good-bye to her at the front door. It took every ounce of self-control not to lean down and finally kiss those ruby red lips, but he didn't want to scare her. Hell, he didn't want to scare himself. He didn't know if he could just stop at one kiss. The sane voice in his head told him that this wasn't the time to woo Callie Hopewell. But the other voice, a reckless voice he didn't recognize, urged him to throw caution, propriety, not to mention good sense, to the wind and give in to the urge to taste Callie Hopewell's lips. In the end, his sanity had prevailed and he'd walked away.

"So, are you falling in love?" The question from Garret's grandmother brought his thoughts back to the present.

Zenna laughed. "Look how he's mooning over her. He looks like a lovesick puppy dog!"

Garret flashed her a look of annoyance, but he wondered if his fascination with Callie was obvious.

"I don't know her well enough to even think about the subject of . . ."

"It's called love." Zenna finished Garret's sentence. "It happens to the best of us."

Garret shook his head. "Not to me. It's never happened to me and if I were you, I wouldn't hold much hope of my falling in love with anyone."

Garret's grandmother took a sip from a steaming of cup of herbal tea. "I wouldn't be too quick to dismiss love out of your life if I were you."

"I'm not exactly dismissing it," Garret replied. "Let's say that I just don't believe in that particular emotion."

Garret's grandmother shook her head. "How did I manage to raise such a jaded grandson?"

Garret looked over at his grandmother. He knew that she was a hopeless optimist. She'd had a great and passionate marriage with a man she still thought about daily. He was lucky to have had the opportunity to experience his grandparents' love firsthand. The only other example he had of love was his parents' marriage, and that was not a ringing endorsement.

As if she could read his thoughts, Garret's grandmother spoke up. "Don't let the mistake your parents made hold you back. You're not your father and I would venture to say that Miss Hopewell is nothing like your mother. Your mother was my own child and I loved her more than anyone or anything else in this world, but your mother had demons that none of us, not even your father, could help."

At the mention of his father, Garret felt his spine stiffen. He never understood how his grandmother was able to forgive his father for everything he put her daughter through. Although there had been times when there was tension, his grandmother and his father had a good relationship. They talked to each other weekly and saw each other for dinner at least once a month. His grandmother had tried inviting him to dinner with them, but Garret had always firmly declined the offer. He didn't have his grandmother's capacity for forgiveness. He knew that his grandmother's faith had a great deal to do with her willingness to put any past grievances she felt against his father behind her. She truly forgave his father for any pain he caused Garret's mother. His grandmother had a bigger heart than he did.

"Could we change this subject?" Garret asked.

"Touchy, touchy," replied Zenna. "That's the first sign of a man in love!"

Garret suppressed a sigh. Once Zenna and his grandmother ganged up on him, he might as well wave the white flag of surrender.

"Look, when I fall in love, you two will be the first to know . . . after the lady in question," said

Garret. "Are you guys ready to drop this ridiculous subject now?"

Garret knew he was attracted to Callie. He knew that his attraction was strong. He'd never experienced this kind of emotion for any woman, but this was not love. True, he'd never experienced love—not the romantic kind—but he'd know it if it happened to him. He was certain of that. Still, he couldn't quite explain what came over him whenever the thought of Callie Hopewell came to mind.

Chapter 18

Two days later Callie found herself sitting in Inspector Mobray's small, stuffy office. He'd summoned her to the Queenstown Police Department for questioning. Callie had been surprised that it had taken this long for the police to get in contact with her. Henry's murder was still the biggest news on the island. The few times she'd watched the local news it was the lead story. She hadn't bothered to read the papers, but she was certain that their coverage of Henry's demise was just as feverish and widespread. Reporters from the *St. Christopher Chronicle*, the island's principal newspaper, had tried to get in contact with her, but Garret had forbidden her from talking to the press. She knew that it was good advice but she wasn't used to taking orders from anyone, even someone who right now was helping to keep her out of jail.

She had to admit that the past few days she'd spent with Garret had been almost enjoyable, despite her current circumstances. They'd followed up on leads and planned strategy together. Callie felt guilty that Garret had apparently put aside his entire caseload and had dedicated himself solely to her case. It was hard to believe that just a few short days ago she was in New York City, blissfully unaware that her life was about to change in such a dramatic and terrible fashion. If Garret and his family hadn't been here to help her, she didn't know how she would have gotten through these days. His grandmother had made sure that every day she was fed, Zenna would come by and talk with her, keeping her spirits up—even Winsome, the domestic engineer, as she referred to herself, tried to cheer her up.

"Never mind, darling, not that I believe you killed the man, but if ever a man deserved killing, well, it was that one," Winsome had told her.

"I didn't kill him, Winsome," Callie had calmly replied.

"If you did, or you didn't—well, that's your business. But all I'm saying is that if you did, you had your reasons!"

The private investigator Ransom Miller had called Garret on their way over to police headquarters. He told Garret that he had some more information, and Garret had made plans for them to meet with Ransom when they were through with Inspector Mobray.

The police headquarters was located in a three story limestone building in downtown Queenstown. For the first time since finding Henry's body back at the hotel, Callie felt nervous. As she walked through the doors of the police station the reality of the situation in which she found herself hit her.

She was a suspect in a murder case. A murder case where she'd had both the motive and the opportunity to end Henry Kincaid's life.

"Do you think they'll arrest me?" Callie asked as she sat with Garret in the crowded waiting area.

Garret shook his head. "If they had enough on you to warrant an arrest, they would have done that first and then asked you questions."

"Oh," Callie replied. Although she was a lawyer, she never did any criminal law work. She was clearly out of her element.

"Don't worry, I'll be there with you."

Callie had felt reassured by Garret's words, but sitting in Inspector Mobray's office, all feelings of reassurance left her quickly. There was a vase filled with roses and two pink Valentine's Day balloons. She'd forgotten that today was February fourteenth—Valentine's Day. She'd planned to spend a romantic Valentine's Day with Henry.

"The curse continues."

"What did you say?" Garret asked. They were waiting for Inspector Mobray who had disappeared forty minutes before with the promise that he'd be right back.

Callie didn't realize that she'd spoken out loud.

"I was just talking about my Valentine's Day curse," said Callie. She was embarrassed that Garret had heard her.

Garret turned and looked at her. "What's the Valentine's Day curse?"

Callie shrugged her shoulders. "It's nothing, really. Forget I said anything."

"Now I'm intrigued," said Garret. "What's this curse about?"

Callie sighed. "I've never really had a great Valentine's Day. For some reason, the past few years have been horrible."

"I think you're exaggerating," said Garret.

"Well, let's see," Callie replied. "Two years ago I was mugged on my way to meet my sisters for a Valentine's Day dinner. Last year, I was stuck in an unventilated elevator for two hours. A few years back I fell down the stairs in my apartment building and broke my leg, that was on Valentine's Day. Back when I was in college my boyfriend broke up with me on Valentine's Day . . ."

"Okay, you win," said Garret. "You weren't exaggerating."

Callie felt the tears well up inside her. She fought the feelings of self-pity that were threatening to come to the surface. She'd had so much hope for Valentine's Day this year. She'd given her heart to someone who didn't care for her. She was now being charged with his murder. Thus far, she'd have to say that this Valentine's Day was the all-time worst.

Garret extricated some tissues from Inspector Mobray's desk and gave them to Callie.

"Your Valentine's Day isn't over yet," he said quietly.

Callie wiped her eyes and nodded her head. *Pull yourself together, girl*, she chided herself. *Now is not the time to fall apart.* Valentine's Day was nothing but an insidious plot of florists and card companies, anyway.

Inspector Mobray entered his office. "Sorry, I got caught up. I apologize for the long wait."

Callie cleared her throat. "I don't mean to be rude but could we get this over with?"

The inspector sat behind his desk.

"Well, I appreciate your eagerness to answer questions. I usually find most people to be much more reluctant," said Inspector Mobray.

"Look, can we cut the sarcasm, and just get on with this?" Garret asked.

Callie placed a restraining hand on Garret's arm.

"It's okay," she told Garret, then she turned her attention back to the inspector. "I have nothing to hide. I didn't kill Henry and I don't know who did. I just want to do everything I can to make that clear, and the sooner I do that, I'll be a much happier person."

Callie spent the next two hours talking to Mobray about her relationship with Henry and the night she found him dead. She explained that Henry hadn't told her much about his family, only vague information about the family business. She reiterated that she'd never known about Henry's marital status. If she'd known that Henry was married she would never have been in a relationship with him, let alone traveled to another country to meet with him. The inspector also asked her about Henry's gambling. Apparently, he'd been doing his homework also. Callie went over in vivid detail the night she found Henry in her hotel. It was still just as difficult to talk about it. She relived the horror of finding Henry in her hotel bed. The inspector was thorough, but he was more gentle with his questions this time.

"Why do you think that Mr. Kincaid wanted to see you?" The inspector had asked.

Callie gave a quick shrug.

"I don't know," she replied. "He wanted to tell me to be careful. He warned me about his wife."

"What did he say?"

Callie tried hard to remember Henry's exact words, but everything was jumbled together. "I just know that he told me I needed to leave the island as quickly as possible. He said that his wife was dangerous. I do remember that."

Callie suddenly remembered something else—a memory that had been pushed aside with everything that had happened since coming to this island.

"Henry tried to give me a ring—an engagement ring."

That caught the inspector's attention, as well as Garret's.

"You never mentioned that before," said Garret.

Callie turned to Garret. "I know. I'm sorry. I'm not sure why I didn't think of it—I guess it was such an odd thing to do in light of everything."

"What did this ring look like?" asked Inspector Mobray.

"It was a sapphire ring with diamonds."

"Where is the ring now?" Inspector Mobray asked.

"I don't know. I never accepted it," said Callie. "I assume it's with his personal effects."

Inspector Mobray shook his head slowly.

"There was no ring found in Mr. Kincaid's possession at the time of his murder," said the inspector.

"That's strange," said Callie. "Maybe someone took it before the police came."

"That's possible," the inspector agreed.

"Things were pretty chaotic after I . . . found Henry, but I don't remember there being a lot of people in the vicinity—only Ma Ruth. Maybe Dara was there also, but I don't remember."

"I'll check with Ma Ruth," said the inspector. "Maybe the ring is still in the hotel room somewhere."

"It looked like a pretty expensive ring," said Callie. "I think if someone had found it, we'd have heard about it."

"Unless they want to keep it for themselves," said the inspector. "I'll look into it."

"Is the ring important?" Callie asked.

"I don't know," Inspector Mobray replied. "It is intriguing—a missing piece of valuable jewelry . . . that could change the direction of this investigation somewhat."

"Are you thinking that perhaps Henry's murder is related to a robbery gone wrong?" asked Garret.

The inspector gave a noncommittal shrug and didn't respond to the question.

"Why do you think Henry wanted to give you a ring?" the inspector asked. "Was he trying to make up with you?"

"I don't know why Henry wanted to give me that ring," Callie replied, trying hard to keep the bitterness out of her voice. Did he set out to hurt her, or was she just collateral damage? Was everything he told her a lie, or was there some truth buried deep in his words? Had he ever cared about her? Was it just a game to pass the time while he was in New York? The most important question she wanted to ask him was "Why me?" Why did he seek her out. Her life had been perfectly fine without having Henry Kincaid and his troubles collide with her perfectly ordered world. It was strange—if she really examined her feelings, she knew that she didn't love Henry. She wanted to love him because of the package he presented and more importantly, because in her perfectly ordered life, she was lonely. Her loneliness had led her to let her guard down and the results were disastrous.

At the end of the interview Callie asked the inspector when she would get her passport back.

The inspector was noncommital. "The investigation is ongoing," he said, "so until we wrap things up here, we're going to hold onto your passport a little longer."

This was not the news that Callie wanted to hear. She'd hoped that after this meeting with the inspector he would see that he'd made a terrible mistake even thinking that Callie could be a suspect. However, despite his more friendly demeanor, in Inspector Mobray's eyes, she was still under suspicion for the murder of Henry Kincaid.

After stopping for a quick lunch in downtown Queenstown, they headed over to Ransom's office. Garret could see that the interview with Mobray had taken a lot out of Callie. She'd been preoccupied and quiet through most of the meal. He tried to keep her spirits up by telling her just how well the interview had gone. Typically, he would have advised his clients not to be so candid, but Callie handled herself well.

Garret pulled the car into a parking space in front of the warehouse. Outside the same two old men who asked him questions about Callie when they first visited Ransom were sitting on overturned crates drinking rum. It was just past three in the afternoon and Garret guessed that they'd probably been drinking since the morning.

"Do you want to stay in the car?" Garret asked. "It's been a tough day for you."

Callie looked at him.

"It has been tough," Callie agreed. "But I'm tougher."

"I'm not questioning how strong you are," said Garret gently, "but sometimes everyone deserves a break, even tough women like you."

"Sometimes," Callie said, "I wonder if I'll wake up and this will all be a bad dream."

"Callie, you're going to get through this," said Garret. "You have to believe that."

"I've always thought that if you play by the rules, then life would be fair in return. I sound so naive, don't I?"

"No, you sound like someone who's going through a rough time," said Garret.

"You are a kind man, Garret Langrin," said Callie.

"I'm not sure anyone's ever described me in those terms."

"Well, they haven't spent the kind of quality time that I've spent with you these last few days," Callie said, her tone light and teasing.

"So we've been spending quality time together?" Garret asked.

He watched as Callie blushed, and the thought came to mind that he could easily spend a lot more quality time with Callie.

Callie cleared her throat, "I think we should go see what news Ransom has for us. Maybe he has some information that'll actually help me."

"Actually, I was kind of intrigued by this whole

concept of spending quality time together," said Garret.

"Well," said Callie, after unbuckling her seat belt, "I think we can spend our quality time with Ransom."

Garret couldn't be certain, but he thought he saw the beginnings of a smile tugging at the corner of Callie's delectable mouth.

He unbuckled his seat belt and got out of the car. After going around the car to the passenger side, Garret opened the door and Callie exited the vehicle.

"Hey, Garret," one of the rum drinkers, Jethro, called out. "Me see you got de same pretty lady with you today."

Garret groaned. He'd known Jethro and Alexander, two best friends whose petty brushes with the law had brought them into his offices on more than one occasion, for years. They were both in their early sixties, although the vast amount of alcohol they regularly consumed made them appear to be much older. As far as he knew, any family they'd had decided long ago to give up on them, and with the exception of those folks who drank with them, all Jethro and Alexander had were each other. Garret had convinced Ransom to give them a job keeping an eye on the building. In reality, they did more drinking than anything else, but Ransom had gotten used to them, and their employment was secure, no matter how drunk they were when they showed up for work.

Alexander chimed in. "This one must be special. Me don't ever recall seeing you with de same woman twice."

Good God, Callie's going to think that he was

some sort of raving Cassanova, squiring different women all around the island. It was true that he enjoyed the company of women, several women in fact, but it was never anything serious. He never broke any hearts. He was up front with each and every woman who he dated. His priorities were his grandmother and his business, in that order—and that left very little time for pursuing a relationship with anyone.

"How do these men know so much about your love life?" Callie asked.

Garret wondered the same thing. It wasn't as if he was used to bringing women to Ransom's warehouse. Still, St. Christopher was a small island, and word got around. He often ran into Jethro and Alexander at odd places—the gas station, the supermarket, he'd even run into them at Hellshire Beach, one of the more popular beaches on the island—but he couldn't remember being with any woman when he ran into the alcohol loving duo. He was going to have to have a private talk with the men about spreading his business, particularly when it made him look like a downright gigolo, around Callie. She already had a right to hold a low opinion regarding men in general, he didn't want her thinking that he was the same as Henry Kincaid.

Before Garret could answer Callie's question the sounds of screeching car tires and four gunshots rang out in the air. Garret reached over to grab Callie but she'd fallen to the ground. A bright red stain darkened the white shirt she was wearing. Callie had been shot.

Garret felt his heart hammer in his chest. He couldn't breathe. Callie had been shot. He knelt down quickly to examine her. She was still conscious but he could tell that she was in a lot of pain.

Garret took the cell phone out of his jacket pocket and handed it to Alexander, who was kneeling beside him.

"Call emergency!" Garret barked, then turned his attention back to Callie.

"Me saw de car!" Jethro called out. "It was a dark blue sedan. Me couldn't see de face of the driver, but it was a woman. A woman with long hair."

"Did you get the license plate number?" Garret asked, his attention still focused on Callie as he bent over to pick her up.

"Car driving too fast, mon!" Jethro called out.

Garret ripped Callie's shirt to expose the wound on her shoulder. It didn't appear that she had any other wounds, thank God. He said a silent prayer. She could have been killed. A shoulder wound was nothing to joke about, but all things considered, it could have been a lot worse.

"Did you call emergency?" Garret yelled at Alexander.

"They coming, mon."

Garret decided that he wasn't going to wait for the ambulance to come. Callie was in too much pain.

"Callie," he said gently, as he carried her towards his car. "I'm going to take you to the hospital."

She nodded her head, but didn't say anything. Instead, she clenched her teeth as waves of pain swept over her.

"What the hell happened here?"

Garret looked over to see Ransom running towards him.

"Somebody shot Garret's girlfriend," Alexander

replied. "And it looks like he's taking her to de hospital, but if you ask me he should just wait here for de ambulance."

"Don't listen to that fool!" Jethro shouted. "If you wait for an ambulance, the angels come and take you home first!"

Callie managed a weak chuckle.

Ransom opened the car door and helped Garret place Callie in the seat.

"Garret," Callie whispered, before he moved away.

"Yes, Callie?"

"I told you that Valentine's Day never turned out well for me."

Chapter 19

"I'm not staying in this hospital."

Callie repeated her words to the people assembled in her hospital room—her not-too-happy doctor, her even less happy nurse, and Garret—who, judging by his stormy expression, shared the opinion of the doctor and the nurse.

The doctor, a thin, tall man with a large afro, shook his head sternly at Callie.

"While you were very lucky that the bullet passed through the shoulder and didn't lodge there, we still need to keep you overnight to make sure that the wound is properly taken care of. We wouldn't want infection to set in," said the doctor.

The nurse was less diplomatic. "It's just plumb foolish of you to leave the hospital now! Your body had just gone through major trauma. You need to just stay here and let us take care of you."

"Now, Mabel . . ." the doctor cautioned

"Beres, someone has to talk some sense into this woman!" the nurse snapped.

They were very informal here in the Caribbean, Callie thought. She'd never heard of doctors and nurses referring to each other by first names.

"We're married," Beres explained. "I know in the States it might be frowned on—husbands and wives working together in the hospital—but things are a little more relaxed here on St. Christopher."

Garret cleared his throat. "Doctor, I don't mean to be rude, but please explain to Callie how . . . unwise she's being—she needs to stay in the hospital."

"He's already explained," said Callie. "Under any other circumstances I'd happily stay put. But someone took a shot at me and I don't want to stay here where they can finish what they started."

"Callie, we've gone over this," Garret replied. "I'm not going to leave your side. Nothing's going to happen to you. I've already arranged for my own personal security detail to be here at the hospital . . ."

Callie sighed. "Garret, my mind is made up. I'm not staying here. I'm going back to your house and we'll go over our strategy—I have some plans . . ."

The doctor spoke up. "Miss Hopewell, you're not going anywhere. We're going to keep you overnight. Please be reasonable. It's for your own good."

"I thought I recognized the name!" exclaimed the nurse. "Callie Hopewell. You're the one in the news about killing that man."

"Mabel . . ." the doctor cautioned again. But it was clear to all those in the hospital room, including the doctor, that Mabel didn't take the doctor's advice even if he was her husband.

"So, did you kill him?" the nurse asked in a conspiratorial tone.

"No!" Callie and Garret answered in unison.

The nurse went on talking as if she didn't hear the response.

"Now if my husband did what that man did to his wife . . . not to mention you . . . well, let's just say . . ."

"Mabel, for heaven's sake!" the doctor roared. "Remember that you're talking to a patient!"

Mabel seemed a little taken aback. It seemed, Callie thought with relief, that Nurse Mabel would finally listen to her husband.

"You're right, pumpkin." Nurse Mabel had the good sense to look chagrined. "She is a patient."

Pumpkin? Who calls their husband pumpkin in public, thought Callie.

"I am sorry," said Nurse Mabel, who now had adopted a stern, professional tone. "Do forgive me. Your story has been intriguing . . . I've been following the news reports about it."

"It's okay," said Callie, anxious to change that particular topic of conversation.

"My dear," Nurse Mabel continued. "I've met the wife . . . quite a nasty woman. I wouldn't have messed with *her* husband, if you know what I mean. She's not the kind of person who would take that sort of thing lightly."

"Mabel!" the doctor roared again.

"All right, Beres—I've got no more to say on the subject. My lips are sealed."

Thank God. Callie gave a silent prayer to the Almighty.

Turning to Callie, the doctor said, "I apologize

for my wife. She's a good woman, but sometimes her mouth gets in a place where it shouldn't go . . ."

Callie heard Mabel mutter, "I hope Beres likes the couch because that's where he's sleeping tonight!"

Garret spoke up.

"If I could get us all back on point, I think that Callie should spend the night in the hospital."

"Of course she should!" said Mabel. "Any fool can see that! If you were my child, I would really give you a lecture on reckless behavior! Leaving the hospital now is nothing short of reckless! Can you imagine the pain you're going to be in?"

"That's it!" said Garret, triumphantly. "Callie, if you don't stay in the hospital—I'm going to call your mother in New York and tell her what's going on!"

Callie felt her heart sink. He'd used the secret weapon—her mother. She'd confided in Garret about her mother's intention to come to St. Christopher. Callie had been clear that as much as she loved her mother, she didn't want her involved in this mess. This whole thing was Callie's doing, and as far as Callie was concerned, she needed to handle her own business without relying on her mother. Her mother had enough to worry about with her other crazy daughters.

"You wouldn't call my mother," Callie said in a small voice.

"Yes," said Garret, with a slow—and Callie suddenly realized—very sexy smile. "I would."

"Then that's settled!" the doctor said. "This is a private room. You'll be very comfortable here. The police have been contacted and they want to talk to you."

"You'll be safe here," said Mabel. Her voice was gentle. "I'll come back tonight to check on you. Believe me, no one's going to shoot you on my watch!"

Ransom stood outside Callie's hospital door and spoke to Garret in a low, urgent tone. The news that he'd given Garret wasn't good, but he'd wanted to give Garret the information as soon as possible.

"Are you certain?" Garret asked, his expression grim.

"I'm dead certain," said Ransom. "Henry owed money to Otis Lorde."

Otis Lorde had been credited with bringing organized crime to the island of St. Christopher. Garret had often thought that this was an exaggeration, but even if Otis didn't bring crime to the island, he had his hands in various illegal activities—gambling, prostitution, guns. The only crime that Otis steered clear of was the trafficking of drugs. His only son had died of a drug overdose several years ago, and Otis had an aversion to selling illegal substances. However, he had no difficulty involving himself with any other criminal activity. He was a nasty man, a man whose enemies regularly ended up dead or in the hospital. Even the police on the island steered clear of Otis Lorde. He was a man who very few people wanted to get close to, which was why Garret never understood how his own father would ever befriend Otis Lorde. His father's friendship with Otis went back many years. They'd met over a business deal and had been close friends ever since that time.

"The word is that Otis put out a contract on Henry Kincaid," said Ransom.

"A contract, as in a contract to kill him?" Garret asked.

Ransom nodded his head.

"So we have another possible suspect," said Garret. "With a strong motive."

"Yes," replied Ransom. "But the police aren't going to touch Otis Lorde. They're too scared of him. We need some evidence . . . something concrete . . . I don't know how the hell we're going to get that."

Garret let out a grim sigh.

"It looks like I'm going to have to give my father a call."

Chapter 20

Inspector Mobray sat down on the chair beside Callie's hospital bed and said, "Miss Hopewell, when you left my office this morning, I didn't think I'd see you again quite so soon."

Night had fallen, and although Callie had taken medicine to help her with the pain in her shoulder, she was still uncomfortable. She hated to admit it, but the doctor and his wife were both right. She belonged in the hospital—at least for the night.

"I've already given a statement to the police," said Callie. The painkillers were making her feel light-headed.

"Mobray, can't this wait until tomorrow?" asked Garret.

The only time that Garret had left Callie's side since the shooting was when the doctors were examining her.

"No," the inspector replied. "It can't."

Turning his attention back to Callie, Inspector

Mobray asked, "Any idea who would want to do this to you?"

Callie shook her head. "I don't know. I have to think that it's somehow related to what happened to Henry."

The inspector narrowed his eyes. "What makes you think that?"

"I hardly think it's coincidence that Henry gets murdered and days later I get shot."

"It is rather strange—I'll grant you that," Inspector Mobray agreed.

The small hospital room felt cramped. It was painted hospital white, with a worn leather chair that had seen better days, and a light blue wooden chair by the window. Garret had spent most of his time in the leather chair beside the hospital bed, but he'd given up his seat, reluctantly, to Inspector Mobray. The overhead light was dim and the bedside lamp didn't give the room much more illumination. The room, Callie decided, was a dreary affair in need of a makeover.

"What were you doing in that part of town anyway?" Inspector Mobray asked. "It's a rough neighborhood."

"We were visiting a business associate of mine," said Garret.

"A business associate?" the inspector asked.

"Yes," Garret replied.

"Does this business associate have a name?"

There was a moment of silence before Garret answered. "Yes, his name is Ransom Miller. He does investigations for me. I asked him to help me find out information about Henry Kincaid."

"Ah." The inspector nodded his head. "I know

him well. He's a good fellow, very competent. Has he found out anything helpful?"

Garret shook his head. "No, but when he does give us any info, you'll be the first to know."

The inspector looked over at Callie.

"Miss Hopewell, you seem to be a magnet for trouble."

Callie was inclined to agree, but at that moment she felt a sharp pain in her shoulder. It was time for another painkiller.

"Are you all right?" Garret asked her.

Callie hadn't realized that she'd reacted to the pain in her shoulder.

"I'm going to need more pain medication," Callie replied as she pushed the button on the side of the bed for the nurse.

"I won't keep you much longer," said Inspector Mobray, standing up. "I've already read the incident report that the investigating officer prepared. According to the report, no one had a clear look at the driver, although one of the eyewitnesses stated that the driver appeared to be a woman with long hair—no one got the license plate number of the car, but it was a dark blue sedan. Anything else you'd like to add?"

The pain had now seared into her shoulder. Callie took a deep breath and closed her eyes.

"There's nothing more to add, Mobray!" Garret snapped. "Can't you see she's in pain?"

"Yes, I can see that," said Mobray. "I'll be back tomorrow."

"I won't be here tomorrow," said Callie. "They're going to release me tomorrow morning—hopefully with a stash of painkillers."

"Well, just check in with me sometime tomorrow," the inspector ordered. "I have some more questions I'd like to ask you. By the way, I checked with the owner of the Pink Hotel and no one reported finding a sapphire ring on the premises."

Callie was in too much pain to care.

"She'll talk to you tomorrow, Mobray," said Garret.

Callie heaved a sigh of relief when Mobray left. Now, where was that nurse with her pain medication?

Garret watched Callie as she slept peacefully. The pain medication had done the trick. Now, if he could only get comfortable in the narrow cot that he'd convinced the hospital to bring into Callie's room. The policeman who stood outside Callie's room had poked his head in the room moments ago to check to see if everything was all right. In addition, Garret had hired the services of a security firm and there were five armed security guards patrolling in front of the hospital. Garret wasn't taking any chances with Callie's safety.

He shifted his frame in the cot but he still couldn't get comfortable. Before she'd fallen asleep, Callie had insisted that he go home to sleep in his own bed. She'd assured him that she'd be fine, but Garret had refused to go. He wasn't going to leave her side while she stayed at the hospital. Someone had already hurt her, and he'd be damned if they finished the job.

Garret heard Callie moan in her sleep and he got out of the cot to check on her. He sat on the edge of her bed and watched her. She was becoming more fitful and he wondered whether even in her sleep the pain from her injury was affecting her. He was debating whether to wake her but she opened her eyes and smiled at him.

"You looked like you were in pain," said Garret. "You were thrashing around a little bit."

Callie sighed.

"I'm not in any pain," Callie replied. "I was having a bad dream."

"Want to talk about it?" Garret asked.

"No," Callie replied. "It involved midgets with guns chasing me."

"Say no more," said Garret. "Do you want me to call the nurse?"

Callie shook her head. "No, I'm okay. I know it's selfish of me, but I'm glad you're here."

"I'm glad I'm here, too," Garret replied. An unexpected feeling of tenderness gripped him. He thought about how close he'd come to losing Callie Hopewell. If the idiot who harmed her had been a better shot... Garret shook his head. He wouldn't allow his mind to go in that direction. Looking at Callie he wondered how any man could have left her. Henry Kincaid was a damn fool. Women like Callie didn't come around often—beautiful, smart, kind, funny, sexy. God, how sexy. Even lying there in a white hospital gown with tousled hair, she was ... well, she was beguiling.

"You know." Callie bit her bottom lip, and Garret felt immediately aroused. What was wrong with him? Callie was in the hospital and all he wanted to do was make love to her until they both lost their breath. "I was really mean to you when I first met you on the plane."

"Yes, you were." Garret smiled at her.

"Well, I was rude and I'm sorry," said Callie as she sat up in the bed. "I just thought you were . . . well, a player."

"A player?" Garret asked, as his arousal deepened.

"Yes," Callie continued, blissfully unaware how close she was to having him make love to her right there on the hospital bed. "A guy who goes out with lots of women . . . you know, a heartbreaker."

"I hate to disappoint you," Garret teased. "But I haven't broken that many hearts . . . at least, not lately."

"Hmmm . . . somehow I find that very hard to believe."

"Why is that?" Garret asked, leaning closer to her. He was playing with fire but he didn't care. He wanted to kiss her. He wanted to kiss her now.

Callie looked directly into his eyes.

"Because I'm sure that many women find you attractive," she said.

"Do you?" Garret asked. "Do you find me attractive?"

She didn't answer him, instead she kept staring at him, as if she were looking at him for the first time. It was her expression of startled wonder that did him in—her widened eyes, her parted lips. There was a recognition in those dark eyes that said *I've been waiting for you for a very long time.* He recognized that expression and knew that his own expression mirrored what he saw in her eyes.

"Callie," Garret said, his voice hoarse. "I'm going to kiss you unless you stop me."

Callie remained silent.

Garret leaned forward until their faces were only inches apart.

"Callie, for God's sake—tell me how inappropriate this is, tell me how wrong this is, tell me that you're my client, tell me anything, Callie—because if you don't, so help me, I am going to kiss you."

Garret inhaled sharply as Callie put her hands gently on each side of his face and pulled him closer.

"I want you to kiss me, Garret," she whispered.

He felt all self-control leave him as he tasted her mouth for the first time. He was gentle at first, exploring her lips, then as she drew him closer he began a more urgent, thorough exploration of her mouth. He thrust his tongue inside her mouth and explored, stroked, and ultimately devoured Callie with his kiss. Callie matched his intensity, pulling him deeper and deeper into a place that he'd never been with any other woman. He wanted to explore each and every inch of her body intimately with his hands, his tongue, his mouth. He wanted to make her his. He'd never felt possessive about any other woman, but he knew that he would hurt any other man who came near her. Callie Hopewell was a part of his DNA. She didn't know it. Hell, until their kiss, he hadn't known it, but he wasn't going to let this woman go. He felt Callie draw him closer, her hands tearing away at his shirt, desperately trying to undo his buttons. Good God, she was like a drug he couldn't resist.

He pulled his lips from hers and began to kiss her lightly at the base of her throat. He felt her body shudder in response to his kisses. Her hands momentarily stilled their movement as she allowed him to taste her. Throwing her head back, she moaned softly as his kisses got more urgent. He felt his desire rise in response to the soft, fluttery sounds that came from her throat. He was ready to make love to her in the hospital room, with the policeman standing right outside. Pulling her closer, he felt Callie wince with pain. His tenuous grip on sanity became stronger as somewhere a small voice inside told him that now was definitely not the right time to make love to Callie. He knew they had unfinished business. He knew one day he would claim her, just as she would claim him—in body and in spirit. But now was not the time to give in to the urges that they both felt. He pulled away.

"Callie, as much as I want this to go farther, this probably isn't the best time for us to do this," said Garret.

Callie looked at him as if she was in a daze.

"Did I hurt you?" Garret asked anxiously.

"There was some pain," Callie admitted, with a slow, sly grin, "but it was worth it."

Garret found that as he buttoned his shirt, his fingers shook slightly. He was still aroused. No woman had ever affected him this way. His desire for her was all-consuming. It robbed him of all common sense, he thought to himself. He was normally a practical individual. Ravaging a woman who'd just gotten shot, in her hospital bed... well, he'd just have to give up any claim at being a responsible person.

"You kissed me," Callie said slowly, her eyes staring directly into his.

"Yeah," Garret agreed. "I did."

"And I liked it," said Callie.

Garret felt a smile tug at his lips. "I'm glad, because I intend to kiss you again."

Callie smiled at him.

"It's five minutes to midnight," she said.

Garret was confused.

"Come again?" he asked.

Callie's smile was triumphant. "It means that the Valentine's Day curse is lifted."

"I'm still not sure what you mean." Garret wondered if the painkillers had affected her sanity. "Maybe I should remind you that you got shot today."

"Yes," Callie agreed. "That is bad, but today I got the best kiss I've ever gotten."

"The best kiss?" Garret asked, feeling unaccountably proud.

Callie nodded her head definitively. "Absolutely. It was the best kiss... I mean it's not like that many men have kissed me, but your kiss was *definitely* the best one I've been involved in."

"Thank you," said Garret. "I think."

"Well, don't get a big head," said Callie. "I was responsible for half of the kiss."

"That's true," Garret agreed.

"Don't get me wrong, it doesn't make up for me getting shot, but it *was* nice."

Catherine Hopewell sat up in bed and let her eyes get accustomed to the dark room. She'd been dreaming about Callie, and the dreams were all disturbing. She couldn't remember them now, but she did remember knowing that in the dreams Callie was fighting for her life. Catherine was not going to stay in New York while her daughter was in trouble. She had to go to Callie. Looking at the LCD clock in the corner of her room, Catherine saw that it was just past midnight. Something was wrong. Something was very wrong. Callie was in danger. Someone was out to hurt her. Catherine felt her chest tighten with fear. She should never have listened to Callie or to any of her other daughters. She should have gotten on an airplane and flown down to St. Christopher to be with her daughter. Forcing herself to take a deep, calming breath, she dialed Phoebe's number. It was time for them to go to St. Christopher to save Callie.

Chapter 21

Callie was discharged from the hospital the following day. The doctor had wanted her to stay one more day, but she'd refused. It was time to get back to the business of clearing her name. As Callie sat in the passenger seat of Garret's car, she thought about the events leading up to her getting shot. She hadn't noticed anything out of the ordinary and neither had Garret. They'd both gone over everything that happened from the time they left the inspector's office until the time they reached Ransom's warehouse. Garret had remembered a dark blue car behind them, but he hadn't thought anything of it. Someone wanted to kill her, or at the very least, scare her. But whoever did this had failed to do either. All they did was make her even more determined to find out who was responsible for killing Henry and shooting her. She was certain that the two events were related.

Garret cleared his throat. "You're quiet this morning."

Callie smiled. "I had a late night, remember? Someone kept me up late."

Despite everything, her heart felt remarkably light this morning, even though her shoulder still hurt like hell. Pushing all thoughts of her near-death experience out of her mind, her mind flashed on the kiss she had shared with Garret the previous night. She hadn't exaggerated when she told him that his kiss was the best she'd ever had. She'd never given herself to anyone, not even Henry, with such abandon. If Garret hadn't pulled away she would've forced him to make love to her right there in the hospital room. She didn't care.

In addition to becoming a murder suspect, she'd become a wanton woman. No man had ever made her want to rip off her clothes and deliver herself to him. She'd done everything but strip naked and wrap herself up in a big, red bow. She remembered the times that certain ex-boyfriends had hinted that she was frigid and she'd believed them. But there was nothing frigid about her response to Garret. She was downright scandalous. After all, her fiancé was murdered a few days ago. Her behavior might be considered callous, and before last night she would have agreed—but that was before someone tried to kill her; and although she mourned her fiance's death, her relationship with Henry was a farce. She was going to do right by Henry. She was going to find out who killed him—but she'd decided that she wasn't going to let Henry stop her from going forward with her life. Besides, it was just a kiss—it wasn't as if she'd just accepted a marriage proposal, she reasoned.

"I've got a vague memory that involved a kiss . . . maybe later you'll be able to refresh my recollection." Garret's tone was light, but there was an underlying note of seriousness. They both knew that their kiss was just an opening act. There was much more to come, but before that, they needed to take care of some unfinished business that involved finding a murderer.

"Hmm," Callie responded. "I might be persuaded to... um, refresh that recollection... at some point."

Garret put on his turn signal and made a left turn onto one of the side streets in Queenstown. It was a busy morning and Callie watched as people made their way to their various destinations. Garret maneuvered the Mercedes into a tight spot between two badly parked cars and placed the car in park.

"Why're we stopping?" Callie asked. "I thought we were going directly back to your home."

Garret didn't answer. Instead, he unbuckled his seat belt and leaned forward, planting his lips on hers before she realized what was happening. She felt an immediate response of desire as a heat she'd never before known existed engulfed her. She kissed him back, tasting him, drinking him, learning him. She felt his hand unbuckling her seat belt and once she was free she drew her body into his. Good Lord, what was happening to her? She was on a crowded street and she was kissing Garret as if there was no one around to witness their display of passion. She didn't care. She wanted more of him as she thrust her tongue deeper into his mouth. Callie felt desire that he'd ignited burst into a raging fire inside her, as she hungrily explored his mouth. Then, just as suddenly as he kissed her, Garret pulled away.

"I think maybe we should talk about this," Garret said shakily.

Callie could see that he shared the desire that she felt for him.

"Okay." Callie took a deep breath and said, "Let's talk."

Garret moved back over to his seat and stared straight ahead. "I want you, Callie."

Callie didn't respond; instead, she listened to what he had to say. She understood that he wanted her just as she wanted him. It scared her, but it also gave her a secret feeling of exhilaration. She was doing something completely out of character, under circumstances that were, at the very least, less than ideal, and she loved it. She felt like a dying woman eating her last meal. Her actions were wrong—foolhardy—scandalous, but she reasoned, who was she hurting? Besides, it was only a kiss. It wasn't like she was going to fall in love with Garret.

"I want you in a way I've never wanted any other woman. Do you understand that?"

"Yes," Callie replied, trying hard not to look at his full lips. "I think I do."

He turned and looked at her. "But I want to do this the right way. I don't want to mess things up before they've had a chance to begin. I also want to make sure that we keep our focus on finding out who killed Henry and who took a shot at you. I'd also like to keep you out of prison."

Callie sighed deeply. Garret was absolutely right. Her neck was on the line; now was not the right time to lose her head, literally and figuratively. Damn, she hated when reality intruded.

"Does this mean no more kissing?" Callie asked.

"Oh, there'll be more kissing," Garret promised.

"But right now, we need to take care of business and get you out of the jam you're in."

Callie nodded her head. No more kissing, damn.

"You're right," she said.

"I know I am," said Garret, "but I don't know how I'm going to keep my focus around you, Callie Hopewell."

"Garret." Callie leaned over and held his hand. "I like kissing you. I like kissing you very much."

"God help me, so do I," Garret replied.

"So, what do we do now?" Callie asked.

Garret started the car.

"We go back to my home where you're going to get some rest. I'm going to follow up on a few leads and then I'm going to come home, tell you everything I know and cook you, my grandmother and Zenna dinner."

"I want to come with you today, Garret."

"No." Garret's response was firm and it was clear that there wasn't anything she could do to change his mind. "This is something I've got to do alone."

"Why?" Callie asked him, perplexed. As far as she was concerned, they'd made a pretty good team. Why wouldn't he want her to help him?

"Because," Garret replied, as he eased the vehicle out of the tight parking space, "this involves my father."

Chapter 22

James Langrin was surprised to see his son. James's office was located in a building in Queenstown, not too far away from his son's offices. Despite the close proximity of the offices, it had been several years since Garret had visited his father's office. The gulf between the two of them had widened over the years and James had come to realize that some wounds would never heal. James knew that Garret blamed him for what happened to his mother. God knew that he blamed himself often enough for not getting his wife the help she needed. Mariah had been beautiful and temperamental—both qualities that had drawn him to her. But Mariah had demons he'd never understood. Today, Mariah's condition would probably be classified as bipolar or manic depressive. But at that time, he hadn't realized how serious things were until it was too late. James had thrown himself into his work, and then later, into the arms of other women, when the pressures of dealing with Mariah had overwhelmed him. He'd run away from his wife and from his son. Both actions were unforgivable. It wasn't until Mariah's death that he realized the magnitude of his mistake. He'd thrown his family away at the time when they needed him most. After Mariah's death, the guilt had driven him even farther away from Garret, and it wasn't until Mariah's mother Dreama had a long and heated discussion with him about the responsibility he had to his son that James started to try to make amends with Garret. But it was too late. Garret had loved his mother and he'd seen firsthand how James had made her suffer.

"What can I do for you, son?" James stood up and walked around the desk to stand in front of his son. He hadn't seen Garret in a few months, although he followed his accomplishments closely. Dreama filled him in with information on his personal life, and he was able to read about Garret's professional success in the newspapers. He was proud of his son—proud of the man he'd become—even though James knew he'd had nothing to do with the strong, principled man he saw standing in front of him. Dreama deserved all the credit for molding his son into the fine man who James saw before him. James ached to hug his son. But the last time that Garret had let his father touch him was at Mariah's funeral. After that, Garret had distanced himself from James—physically and emotionally.

James extended his arm for a handshake, which Garret ignored. Dropping his arm to his side, James asked his son, "Is everything all right?"

"May I have a seat?" Garret asked.

James nodded and watched as Garret sat down. His son looked uncomfortable. It was ironic to see him here in his office. He'd convinced himself that he was building a career for his family. In the end, his career had flourished, but his wife was dead and his son had turned his back on him and on his business. James sat in the chair beside his son.

Garret got right to the point. "I need a favor."

James responded without hesitation. "Name it."

"Dad, it's not that simple," said Garret.

James forced himself to look away from Garret. He didn't want him to see the tears that glistened in his eyes. It had been a long time since Garret had called him "Dad." In that one moment, everything that he'd lost came crashing down on him. He wanted those years back. He wanted his son back. After what he did to his family, James knew that he didn't deserve a second chance, but, by God, he wanted it so badly he could taste it.

James quickly composed himself. "Why don't you tell me about it?"

"This involves Otis Lorde," Garret said quietly.

James felt his heart quicken. Was his son mixed up with Otis? Although Otis was a friend, James knew just how dangerous Otis could be and he didn't want Garret anywhere near him or his business dealings. There were many who questioned James's friendship with Otis, but long ago Otis had done a favor for James—a favor which saved his life—and James had remained loyal to his friend, even though he knew that sometimes friendships with Otis could turn deadly.

After taking a steadying breath, James asked, "How are you involved with Otis?"

"I'm not involved with him, but I need some information from him."

Thank God, thought James. "What sort of information?"

James listened as Garret told him the story of his involvement with Callie Hopewell's case. Like the rest of the island, James had read about the murder of Henry Kincaid with interest. He'd known Henry Kincaid and his beautiful wife, Josephine, fairly well. Once, at a party a few years ago, Josephine had come on to him but he'd been repelled by her advances. She was beautiful, but to James, Josephine Kincaid was about as cold as a dead fish and just as appetizing. Garret told him about Henry's involvement with Otis Lorde, and the threats Otis Lorde had made when Henry couldn't repay his gambling debts.

"I need to talk to Otis, but I'm sure he won't talk to me," said Garret.

"You're right about that," James said. "But he will talk to me. Let me just say, if he did kill Henry, he's not about to tell me about it."

"I know that," Garret replied. "But any information you can get about Henry's gambling would help me."

"I'll go see him today," James decided. "Then, I'll call you and let you know what I found out."

Garret cleared his throat. "I'd like to go with you, if that's okay."

James looked directly at his son. "Garret, Otis is not a man to fool with."

Garret nodded his head slowly. "I know that, but I want to be with you when you talk to him."

"Why?" James asked.

"This case is very important to me." Garret stared into his father's eyes.

"Callie Hopewell is very important to you," James said slowly, as a full understanding of his son's feelings for Callie Hopewell became clear.

"Yes," said Garret. "She is."

James got up and walked to his desk. He picked up the telephone receiver and hit the intercom button that signaled his assistant, Maryce.

"Maryce, I need you to call Otis Lorde and tell him that I need to see him this morning. Yes, that's right . . . this morning."

"I don't care what his family says," Josephine Kincaid repeated her words slowly. "I want a closed casket. I didn't want to see Henry when he was alive, and I *damn* sure don't want to see him now that he's dead."

She was sitting in a Queenstown restaurant with her father, having lunch. It was just after noon and the small restaurant, *Palmetto's,* was filled to capacity. Josephine loved coming here—this was the place where those who were well acquainted with power and notoriety lunched. Many of her friends came here, and the food was wonderful—a mixture of Caribbean and French cuisine. Her father had wanted to go to another restaurant—somewhere more discreet, in light of the emerging scandal surrounding Henry's death, but Josephine had never run from getting attention, even when the attention was negative.

"Josephine," hissed William Hawthorne, "keep your voice down, for God's sake!"

Josephine stabbed her fork into a slice of mango from her fruit salad plate. "Daddy, I don't care *who* hears me. Everyone knows that Henry played me for a fool! Why should anyone expect me to be sad now that the bastard's dead?"

William shook his head. "Show some decorum, Josephine."

After eating another mango slice, Josephine said, "I'm not going to act like the bereaved widow, if *that's* what you mean. I won't do it, Daddy."

Sighing, William looked at his daughter, disappointment showing clearly in his eyes.

"Let's get back to the subject we were discussing," he said. "Henry's father wants an open casket."

Josephine shook her head vigorously. "I already told them that the casket is going to be closed. If they want to take a look at him before he meets up with the devil, then they can look at him at the funeral home."

"Be *reasonable*, Josephine," William implored his eldest daughter. "How could it hurt to grant them this last request?"

Josephine gave a bitter laugh. "There's nothing I would do to help anyone in the Kincaid family. I wouldn't spit on them if any of them were on fire. They were always against our marriage—although it turns out that they were right on that score. They never did anything for me, so why should I care what they want?"

William shook his head. "You shouldn't be like that, Josephine. I'd hoped that I'd raised you better than this."

"For heaven's sake, Daddy, you hated Henry just

as much as I did! Why do you care if his casket is open or closed?"

William lowered his voice. "You're right. I didn't care for Henry. I think he was a terrible husband to you and if I knew then what I know now, I never would've advised you to marry him. Still, I've brought you up to do what's right—what's proper. You need to respect his family's wishes."

"Daddy, I'm not discussing this any further. The conversation, like Henry's casket, is closed."

"Well, let's talk about another subject, then— let's talk about what's going on between you and Esme."

Josephine pushed away her fruit plate angrily. "I don't have anything to say about that whore."

William Hawthorne raised his hand in the air as if he were going to slap Josephine. All conversation in the restaurant ceased. It was clear that William and Josephine now had the attention of the patrons in the restaurant. He saw Josephine flinch as if she expected him to land a heavy blow— instead, he put his hand down slowly.

When William finally spoke, his voice was hoarse.

"Remember, Josephine, if I've taught you nothing else. Blood sticks by blood. Esme is your sister. I don't care who she slept with . . . she's still your sister. She's your blood."

William stood up to leave.

"Daddy, I . . ." Josephine's voice trailed off. She'd been frightened by her father's outburst.

"You need to rethink your position on opening Henry's casket," William cut her off. "After all, it's the decent thing to do."

Chapter 23

Otis Lorde lived in a well guarded mansion in the hills surrounding Queenstown. Although he had an office in Queenstown, he conducted most of his business in his home. Garret had never been to Otis's property but he'd heard about its magnificence. Otis lived on a property that had three Spanish-style villas with panoramic views of the Atlantic Ocean and nearby islands. Set in a leafy garden of exotic trees, flowers, and coconut palms, Otis lived in the largest of the three villas. As Garret and his father walked up the sweeping front entrance to the main house, he could see men holding guns and wearing bulletproof vests patrolling the grounds.

Otis had agreed immediately to see them although James had been vague about the reason for this visit during the brief telephone call. On the drive to Otis's home, the conversation with his father had been strained. Garret was grateful for his father's help, but that didn't change how he felt about the man. Garret now understood the phrase "desperate times call for desperate measures." Callie was in trouble and no matter what his feelings were about his father, he needed his help to get the information he needed from Otis Lorde.

They were met by an extraordinarily beautiful woman at the front door. She was at least six feet tall and she looked as if she was a mixture of both East Indian and African descent. Her long black hair was pulled back from a face that looked as if it had been chiseled by an artist—oval, with large dark eyes her dominant feature. Her face was a mixture of full lips, aristocratic nose, sloping cheekbones that all came together to form a look that Madison Avenue modeling agencies would die for.

"Mr. Lorde is expecting you, Mr. Langrin."

His father smiled at the woman. "Syreeta, I'd like you to meet my son, Garret."

Syreeta turned and looked at Garret. She wasn't friendly or aloof—just very matter-of-fact. "Pleased to meet you," she said.

Walking briskly through the first floor of the house, Syreeta directed them to the veranda in the back where Otis Lorde and four armed bodyguards who looked as if they were former bouncers in a bar waited for them. After depositing them on the veranda, Syreeta left the men to their business.

Otis rose from the chair on which he sat, to greet them. Shaking James's hand, he asked, "Who is this man who looks as if he's a younger and more handsome version of you?"

Otis was not a physically imposing man. He was slight in stature, and if Garret didn't know the crime history of Otis Lorde, he'd think that this thin, brown, bespectacled man in a tan seersucker suit and button-down shirt was an accountant, or a librarian—not the cold-blooded crime lord he was reputed to be.

"I've heard a lot about you," Otis said, looking at Garret with a disconcertingly direct stare. "I've heard that you're a good criminal lawyer. Perhaps one day we'll work together."

James cleared his throat nervously.

"Garret doesn't do much criminal work," he said quickly. "His specialty is corporate law."

Otis sat down.

"But he does do some criminal work," Otis said, his tone mild. "Isn't he involved in that whole Henry Kincaid mess?"

"That's what I want to talk to you about, Mr. Lorde," Garret spoke up. "I represent a lady named Callie Hopewell."

Otis nodded. "Yes, I know. Why don't you two men have a seat."

James sat down, but Garret remained standing.

"So what is it you want to know about the unfortunate Henry Kincaid?" asked Otis, wiping his forehead with a handkerchief proffered by one of his beefy bodyguards.

"I want to know if you had anything to do with his death," Garret said.

One of the bodyguards let out a low laugh but the rest of the group remained silent. Maybe he should have warmed Otis up a little and not gone in for the kill immediately—but Garret had always prided himself on being a good judge of character and his instincts told him that the direct approach was the best approach with Otis Lorde.

"You know"—Otis turned to James—"I rather like your son's style. I can see why he's so successful."

James smiled wanly and agreed. "He's a good lawyer."

Turning his attention back to Garret, Otis said, "Most men wouldn't have dared to ask me that question."

Garret replied, "I'm not most men."

"So, I see."

"My client, Miss Hopewell, is accused of killing Henry Kincaid."

"Has she been arrested?" Otis asked.

"Not yet," Garret replied, "but the police have her pegged as their number one suspect and she didn't do it."

Otis smirked. "Maybe she did kill him. After all, he'd certainly played her for a fool."

Garret felt the blood rush to his face. He could happily and easily throttle Otis Lorde, but common sense and the four armed bodyguards made him resist the urge.

Forcing himself to remain calm, Garret said, "I believe in my client."

James spoke up. "Otis, it would help Garret if you could give him some information—any information on Henry Kincaid. What do you know about him?"

"I know that he was a weak man," Otis said. "I also know that he deserved to be killed, but I didn't do it."

"Can you prove that?" Garret's tone was sharp but he didn't care. He suspected that Otis was telling the truth, that he hadn't killed Henry. When Otis Lorde murdered someone, it was years, if ever, before a body was found—that was his reputation. Still, Garret needed to know if there was any information that Otis could give them to help him clear Callie from suspicion.

Otis narrowed his eyes and looked at Garret for a long moment, then he said, "No, I can't prove it. I don't have to prove it, young Mr. Langrin."

"Look, Callie Hopewell is an innocent woman caught up in something I suspect is far bigger than anything she's ever been involved in," said Garret. "Someone took a shot at her yesterday. All this woman ever did was give her love to the wrong man."

"And are you the right man?" Otis observed mildly.

"That's none of your business," Garret replied.

James put a restraining hand on his son's arm.

"Otis, it's obvious he cares for the lady. It's equally obvious that he doesn't believe she killed Henry. If he did, he wouldn't be here and neither would I. Can you help him out? As a favor to me?" James asked.

Otis stood up slowly. Then, he walked directly in front of Garret.

"I'm only doing this because of my friendship with your father," he said.

"Henry Kincaid was a gambler who loved whores. Gambling and women—those were his two weaknesses. He wasn't a very good gambler and from what his wife told me, he wasn't much good in bed either. Anyway, Henry had a business proposition for me—he wanted me to help him set up a casino here in Queenstown. I thought he was crazy. Although gambling is legal here—there really hasn't been much interest in it and the only casinos that do well are run by American businessmen—but Henry was convinced this would be a good thing. He got his family to put up some money and I put up the rest and we became the silent owners of Skylight Casino in Lime Key. No one knew who the real owners of Skylight were. Anyway, it turned out that not only was Henry losing money there at the blackjack table, but he was skimming money as well. The authorities were starting to look into it and that's the real reason that Henry left the island. As it stands, Henry owed me at least three million. But it wasn't just the money that upset me—Henry knew how I felt about drug trafficking. I lost my son to drugs and it's a business I would never get into, but Henry was apparently into that line of business and he was trying to launder his dirty money with the money from the casino. When I found all that out I did threaten to kill him, but his father repaid the loan with interest. As for the drug business—I think it was cocaine, or so I heard—his other partners were pretty unhappy with him. Who knows, maybe they bumped him off. If they did, they did society a favor. Henry Kincaid was scum."

After Otis finished speaking, Garret sat down heavily on the empty chair beside his father.

"Have you talked to the police about the drug connection and Henry?"

"No," Otis replied, going back to his seat. "And I don't intend to. This is the kind of information that I don't want to share with law enforcement. I'm not trying to bring that sort of attention to my doorstep."

Garret spoke up. "Then, I'll have to go to the

police myself. There's an innocent woman whose freedom is at stake here."

Otis's words were spoken in a quiet tone, but the menace behind those words was clear. "Those who threaten me usually don't live to carry out their threats."

James got out of his seat and walked over to where Garret stood. Then, he turned and said to Otis, "This is my son, and I stand behind him, Otis."

Otis looked at James and shook his head slowly. "James, you've been a close friend for over thirty years, but I'll do whatever's necessary to protect myself."

"I understand that," James said. "But you're not involved in Henry Kincaid's schemes. All Garret is asking is that you tell the police that there are others who have very good motives for killing Henry."

"Including me," said Otis. "But I didn't kill him."

"Then you have nothing to worry about," said Garret.

"What about the associates of Henry . . . the ones who were involved in his drug trafficking? If I go to the police they'll come after me," Otis snapped. "James, your son is putting me in a no-win situation. I'll be bringing heat on my business . . . heat from the police and heat from some pretty unsavory folk."

"I know that," James replied, "but my son is right. There's an innocent woman who also has a lot at stake here."

"You know the police are going to treat you with kid gloves, they always have," said Garret.

Otis laughed. "You must know something that I

don't. Right before you guys got here, a gentleman named Mobray... came to visit me. Apparently, the police are already looking at other persons of interest in the case. According to Mobray, there's been some discussion that I might have had a good reason to kill Henry Kincaid."

"Did you tell Mobray about Kincaid's involvement with drugs?"

"No." Otis shook his head. "I already told you that I don't want that kind of attention on me."

"Otis, please help my son," said James.

Otis stood up. "Do you understand what you're asking me to do?"

"Yes," James replied. "I wouldn't ask you to do this if there was any other way. I understand that once the police start looking into your involvement with Kincaid, they might start looking into other parts of your business."

"You're damn right," said Otis.

"You have my word that I'll help you deal with any heat that might come your way. You know that I did it before, and I'll do it again for you."

Garret had no idea what his father was talking about, but his words apparently had a strong effect on Otis.

"I know what you've done for me," Otis said quietly.

"Then you know I would only ask you to do this because it's important to my son."

Otis looked at Garret and James for what seemed like an eternity. Then, he walked back to his seat and sat down heavily.

"Okay," Otis finally said. "I'll go to the police. I'm only doing this for you, James... because of what you've done for me."

On the drive back to his father's office, after they left Otis's home, Garret asked his father, "What favor did you do for Otis?"

"I saved his life," James replied. "Years ago, Otis was accused of murder. There was some very strong evidence against him. I gave him an air-tight alibi."

"Was he guilty?" Garret asked.

"Yes," said James.

"Why'd you give him the alibi?"

"He took care of a man who hurt your mother."

Garret felt the blood in his face drain away. He was aware of a rushing sound, the sound of waves, only louder.

"Who hurt my mother?"

James looked out of the window. "It was a long time ago. Let it drop, Garret."

"Who hurt my mother!" Garret's roar made his father flinch.

"Your mother was raped. It happened before we were married. Otis took care of the guy who did it . . ."

"How did Otis know about what happened?"

"Because I told him. Before I married your mother, both Otis and I were in love with her. I think he still loves her, if you want to know the truth. Your mother chose me. But there was a man who was fixated on her. Your mother was a very beautiful woman and she caught his attention. He tried to get her interested in him, but she refused. She was seeing me at the time. Well, this individual couldn't deal with the answer no. He raped her. When I found out about it I nearly went crazy. I told Otis about it. But I didn't intend for him to kill the guy. I told Otis to find the guy because the police couldn't do it. Well, after Otis got involved, the man showed up dead. The prosecutor thought it was an open and shut case. I felt responsible and I gave him an alibi."

"So, Otis owes you."

"Yes," said James. "We owe each other."

Chapter 24

It was just past midnight when Garret showed up at Callie's door. She'd been worried all day when she hadn't heard from him. An overactive imagination had plagued her all her life and it went into overdrive while she waited for Garret. Thoughts about the danger that he might be in as a result of taking her case had added guilt to the worry that had gripped her the entire time that he was away. Not even the calming words of Dreama, who assured her that nothing bad was going to happen to her grandson, had helped to ease her anxiety. When she opened the door and saw him standing there she felt relief wash over her. *Thank God,* she made a silent prayer of gratitude that he was all right. After what happened to Henry, and her own recent brush with danger, she didn't take Garret's safety for granted. An urge to grab him and hold him tight swept over her.

"Can I come in?"

His voice was strained, and when she looked closer she saw something she hadn't seen before when she looked at him. She saw raw pain in his eyes.

She stepped aside and let him enter. Closing the door behind her, she turned and faced him. He stood in front of her, not saying a word. Instead, he looked at her with pain and yearning. What had happened that caused the look of despair that he now carried?

"Garret, what's wrong?"

Shaking his head, he pulled her close and buried his face in her hair. He was trembling and Callie held him tight. Her shoulder still ached, but she ignored her own pain and she held him. She could feel his thundering heartbeat as she held him. Whatever had happened to him had been terrible. She was certain of this.

Garret suddenly pulled away and looked at her intently. "Callie, I don't want to hurt you."

Callie didn't respond. Instead, she let him speak.

"I don't want to hurt you the way my father hurt my mother. I don't want to be like the other men that hurt my mother." His voice was as raw as his emotions.

"You won't hurt me, Garret."

"How can you say that after everything you've been through? How do you know I won't do what Henry did to you?"

"I believe in you."

Garret shook his head. "My mother believed in my father, and she was hurt. She was a kind woman, like you . . . but she was hurt . . . badly."

"I'm so sorry," Callie whispered.

Garret grabbed her and crushed his lips on hers. This was a different kiss from the other ones they'd shared. There was a desperation in this kiss; he hungrily sucked her tongue—his mouth bruising hers. Dragging his lips away from hers, he pulled away and said, "I need you, Callie."

Callie pulled him closer.

"But I can't promise you anything. I know that my parents loved each other at one time, but that love turned into something bad. My father's blood runs through my veins. I can't tell you that I won't turn out to be like him."

"I don't know your father . . . but I know that you have the choice to live your life in a way that you'll be proud of. Your father made his choices and he has to live with the consequences. You have the same choice to make . . . how to live your life," Callie said. "And I don't want any promises from you, Garret."

"Callie, I never thought my father ever loved my mother. He was unfaithful to her."

Callie closed the space between them. When she was standing directly in front of him, their bodies touching, she said, "You're not your father."

Then she brought two hands to his face, and lightly touched his lips with hers. That was all Garret needed before a flame of desire was ignited. He pulled at the sash of her dressing gown, letting it fall away. He pushed down the straps of her silk nightgown, as she hungrily devoured his mouth, his throat, his face . . . Closing her eyes, she let the feelings wash over her. She heard him murmuring her name over and over again, like a mantra. Her nightgown fell to the floor and she stood naked before him. All of the insecurities about her body came flooding over her as she placed her hands over her breasts as if to shield herself from him.

Garret moved her hands away. "Let me see you, Callie. All of you."

She dropped her hands and stood in front of him.

"You're beautiful, Callie," he whispered.

Whenever she'd been intimate with Henry, she'd never felt comfortable. His comments about her lush figure had carried with them a hint of disapproval that she hadn't lost weight. On occasion, he'd made comments about her full figure. Callie wasn't overweight, but she wasn't stick thin, either. She had curves and everything that came with them—large breasts, wide hips, her stomach was not flat but didn't have a six-pack bulge. Callie now realized that Henry didn't want the woman she was. He wanted some ideal that she couldn't live up to, but from what she now knew about the many women Henry had been with, there wasn't anyone who was going to live up to Henry's ideal. Staring at the unabashed admiration in Garret's eyes as he looked at her, she realized that she'd sold herself short with Henry. There were men who looked at her and liked what they saw without a complaint. She wanted to shout hallelujah as she felt her shyness disappear. Instead, she let him carry her to the bedroom where she knew that they were going to make love.

She'd known that they would come to this place after their first kiss. The kiss had a promise of things to come. But she hadn't thought that things would happen this soon. However, as she'd found out, sometimes life brought you to unexpected places—some good, and some bad. The old Callie would have talked herself out of making love to Garret. She'd have reasoned that until a few days ago she was engaged to another man. She would have chided herself for being in such an intimate position with a man she'd only just met. She would have been appalled at the thought of sleeping with a man who was representing her in a serious legal matter. She had lived her life being cautious, and she'd still ended up getting hurt. Maybe now it was time to let go of the old and start something new. Maybe now it was time to run with her heart, and if she got hurt again, she'd deal with the consequences—but right now, right this very moment, she was going to make love to Garret.

Garret placed her on the bed and began to undress. She watched him as he took off his clothes slowly. With each disrobing, she got more and more of a view of a glorious, hard brown body. This was a man who believed in taking care of his body. From his broad shoulders to his long, sinewy arms and taut stomach, she drank in every beautiful part of his body. Holding her breath, she watched as he took off his jeans, then the last article of clothing. Exhaling slowly, Callie stared at him with wonder in her eyes. *Good Lord,* she thought, *I'm going to have a very, very good time.*

She watched as he lay down next to her and for a brief moment she felt panicky. This man had been with a lot of women. What if she didn't live up to his expectations in bed? She'd had a suspicion that Henry hadn't been all that thrilled with their lovemaking; she knew she hadn't exactly been bowled over herself during their over-too-quickly interludes. Pushing all thoughts of Henry and his lovemaking out of her head, she took another deep breath. She might not have had a lot of experience in this particular department, but she could learn . . . and judging by his obvious attraction to her, she knew that Garret was going to enjoy teaching her.

He pulled her on top of his naked body. "What about your shoulder?" he whispered.

Callie barely was able to get the words out. The surge of heat she felt inside at the contact of their naked bodies literally took her breath away. *Calm down, Callie.* "Painkillers," she whispered. "I'll be fine."

With one free hand he pulled her mouth down on his, while his other hand roamed freely over her body. Their bodies moved in sync with each other, as they explored with hands, tongues, lips, fingers. . . . Any bashfulness evaporated as a wanton woman whom Callie had never previously encountered took over her body. Who was this woman who told Garret exactly what she wanted him to do, where she wanted him to do it, and how she wanted him to do it? She'd always been quiet in her lovemaking; now she was gloriously abandoned and free as she experienced lovemaking, true lovemaking, for the first time in her life.

While they were still entwined, he gently maneuvered her until he was lying on top of her. His kisses went from her mouth to her neck and when he reached her breasts, she thought she would lose whatever tenuous grip she had on sanity. She let out a low moan as he used his tongue to tease each breast. She began to move her hips frantically as the sensations within her started to surge. "Please," she begged, not certain what exactly it was she wanted him to do. "Please."

He stopped for a moment and stared at her with such tenderness she thought she would cry. "Be patient," he said softly. "I'm going to give you everything that you want."

"Everything?" she whispered.

"Everything."

He began to kiss her again, but this time his kisses trailed from her breasts to her stomach, where he lingered for a while, his tongue playing with her belly button while she writhed with the indescribable pleasure this gave her. Then he moved lower and lower until he was at her most intimate place. At that point, her senses spiraled out of control as he used his tongue and then his mouth to bring her to a shattering climax. She was dimly aware that the voice she heard screaming as the emotions poured out of her was her own. Afterward, she lay sated and drained as he lay next to her—staring at her with a satisfied smile.

"So this is what all the fuss is about," Callie said, when she finally reclaimed her voice.

He leaned over and kissed her on the forehead. "You're a very passionate woman, Callie Hopewell."

"You're the first man who's ever said that to me."

"The other men were damn fools."

Callie leaned over and started to kiss Garret. At first, the kiss was slow and languid, but soon, the passion she now recognized flared up again between them. Once again he pulled her on top of him as their bodies simulated the lovemaking that would soon occur. Somewhere in the midst of the haze, she heard Garret ask about protection. She'd come to St. Christopher with a box of condoms in her suitcase. After she'd discovered Henry's lies, she'd intended to throw them away, but now she was glad that she hadn't. She'd placed them in the top drawer of the bureau along with her underclothes. Somehow she managed to communicate this to him in the midst of a feeling of such intense desire to make love to him that she could taste it. Her shoulder ached from the bullet wound, but her need to finish what they'd started overcame any discomfort she felt.

He got up and walked over to her dresser. Opening the drawer she'd indicated, she watched as he pulled out the small silver wrapper. He tore it open and brought it back to her. A feeling of brazenness came over her as she asked, "Can I put it on for you?"

She'd always fantasized about doing this, but she'd never had the nerve to ask.

He handed her the condom, and with surprisingly steady hands she completed the task. He knelt over her, kissing her lightly on the lips. "God, Callie, what are you doing to me?" he groaned.

She smiled and said, "Hopefully the same thing you're doing to me."

The time for foreplay was over and she opened up to receive him. He lowered himself into her and they both gasped when he finally entered her. She closed her eyes and let the waves of pleasure engulf her as she matched his rhythmic thrusts. "Open your eyes, Callie," he ordered gently. She stared at him as he bit his bottom lip, his thrusts harder and more forceful. "Look at me."

"Am I hurting you?" he asked.

She shook her head.

"Callie, I'm not going to let you go. I can't."

I don't want to go, Callie answered silently, as she wrapped her legs tighter around him. She felt her climax building up again and she saw that he was also close to reaching the peak they were both climbing. His breath came in ragged gasps as he called her name over and over and over again until they both reached the place they'd been straining to get to at the same, earth-shattering, time. Afterwards, Garret held her close until they both fell asleep entwined with each other.

They slept until the next morning when they were awakened by a high-pitched scream. Callie opened her eyes and blinked twice. This had to be a dream. Standing in the doorway to her bedroom were two shocked women: her mother and her sister Phoebe. *Oh, my God,* a voice inside her screamed, but under the circumstances, she remained as calm as she could. "Mom, what are you doing here?"

"What am I doing here!" Catherine Hopewell's voice rose to a point just beneath hysteria. "The more important question is, what are you doing in bed with this man!"

Garret sat up in bed and said, "My name is Garret Langrin and I'm in love with your daughter."

"What!" Both Catherine and Callie exclaimed at the same time.

"I'd love to get up to greet you properly," said Garret, "but under the circumstances . . ."

"Callie, I'm just scandalized!" said Catherine. "Here I come rushing down here to help you and I find you in . . . in . . . I can't even say the words!"

Callie looked over at her sister Phoebe for some help but all she got was a big smile. She knew that within the hour, three scandalized telephone calls would be made to her remaining sisters in New York. Goodness, how was she ever going to face them?

"Callie, surely you must have some explanation for this . . . this behavior! I understand that you've been through a lot these past few days, but that's no reason for this . . ."

Callie decided it was time to take control of the situation before her mother completely lost it.

"Mom, I'm an adult. I'm old enough to make my decisions. I chose to sleep with Garret, and what's more, I'm going to do it again."

"Damn, sis." Phoebe grinned. "You didn't waste any time, did you?"

"No," said Callie. "I wasted enough time on Henry."

Catherine shook her head. "Your father's probably spinning in his grave right now!"

"Mom, Dad's in heaven and hopefully he's happy that his daughter, after all this time, finally got lucky."

"Callie!" Catherine cried out. "What on earth has gotten into you!"

"I think we can see what's gotten into her," Phoebe murmured loud enough for everyone to hear.

"Phoebe Hopewell, there's no need for this crass talk from you!"

"Mom," Callie said. "Don't be angry at Phoebe. I make my own decisions. I'm sorry that you're disappointed in me, but I'm not going to be sorry about what happened between Garret and myself."

Sensing that Callie was not going to budge on the subject, Catherine turned to Garret and said, "Well, young man, what do you have to say for yourself? Now that you've compromised my daughter, do you intend to marry her?"

"Mom!" Callie wailed. "This isn't Elizabethan England! He hasn't compromised me.... if anyone did the compromising, it was me!"

"I've heard enough!" Catherine declared. "I'm going to wait for you in the living room, Callie Hopewell. When you're dressed and decent, you and I are going to have a serious talk!"

Catherine marched out of the room, with Phoebe following close behind.

After they left, Garret turned and looked at Callie. "I think your mom likes me." He grinned.

"She has a funny way of showing it," Callie replied.

"It took you a little while, too... remember?" Garret teased.

Callie marveled at his good humor. Most men wouldn't have been quite so cheerful under the circumstances. Being caught in bed by your partner's parent was usually not a happy situation, but Garret refused to let that little detail dampen a rosy mood.

Callie turned to another subject. "Why'd you tell my mother than you loved me? I appreciate your trying to save my honor, but believe me, after what my mother saw, my honor's pretty well ruined."

Garret kissed her lightly. "I said it because I meant it. I'm in love with you, Callie."

"You've known me for exactly five days."

"That's true."

"You can't fall in love with somebody in five days."

"I did," Garret said. "So I know it can happen."

"What am I going to do with you?" Callie asked.

"You're going to give me another kiss, then you're going to get dressed and talk to your mother."

Chapter 25

Callie waited until Garret left the guest house before going to the living room to face her mother and sister. Her mother was sitting on one of the chairs in the living room area, her face a rigid mask of disapproval. Her sister was sitting on the couch, a broad smile on her face. Callie took a deep breath. Talking to her mother about her recent foray into debauchery was the last thing Callie wanted to do, but she was a big girl. She would handle it.

"Callie, you've always handled yourself with decorum," her mother said quietly.

"That's true, Mom."

"And you've always behaved like a lady."

"That's also true."

"So, how do you explain your recent behavior?"

Callie took another deep breath. "Mom, I'm thirty-four years old. With all due respect, I don't have to talk about my love life with you. I don't want to be rude . . ."

"Too late for that!" said Catherine.

"Mom, please . . ."

Her mother's voice softened. "Callie, I know that you've been through some tough times. I know how much Henry hurt you. I know what it's like to love someone and have them treat you badly. . . . Before I met your father, my heart was broken too . . ."

"My heart's not broken, Mom." As soon as Callie said the words she knew that it was true. No matter what Henry had done, he hadn't broken her heart. She'd never really loved him. If she did, she wouldn't have spent the night with Garret. She wouldn't have given herself to him so freely. Whatever she'd felt for Henry, it wasn't love.

"Callie, you were engaged to be married to the man . . ."

"And you said the engagement was too soon."

"I was right about that," Catherine Hopewell said indignantly. "Still, jumping from one man to another, so quickly . . . and under these circumstances, well, it just isn't wise, Callie."

"You're right, Mom," Callie replied. "It isn't wise. But I'm going to continue seeing Garret."

"What if he ends up hurting you?"

"Then, I'll be hurt," said Callie. "But I'll still live. Mom, Garret put everything aside—his business, everything—to help me. He's been with me from the time I found out about Henry. He stayed with me after I got shot . . ."

"Merciful Father in heaven!" Catherine gasped. "You got shot!"

"Callie, what on earth happened?" Phoebe asked.

At that moment, there was a knock on the front

door. *"Thank You, God,"* Callie whispered. Whoever was knocking had spared her, at least for the moment, from having to go over her recent brush with death.

"Who is it?" Callie called out. Although Garret's home was patrolled by security, Callie had learned to be cautious. She took nothing for granted.

"It's me, Ransom."

She opened the door, and Ransom bounded in. He looked impossibly cheerful at eight o'clock in the morning. He was wearing a brightly colored dashiki and khaki pants.

"I'm sorry for the interruption, Callie," said Ransom.

Callie made quick introductions. "Ransom, this is my mother, Catherine Hopewell, and my sister Phoebe."

"Pleased to meet you," said Ransom.

"I'm afraid to ask," Catherine said to Callie, "but who is *this* man?"

"Ransom is helping us with the case," Callie explained.

Seemingly satisfied with the answer, Catherine mumbled a greeting to Ransom. Phoebe just kept staring at Callie with a wide smile. Lord, her sisters were going to get an earful from Phoebe.

"Would you like to have a seat?" Callie asked Ransom.

"Don't mind if I do," he replied. Sitting down on one of the wicker chairs in the living room, Ransom began talking. "I had a very interesting meeting with Reynalda Chin's mother. She came to visit me yesterday."

For a moment, Callie forgot who Reynalda Chin

was, then she remembered. Reynalda was the woman who committed suicide when Henry wouldn't leave his wife.

"What did she want?" Callie asked.

"She had some information she wanted to give me. She told me that before Henry's wife married, she had an affair with Max Chin—Reynalda's husband."

Callie shook her head. "The plot thickens."

"You've got that right," Ransom continued. "Reynalda told her mother about it. She used the affair as a reason to have her own affair with Henry, at least that's what she told her mother. Apparently, along the way she fell in love with Henry and paid for it with her life."

"Who is Reynalda Chin?" Catherine asked. "And what does she have to do with Henry?"

"She was one of Henry's women," Callie replied. "Apparently, he had quite a few."

"I told you that man was no good," Catherine declared, folding her hands across her chest.

"Mom, give it a rest," said Phoebe. "Callie needs our support."

Callie flashed her sister a grateful smile.

"Here's the thing," Ransom continued. "Josephine knew about Reynalda and Henry. Reynalda told her mother that Josephine had laughed about it—went as far as suggesting that maybe she and Max would get back together for old's time sake."

"Damn, she's cold," said Phoebe.

Callie agreed.

"Josephine didn't care, but her sister Esme did. I've heard some rumors about Esme and Henry, but it wasn't confirmed until Reynalda's mother talked to me yesterday."

"Is there anyone on this island who Henry didn't sleep with?" asked Phoebe.

"Phoebe Hopewell, you know I don't much care for that kind of talk," Catherine declared stoutly.

"Well, the lady does have a point about Henry," said Ransom. "Anyway, Esme threatened Reynalda. Reynalda's mother told me that Esme threatened to kill her if she didn't stop seeing Henry. That was three days before she died. Her mother thinks that Esme was involved in Reynalda's death."

"I thought Reynalda killed herself," said Callie.

"That's what the authorities determined," said Ransom. "But her mother's convinced that Reynalda was murdered. She's also convinced that Esme is responsible."

"No mother wants to think that her child is capable of taking her own life," Catherine said quietly.

Ransom turned and said to Callie, "She thinks that Esme may have killed Henry."

"Why does she think that?" Callie said

"She said that Esme told Reynalda that she was going to kill her and Henry. Reynalda's mother thinks that she carried through on her threats."

"Have you told this to Garret?" Callie asked.

"No," Ransom replied. "Zenna said that he left the house about half an hour ago, but she wasn't sure where he was going. I tried him on his cell phone, but I got his voice mail so I left a message. I also left a message at his office. His secretary gets in early, but she hadn't received any word from him since yesterday when he told her to clear his schedule for the next few days."

Callie wondered where Garret had gone, but pushing those thoughts out of her mind, she said to Ransom, "Where can I find Esme?"

"She works in Queenstown," said Ransom. "But when I went by her office yesterday, her assistant said that she's on an indefinite vacation."

"Do you think she's left the island?" Callie asked.

"Maybe, but I doubt it. Henry's funeral is tomorrow. I have a strong suspicion that she'll be there."

Henry's funeral. The thought that Henry was dead finally hit home. No matter what he'd done to her, she felt an acute sadness. He was a terrible person, but he was someone's child. She had never met his family but she could only imagine their pain. She said a quick prayer for Henry that wherever he was, he would find peace, then she asked Ransom, "Where does Esme live?"

"In Pike's Way, a suburb of Queenstown."

"Can you take me there?" Callie asked.

"Callie, no! This woman sounds dangerous!" Catherine exclaimed.

Ignoring her mother's outburst, Callie repeated her question to Ransom. "Can you take me to Esme's house?"

"I think we should wait until Garret gets back," said Ransom.

"I can't wait for Garret on this," said Callie. "I have a lot at stake here, Ransom. My antennae are telling me that Esme's involved and if she's the person who killed Henry and took a shot at me, then the quicker I get to the bottom of this, the better for me. I want my life back, Ransom."

"I understand that," Ransom replied. "But Garret may be coming back soon."

"You've already left him a message," said Callie. "He can always meet us there."

"Callie, why don't you let the police handle this?" asked Catherine.

"No offense," said Callie, "but I'm not impressed with how the police have handled things so far. Mom, I've sat by on the sidelines all my life..."

"That's not true!" said Catherine. "You're an accomplished lawyer. You've done great things in your life."

"For other people, Mom. I've got to do this for me. I can't wait for anyone else to come and save me. I have to save myself."

"Then I'm coming with you," said Catherine.

"Me too," said Phoebe.

"I haven't said that I was going to take her to Esme's house," Ransom said weakly, but he was a wise man. He knew that he was no match for three determined women. "Okay, come on. But if anything happens, Garret's going to kill me."

As they walked out of the guest house to Ransom's car, Catherine turned to Callie and asked, "What's this business about you getting shot?"

Callie sighed. She'd hoped that it would take her mother longer to get back to the original subject. She should've known better. "I'll tell you in the car, Mom."

Garret sat down in his father's living room. Although his father had lived in this house for almost eleven years, it was the first time that he'd ever been there. His father's house was small compared to the other homes in this high-end neighborhood of Chelsea, a seaside town twenty miles south of Queenstown, but the furnishings were exquisite. His father shared Garret's love of antiques. Looking around the living room at the mahogany furnishings, antique paintings and thick Persian rug, Garret was surprised. He'd thought his father would have a swinging bachelor pad, complete with obligatory black lacquer furniture and a huge painting of himself hung in prominent display. Instead, he noted the only pictures in the living room were of Garret and his mother. He was taken aback by the pictures. He'd never figured that his father would be the sentimental type. He picked up a black and white photograph of his mother. She was standing in a garden, looking in the distance. He blinked back tears as he thought about everything she'd had to endure in her short life.

"She was very beautiful, wasn't she?"

His father's voice startled him. Garret hadn't heard him enter the room. James hadn't seemed surprised to see his son. He'd shown him to the living room and then he'd excused himself for a few moments to take a telephone call.

Garret turned and looked at his father. "Yes, she was," he agreed. "She was beautiful."

"Sit down, Garret," said his father.

"I'd prefer to stand," said Garret.

"Yes, I know you would," his father said gently, "but I'd like you to sit down. Please."

Garret shrugged his shoulders, then sat down. He didn't know what difference it made to his father, but he sat down anyway.

"What can I do for you, son?"

James sat down on one of the two Sheraton-style mahogany armchairs with pale green dralon seats. Garret recognized these chairs from when his mother bought them on a trip to Martinique. This house that his mother had never set foot in was filled with her presence. He recognized two large porcelain vases in the corner of the room that his mother had also bought years ago. The memories of the joy antiques brought her came flooding back. He knew that his love of antiques was based on a desire to always keep his mother's memory alive. She'd tried to teach him about antiques but it wasn't until long after her death that his appreciation finally blossomed. Turning his attention back to his father, he said, "I need to ask you some questions."

James took a deep breath and then said, "Go ahead."

"I want to know about you and my mother."

His father grew visibly uncomfortable. Long seconds went by before he said, "Why bring up the past?"

"Are you going to answer my questions?" Garret asked.

"Yes, Garret, I'll answer your questions."

"Why did you cheat on my mother?"

"Because I was weak," James replied.

"I already know that," Garret spat out. "But why'd you leave her like that? You know she couldn't make it without you."

"I always came back," said James. "She knew I wasn't going to stay away forever."

"How'd she know that?"

James kept looking at his hands. "Son, I'm sorry. You can't make me feel any worse than I already feel."

"I'm not trying to make you feel bad. I just want to understand."

"There's nothing to understand, Garret. I was weak. I loved your mother, but I couldn't handle her problems."

"What about me?" Garret asked. "I was a child. What was I supposed to do with an absent father?"

"I didn't walk out on you. I never divorced your mother."

"But you weren't there when she needed you."

"You're right about that," James agreed.

"Dad, I need to know... did you love my mother?"

James answered without hesitation. "She was, and is, the love of my life."

"Then why'd you cheat on her?" he asked again.

James looked up at Garret and said, "I'm sorry, son. I couldn't handle her pain and I ran away from that."

"Dad, I've met someone who means a lot to me."

"Callie Hopewell."

"Yes," Garret replied. "After Mom died, I stopped being scared. Yesterday I got scared, Dad. I got scared that I'd turn out like you and I'd end up hurting Callie the way you hurt Mom."

"That's not going to happen, Garret."

"How do you know that?"

"Because you're stronger than me, and because you know what it's like to lose your family. You lost your mother and you lost me. You're not going to make the same mistakes I made."

"That's what Callie said," Garret mused. "She said that I would make different choices than you did."

James gave his son a rueful smile. "She's a smart woman," he said. "And a lucky one, too."

Garret looked over at his father and he remembered that there was a time, long ago, when he'd loved this man; a time when he'd wait excitedly to hear the sound of his footsteps when he came home from work. There had been some laughter in their home, before his mother's depression had gripped her the last, final time.

"Dad," Garret said. "I know we can't erase the past, but do you think we could start over?"

The tears ran freely down James Langrin's face. "Yes." He nodded. "We can start over."

Chapter 26

Esme Hawthorne lived in a beige town house in a subdivision where each town house looked exactly the same. Unlike the wild, tropical foliage that surrounded Garret's home, the impeccably manicured lawns, with their symmetrically planted palm trees, looked positively antiseptic to Callie. Ransom pulled his Jeep into the driveway. He was a good driver, but the narrow winding coastal highway that led to Pike's Way coupled with the excessive speed he drove at caused Callie a deep feeling of gratitude that they'd made it to Esme's subdivision safely.

"Now what?" Catherine asked.

"I'm working on that," Callie asked. During the forty minute drive, Callie tried to figure out a strategy, but all she could come up with was a plan to knock on the front door and introduce herself.

"Why don't you just knock on the front door?" Phoebe asked.

"It sounds like as good an idea as any other," was Ransom's comment. "I'll go with you."

"Me, too," said Catherine.

"I'll hold down the fort right here," said Phoebe. "But you all call me if you need me."

"Phoebe Hopewell, you're coming with us. Your sister needs you."

"That's all right, Mom," said Callie. "Actually, I'd rather do this by myself."

"Not on your life," said Ransom. "Garret would kill me."

Callie shook her head. "Garret would understand. Some things you have to do alone and this is one of them. You guys are outside, what could possibly happen to me?

A look of disbelief passed between Catherine and Ransom, but neither said a word.

Callie got out of the car. "Give me a few minutes. I want to talk to Esme."

"Look, this woman isn't going to confess that she murdered Henry," said Ransom.

"I know, but I want to see if I can shake her. Maybe she'll slip up and say something."

Ransom didn't look convinced.

"My gut tells me that she's involved. One way or the other, I'm going to get some information from her."

Ransom shook his head slowly. "Garret is going to kill me."

"An unfortunate choice of words," Catherine muttered. "But I understand the sentiment. Callie can be very stubborn at times. She doesn't get *that* quality from me!"

* * *

Garret dialed Ransom's cell phone number and got the same message he'd gotten the last three times he'd called. The user of the cell phone had turned off the phone or was out of the service area. He'd spent the morning with his father, talking about Callie's case and getting advice from him. Past grievances hadn't disappeared but for the first time in years, he'd been able to talk to his father without resentment. They were on their way to building a relationship. When he left his father's house, he'd checked his phone messages. The first message didn't cause him too much concern. Ransom's message informed him about the connection between Esme, Henry, Max, Reynalda, and Josephine. That had been interesting and potentially helpful. The next messages were downright disturbing. Callie, her mother, sister, and Ransom were on their way to Esme's house. Had Ransom lost his mind? He knew that Callie could be persuasive but Ransom typically had good common sense. To allow Callie to go to Esme's house when he suspected that Esme might be involved in Henry's murder was sheer lunacy. When he couldn't reach Ransom, Garret had called his secretary to get Esme's home address. The address was unlisted, but his secretary had managed to get the information within ten minutes of his request. She was worth her weight, which was considerable, in gold and then some. He drove like a demon possessed to Pike's Way, which was about half an hour away. *Please, God,* he silently pleaded with the Almighty, *keep Callie safe.*

Callie knocked on the door and a stunningly beautiful woman opened it. Esme Hawthorne was a younger and much prettier version of her sister. She didn't have Josephine's coldness. Although Callie wasn't sure what to expect, she didn't expect to see this slim, vulnerable woman with golden skin and golden eyes. Her light brown hair was pulled on top of her head and tied in a messy knot, with wisps of hair falling around her heart-shaped face. Was this the woman who killed Henry? Had she killed Reynalda? Was this the person who shot her?

"I'm Callie Hopewell."

"I know who you are," said Esme. "Your picture's been in the news. What do you want, Miss Hopewell?"

"I'd like to talk to you, and please call me Callie."

Esme hesitated for a moment, then she let her in. She followed Esme into a small sitting room. Esme sat on one of the two pale cream love seats. She motioned to Callie to sit down.

Shaking her hair free from its knot, her long hair tumbled down her back. *Long hair.* The woman who'd shot her had long hair. *Steady girl.* Callie forced herself to be calm even though her heart was hammering in her chest.

"Did you kill Henry?" Esme asked.

"No," Callie replied.

Esme gave her a hard, direct stare. "I didn't think you did, but I wanted to look in your eyes when I asked you the question."

"I was angry about what he did to me, but I could never kill him."

Esme crossed her long, golden legs.

"So," said Esme. "I finally get to meet the competition."

Callie shook her head emphatically. "I was never your competition."

"Yes, you were. In his own way Henry cared about you, as much as he could have cared about anyone. Henry was . . . damaged."

That's one way of looking at things, Callie reasoned. "I was no competition to you. If anyone was in competition with you, it was probably his wife." *Your sister.*

Esme let out a short laugh that didn't reach her eyes. "Josephine? They never loved each other. She was no competition."

Callie decided to go in for the kill. "What about Reynalda Chin? Was she your competition?"

Esme blinked her eyes rapidly. She looked visibly shaken. Licking her lips, she said, "What happened to Reynalda was unfortunate, but Henry never loved her."

Unfortunate. What sort of person referred to a suicide as unfortunate? What sort of person slept with her sister's husband?

"Would you care for a drink, I think I'm going to have a rum and coke."

"No, thanks," said Callie as the word POISON flashed through her mind. "I don't touch alcohol before noon."

Esme smiled at her. "Are you always such a girl scout, Callie?"

Callie shrugged one shoulder. "Afraid so."

Esme got up and walked to her kitchen. In a few moments she returned with a highball glass filled with her drink of choice. Sitting back down on the love seat, she said, "Are you sure about the drink? It's eleven forty-five . . . surely you can bend your rules a little bit."

Callie shook her head emphatically. "I'm afraid I'm not much of a drinker."

"How about something softer. A soda, perhaps?"

Once again the word POISON flashed in her mind. "No, thanks," Callie said cheerfully. "But I appreciate the offer."

Esme took a long sip of her drink. "I hate to drink alone."

Callie decided to get back to the subject that she'd come to discuss. "What makes you think that Henry didn't love Reynalda? From what I heard, she was a very desirable woman."

Callie hadn't heard anything like this but she wanted to see what reaction she'd get to those words. She watched as Esme drained the glass. Callie didn't know a lot about alcohol but it seemed strange to her that Esme was drinking this early in the morning. Either she was very, very stressed or she was a candidate for rehab.

"Henry used Reynalda. He wanted to get back at her husband for sleeping with Josephine."

"I thought you said that Henry didn't care about Josephine."

"He didn't, but he never liked Max and it bothered him that he was sleeping with Josephine. He felt it was a sign of disrespect."

"But you and I both know that Henry cheated on his wife."

"Like I said, he was damaged."

Esme stood up and started pacing the room in an agitated manner. Callie suddenly had the very real sense that she was in danger. As Esme paced Callie became aware that this was a woman who despite all outward appearances was coming unhinged.

"I know that this is a bad time for you," said Callie, standing up. "Maybe I shouldn't have come."

Esme gave a short, harsh laugh. "You're right about that, Callie. You probably shouldn't have come. But since you're here, let's talk."

"Maybe I should leave," said Callie, trying to hide her nervousness. Esme had a wild look about her that hadn't been there moments ago.

"Sit down, Callie."

Callie's instincts told her to get the hell out of Esme's house but she didn't want to push Esme any further into the descent of madness that she seemed to be taking. She sat back down, but she determined that at the first possible opportunity she was going to get out of there. She still couldn't be sure that Esme killed Henry, but in her mind there was enough cause for concern and enough cause to go to the police, which in retrospect was probably the wisest course of action. *Too late to worry about that now,* Callie chided herself.

"I bet you're wondering why I agreed to talk to you."

"The thought had crossed my mind," Callie admitted.

"Like I said, I wanted to meet the competition. Though if you don't mind my saying this, you aren't exactly his type."

"So I gather," Callie said neutrally.

"Don't misunderstand me," Esme continued. "You're a beautiful woman, but you're not as hard as his other women have been. He told me about you. He actually thought that he was starting to care for you . . . he told me he was thinking of leaving Josephine."

"Why would he tell *you* this?"

"Henry could never have been with me openly. My family wouldn't have allowed that kind of scandal. I knew that to be with him I'd have to stay in the background, which was fine with me. Henry wasn't the kind of guy you'd want to marry... God knows he'd never be faithful, plus he had *other* weaknesses... weaknesses that would end up costing me a lot of money. He liked gambling and I wasn't about to be with a man who'd be loose with my money. Fooling around with women is one thing, but fooling around with my money... well, I just wouldn't have that."

Callie reassessed her original impressions of Esme. She might look vulnerable but she was just as callous as her sister.

"I did love him," Esme said, as she started to weep. "I was the only one of his women who really knew who he was and I loved him in spite of himself."

Callie stood up. "Esme, I'm sorry. This is a bad time for you. It was a mistake coming here."

"That's right, Miss Hopewell. It was a mistake."

Callie turned to see a distinguished-looking man with graying hair striding into the sitting room. She had the impression that he'd been by the door to the sitting room listening to her entire conversation.

"I can handle this, Daddy," said Esme.

"No Esme, you can't handle this." Turning his attention back to Callie, William Hawthorne said, "I think you should leave."

Good idea, thought Callie. "I'm sorry to have disturbed your daughter," she said to Esme's father, "and I'm sorry for your loss."

William's laugh was harsh. "What loss? I'm only sorry he didn't die sooner."

"Daddy, don't say that!" Esme called out.

"Well, I'll just be going . . ." said Callie.

"I'll see you out," said William Hawthorne. "Esme, I'll be back, I have some business to take care of."

Callie watched as William picked up a sports jacket that was draped over the back of a brown leather chair. As William picked up his jacket, a ring fell out. A ring that looked exactly like the ring Henry tried to give her on the night he died—a sapphire surrounded by diamonds.

Oh, my God. Callie felt her heart thundering in her chest. How did Esme's father get Henry's ring? No one found the ring after Henry was murdered because, Callie reasoned as the sound of rushing water filled her ears, the murderer took the ring.

Callie was aware that William was watching her closely.

Stay calm. Stay calm. Why hadn't she listened to Ransom? Damn. Damn. Damn. Stay calm. "Listen, I really need to be going. My mother is waiting for me outside and she's going to get worried. She's right outside in the Jeep. I have to get going."

She knew that she was babbling, but she didn't care. She needed to get out of Esme's house as quickly as possible.

"What's the rush?" William said calmly.

"Look, I know you're busy and you were just about to leave . . ."

William walked over to her and smiled. "You've seen this ring before, haven't you?"

Callie shook her head vigorously. "No. I've never seen that ring."

"You're a terrible liar, Miss Hopewell."

"Daddy, what's going on?"

"Never mind, Esme," said William. "Miss Hopewell and I are going out to conduct some business."

"I'm not going anywhere with you!" To her mortification, Callie felt herself start to tremble. William felt it, too.

"Daddy, what's gotten into you?" Esme asked warily.

Callie felt something sharp by her side. She looked down to see William holding a gun by her left hip. *Sweet Jesus, help me,* she prayed fervently. *If you get me out of this mess, I promise that I'll never do anything foolish again!*

"Esme," Callie said calmly. "Your father killed Henry and he's going to try to kill me."

"You're lying!" Esme spat out, even as her eyes took in the gun that her father was holding. Turning to her father Esme said, "Daddy, you didn't kill Henry, did you?"

"This is the woman who killed Henry," said William. "You know I wouldn't do anything like that."

"What're you doing with the gun?" asked Esme.

"This woman is dangerous," said William. "She's the one who killed Henry."

"Mr. Hawthorne, there are three people outside who are waiting for me. There's no way you're going to get away with killing me," said Callie in her best let's-be-reasonable voice.

"That's true, Miss Hopewell. I won't get away with murdering you, but I will get away with killing you because when I shoot you it will be in self-defense."

"Daddy!" Esme cried out.

William's voice was deadly calm when he spoke. "You see, Miss Hopewell, you came here determined to hurt my daughter. You pulled a gun on her and I had to shoot you."

"Did you shoot me?" Callie asked.

William smiled at her. "Guilty as charged."

"But the person who shot me had long hair."

"A wig, Miss Hopewell. I was wearing a wig."

"Why me?"

"I needed to tie up loose ends, Miss Hopewell, and you were a loose end. You knew about the ring. Henry told me before I shot him that he'd intended to give you the ring, and you'd refused."

"Why would Henry tell you that?" Callie asked, stalling for time.

"He was taunting me . . . even at the end . . . telling me that one day he would leave my daughter and marry you . . . He told me that he'd tried to give you the ring, but you were so honorable you wouldn't take it . . . He tried to tell me that you were different from my daughters . . . better . . ."

"Why would he taunt you if he knew you'd come to kill him?" Keep him talking, Callie. Keep him talking.

"Daddy, you can't do this," said Esme. "I'm not going to lie for you."

William turned to face his daughter. "Yes, you are. Blood sticks together, Esme. I killed him for you, for Josephine, for what he did to this family. I went to him and begged him to break things off with you. I saw what your relationship was doing . . . it was destroying us. After your mother left, you girls were the only things I had left . . . I wasn't going to let him destroy our family. I begged him to leave you alone, but he laughed at me. Told me to mind my own business. Told me that he wasn't going to leave you alone. He told me that he was going to divorce Josephine and marry Miss Hopewell . . . he told me that he was still going to keep you, too, Esme. I couldn't let him do that. Blood sticks together, Esme. Henry's blood is on your hands, just like it's on mine . . ."

Callie had heard enough. If he was going to shoot her, she would at least give him a moving target. She bolted for the door.

"Stop!" William screamed.

But Callie had no intention of stopping. It would be hard to prove self-defense if he shot her in the back. As she reached the front door two shots rang out. Callie turned to see William crumple to the floor. Esme had a gun in her hand. William lay on the floor, a pool of blood spreading out around him, staining the carpet. He wasn't moving.

Looking over at Callie, Esme said, "I couldn't let him hurt you like he hurt Henry."

"Where'd you get the gun?" Callie asked.

"I've always kept a gun in my desk," she said calmly. "A lady can't be too safe."

Garret heard the shots as he took the stairs to the town house entrance three at a time. *Please God, let her be okay*, he prayed as he bounded up the stairs. He heard the cries of Callie's mother and sister, who were running up behind him. Throwing the unlocked door open, he saw Callie and Esme kneeling over the body of a man lying on the pale beige carpet. It was clear that the man was dead. Callie stood up and ran over to him, throwing her arms around him. She was shaking and crying as he held her close until her tears ceased

"What the hell is going on here!" Ransom barked as he entered the sitting room.

Esme looked up from where she was kneeling beside her father.

"My father's dead. He killed Henry and I killed him."

Later, much later when they'd all returned to Garret's house, he was able to relax. Callie was finally out of danger. Mobray had shown up and authorized the release of Callie's passport. Callie and her family had shared dinner with Garret, Ransom, Dreama, and Zenna and although the past few days had been filled with danger and intrigue, everyone had managed to relax. After dinner, the group moved to the living room for coffee and dessert.

Garret could hear the commotion around him, but everything else fell away... all he concentrated on was Callie. When he thought about how close he'd come to losing her... He pulled her back into his arms and said gently, "If you ever do anything crazy like this again..."

Callie looked up at him, and under the most unlikely of circumstances, smiled. "I promise, I will never, never, never do anything foolish again. I'm going to back to my regular, dependable, boring life. No more drama for me."

"Is that a promise?" Garret asked.

Callie looked at him with a sly smile. "That's a promise."

Catherine Hopewell shook her head and said to Garret, "Now, if you believe that, I've got some other tall tales to tell!" Catherine then gently pulled Callie from Garret's arms and hugged her daughter. "I love you, Callie. And whatever decisions you make, I know they'll be the right ones for you."

Callie kissed her mother on the cheek. "I love you, Mom."

Catherine then turned to face Garret and said, "I don't know you, Garret, but from what I can see, you care about my daughter and she seems to care about you. Now, I want you to know something. I'm a God-fearing woman, but if you ever hurt my daughter, I will come down here and put my foot in your . . ."

"Mom!" Callie wailed. It wasn't enough that she narrowly escaped death, but now her mother was embarrassing her, too!

Garret pulled Callie back into his arms and gave her a long kiss. Then, he said to Catherine, "Don't you worry, Mrs. Hopewell. I'm going to hold onto this woman like my life depends on it."

"Good!" Catherine declared. "It does!"

"So," asked Dreama, "are you guys getting married?"

Phoebe weighed in. "Callie doesn't believe in long engagements."

"Well, Callie," said Garret. "Is five days too soon to become married?"

"For normal, sensible, reasonable people, it would be much too soon," Callie replied. "But I've heard that being that way is somewhat overrated."

"So, is that a yes?" Catherine asked.

"Why don't we give it some time?" Callie asked. "After all, I've only known Garret five days."

Callie married Garret exactly two weeks later. Garret's father was the best man and Callie's mother was a matron of honor. Both parents cried through the ceremony, but the tears were tears of joy.

*Valentine's Day,
A year later*

"Callie, you're being silly," Garret gently chided his wife, who'd refused to get out of bed on February fourteenth.

"Last year I got shot on Valentine's Day, remember?" Callie asked, looking at the wonderful man she'd married. She'd always heard that the first year of marriage was the most difficult, but for her, the past year had been a glorious time of discovery and love. She'd moved to St. Christopher and after passing the bar, had joined her husband's law firm as a partner. The hours and the perks were much better at Langrin and Associates, Callie reflected happily. Although she missed her family, they visited the island often and she'd managed to get back to New York twice during the past year. She missed her family, bagels, and sliced pizza, but other than that, the transition from New York to St. Christopher had been smooth.

The notoriety about her involvement with Henry had died down and life had returned to normal for all involved. Esme left the island after being cleared of her father's murder. No one knew where she went, but it was rumored that she had a lover in Martinique. Callie hoped it was true. Esme deserved a chance to start over. She'd been damaged by the man who raised her, and Callie hoped that distance away from the island and her sister Josephine would help Esme. Josephine had married Otis Lorde six months after Henry's death, and from all accounts, being the wife of a crime lord suited her just fine . . . although Callie hoped that

Josephine would have the good sense not to cheat on him. She couldn't see a cheating wife with a long life ahead of her . . . not if she were married to Otis.

"Yeah, but we shared our first kiss on Valentine's Day," said Garret, as he pulled her closer to him.

"Well, the kissing part was definitely nice . . ."

"Nice! I think you said it was the best kiss you'd ever had."

"True, but I did get shot."

"Callie, you can't stay in bed the entire day."

Callie snuggled closer to her husband. "Why not?"

"Well, because you have work to do."

She pulled one strap down from the peach silk nightgown she was wearing, revealing a shoulder. "I've cleared my schedule."

Garret leaned over and kissed her shoulder. "Did you clear it with the boss?"

Callie pulled the other strap down, revealing her other shoulder. "Well, no . . . but I was certain he wouldn't mind."

Her nightgown fell away as she pulled her husband towards her. Her husband put his lips close to hers but before he kissed her, he asked, "But what about my schedule?"

Callie gave her husband a long, deep kiss. "It's been cleared."

Grab These Other
Dafina Novels
(mass market editions)

Some Sunday by Margaret Johnson-Hodge
0-7582-0026-9 $6.99US/$9.99CAN

Forever by Timmothy B. McCann
0-7582-0353-5 $6.99US/$9.99CAN

Soulmates Dissipate by Mary B. Morrison
0-7582-0020-X $6.99US/$9.99CAN

High Hand by Gary Phillips
1-57566-684-7 $5.99US/$7.99CAN

Shooter's Point by Gary Phillips
1-57566-745-2 $5.99US/$7.99CAN

Casting the First Stone by Kimberla Lawson Roby
0-7582-0179-6 $6.99US/$9.99CAN

Here and Now by Kimberla Lawson Roby
0-7582-0064-1 $6.99US/$9.99CAN

Lookin' for Luv by Carl Weber
0-7582-0118-4 $6.99US/$8.99CAN

Available Wherever Books Are Sold!

Visit our website at **www.kensingtonbooks.com**

Check Out These Other
Dafina Novels

Sister Got Game
0-7582-0856-1

by Leslie Esdaile
$6.99US/**$9.99**CAN

Say Yes
0-7582-0853-7

by Donna Hill
$6.99US/**$9.99**CAN

In My Dreams
0-7582-0868-5

by Monica Jackson
$6.99US/**$9.99**CAN

True Lies
0-7582-0027-7

by Margaret Johnson-Hodge
$6.99US/**$9.99**CAN

Testimony
0-7582-0637-2

by Felicia Mason
$6.99US/**$9.99**CAN

Emotions
0-7582-0636-4

by Timmothy McCann
$6.99US/**$9.99**CAN

The Upper Room
0-7582-0889-8

by Mary Monroe
$6.99US/**$9.99**CAN

Got A Man
0-7582-0242-3

by Daaimah S. Poole
$6.99US/**$8.99**CAN

Available Wherever Books Are Sold!

Check out our website at www.kensingtonbooks.com.

Look For These Other
Dafina Novels

If I Could by Donna Hill
0-7582-0131-1 **$6.99**US/**$9.99**CAN

Thunderland by Brandon Massey
0-7582-0247-4 **$6.99**US/**$9.99**CAN

June In Winter by Pat Phillips
0-7582-0375-6 **$6.99**US/**$9.99**CAN

Yo Yo Love by Daaimah S. Poole
0-7582-0239-3 **$6.99**US/**$9.99**CAN

When Twilight Comes by Gwynne Forster
0-7582-0033-1 **$6.99**US/**$9.99**CAN

It's A Thin Line by Kimberla Lawson Roby
0-7582-0354-3 **$6.99**US/**$9.99**CAN

Perfect Timing by Brenda Jackson
0-7582-0029-3 **$6.99**US/**$9.99**CAN

Never Again Once More by Mary B. Morrison
0-7582-0021-8 **$6.99**US/**$8.99**CAN

Available Wherever Books Are Sold!

Check out our website at www.kensingtonbooks.com.

Grab These Other
Dafina Novels
(trade paperback editions)

Every Bitter Thing Sweet by Roslyn Carrington
1-57566-851-3 $14.00US/$19.00CAN

When Twilight Comes by Gwynne Forster
0-7582-0009-9 $15.00US/$21.00CAN

Some Sunday by Margaret Johnson-Hodge
0-7582-0003-X $15.00US/$21.00CAN

Testimony by Felicia Mason
0-7582-0063-3 $15.00US/$21.00CAN

Forever by Timmothy B. McCann
1-57566-759-2 $15.00US/$21.00CAN

God Don't Like Ugly by Mary Monroe
1-57566-607-3 $15.00US/$20.00CAN

Gonna Lay Down My Burdens by Mary Monroe
0-7582-0001-3 $15.00US/$21.00CAN

The Upper Room by Mary Monroe
0-7582-0023-4 $15.00US/$21.00CAN

Soulmates Dissipate by Mary B. Morrison
0-7582-0006-4 $15.00US/$21.00CAN

Got a Man by Daaimah S. Poole
0-7582-0240-7 $15.00US/$21.00CAN

Casting the First Stone by Kimberla Lawson Roby
1-57566-633-2 $14.00US/$18.00CAN

It's a Thin Line by Kimberla Lawson Roby
1-57566-744-4 $15.00US/$21.00CAN

Available Wherever Books Are Sold!

Visit our website at **www.kensingtonbooks.com**